Heywood Gould le[illegible] a newspaper reporter.[illegible]V script writer, freel[illegible]g screenplays for *Fort*[illegible]*m Brazil*) and barma[illegible]so features Josh Krale[illegible]k. Heywood Gould liv[illegible]

By the same author

Glitterburn

HEYWOOD GOULD

Deadline for Murder

GRANADA
London Toronto Sydney New York

Published by Granada Publishing Limited in 1983

ISBN 0 586 04639 9

A Granada Paperback UK Original
First published in the USA by St Martin's Press, Inc.
in 1975 under the title of *One Dead Debutante*

Granada Publishing Limited
Frogmore, St Albans, Herts AL2 2NF
and
36 Golden Square, London W1R 4AH
515 Madison Avenue, New York, NY 10022, USA
117 York Street, Sydney, NSW 2000, Australia
100 Skyway Avenue, Rexdale, Ontario, M9W 3A6, Canada
61 Beach Road, Auckland, New Zealand

Printed and bound in Great Britain by
Cox & Wyman Ltd, Reading
Set in Times

CHAPTER ONE

I blame it all on Thanksgiving. It's an ersatz holiday to begin with, invented by Roosevelt to keep the banks closed for a couple of days. It's got a real imperialist mythology to it too, complete with sour-faced Pilgrims and Noble Red Men who show them the way. Historically, all I can remember about it is that the Pilgrims were starving in the wilderness until Chief Squanto and the Algonquins happened by and invented corn on the cob. The Pilgrims showed their gratitude by running the Indians over Niagara Falls without barrels, and the Algonquins got a hotel named after them. When I was in P.S. 154, we used to bring in funky canned goods for the poor kids in the orphanages. To this day I have a picture of some smudge-faced Mickey Rooney type in Father Flanagan's Boys Town subsisting on my Chef Boyardee ravioli and Krasdale grapefruit sections. Why, I may have kept a future Monsignor healthy and devout with my culinary rejects. Still, on Thanksgiving Eve, I was looking forward to the day's festivities at the ancestral home in Brooklyn, reunions with crotchety relatives, epiglottal battles with parboiled turkey, and asphalt potatoes, tonics for my jaded soul. I'd been drinking, wenching and working for months, in that order, and I needed a break. I was definitely not looking for adventure. If anyone had told me that ten days hence I would have a broken nose, a warrant out for my arrest and a case of blue balls, I would have immediately fled the country. But nobody told me.

While I slumbered in my bachelor's bed, visions of Alka Seltzers fizzing in my brain, an Israeli ship called the 'Ben-Gurion' was heading back to port with a cargo of Caribbean cruisers, their waistlines expanded, their libidos quiescent, their suitcases bulging with duty-free booze and perfume from the exotic ports of Curacao, the Dutch Antilles, Montserrat, etc., which they would all invariably claim looked no different from Miami. Meanwhile, unbeknownst to my seagoing *landsmen,* as well as my manifest content, a Swedish freighter, the 'Charles XII', was also steaming in the same direction, loaded with blondes, Volvos, meatballs, or whatever Swedish freighters carry. Although the two boats were coming from different directions, they were heading for the same point, inscribing a huge isosceles triangle in the choppy coastal waters. And then they met with a crunch somewhere beyond the entrance to the Narrows.

There were cries and curses and the cranking of lifeboats being lowered. Some of the cruisers lost their midnight snacks, which explained the quantities of disgorged lox and cream cheese that fouled the propellers of other boats for weeks to come. One Swedish sailor locked himself in the galley, drank great quantities of Norwegian beer, and mounted the decks, announcing his intention to go down with the foundering ship. When no one discouraged him, he lurched meekly to the lifeboats, but slipped as he climbed down, and disappeared without a bubble. He was the only casualty.

Both ships sent out distress signals, and the Coast Guard responded forthwith. Every commercial ship in the area came to the rescue, according to marine etiquette. Unfortunately, so did every other boat owner who had a ship-to-shore radio and a social conscience. The Coast Guard was so busy plucking these hardy seamen out of the water and towing their boats back that the victims had to wait patiently in their lifeboats for aid.

The New York Police Harbor Patrol also got the call and launched its rescue operations. The emergency call was put on the police department ticker, which records all calls in a given borough and feeds them into police headquarters. The press shack at Manhattan police headquarters has a ticker of its own, put there to alert reporters to juicy stories. But the news hounds who work the lobster shift, from midnight to eight, have an unspoken agreement that they will ignore all incidents, short of national emergency, thus giving their editors and the public the illusion that there are no miscreants abroad during the wee hours. This is management of the news at its most altruistic, and I heartily endorse it.

But someone neglected to tell a young AP man fresh from the Wyoming bureau about this policy of benign neglect. He let out such a squawk when he saw news of the collision on the ticker that he woke up the UPI man and distracted the *Times* and *News* men from their gin game. Refusing to listen to reason, he actually called his desk to inform them of this occurrence, which meant that the other reporters had to do the same. And then, with good journalism-school precision, he proceeded to call the Coast Guard, the shipping line, the Harbor Patrol and all the interested parties he could think of, forcing his by now highly irate colleagues to follow suit.

The wire services interrupted their usual transmissions, which consisted at that hour of Ecuadorian soccer scores and reports of an eight-foot eggplant that attacked three peasants in Abruzzi. Bells rang, and URGENT was flashed on the ticker. This served to alert the editors of the nation that a story of unusual interest was about to be transmitted. Before any of the details were in, the first lead on the story ringingly announced: 'ISRAELI CRUISE SHIP SWEDISH FREIGHTER IN COLLISION'. And that was enough to galvanize the entire apparatus of a major American newspaper into action, the main thrust of which involved a telephone call to me.

I am a reporter for the New York *Event*. I have eight years on the job. In addition to seniority, I've accrued goodly amounts of boredom, bitterness and incipient cirrhosis – none of which is listed as a fringe benefit in the union contract. I shouldn't have to be awakened at all hours and sent to cover murders and mishaps and all manner of uncivilized occurrences. There should be some young Jack London on our staff, an eager beaver with a police radio attached to his contact lenses, who will leap at the chance to show his reportorial mettle. There must be somebody on our staff who likes to run around on cold, dark nights, asking silly questions, getting the wrong answers, and misquoting them to boot. I certainly don't. And yet I'm always called to do it. Is this because I'm an ace reporter, dependable, persistent, incisive, the only man for the job? No. It's because management hates me.

Larry Persky, the assistant night city editor, doesn't understand why I should be allowed to sleep while he works. Sometimes he just wakes me up and blows raspberries over the phone before hanging up. This time he had a reason.

'Did I wake you, Krales?' he hollered gleefully.

'No.' I croaked. 'I was just going out to slop the hogs.'

'Gotta bimbo in there with you, Krales?'

'Yeah, as a matter of fact, I do.'

'You're full of crap, Krales. You couldn't get laid in a cat-house.' I could hear Persky's co-workers laughing in the background. 'Get up and earn your keep.'

It was 4:35. Almost exactly at that moment, the 'Charles XII' began to list. With scores of boats encircling it 'like hunters surrounding a downed animal', I would later write, it turned over on its side and sank.

'What's goin' on?'

'Boat collision off the Narrows. One's a Swedish freighter, the other an Israeli cruise ship coming back from the Caribbean.'

'What am I supposed to do, swim out there and say Kaddish?'

'They're bringin' the survivors back to the Brooklyn docks,' Persky said. 'Over by the First Army Terminal. Big rescue operation. Go cover it. You got Ianelli and Jill Potosky. She'll do the feature stuff. You concentrate on the breaking story. We wanna know whose fault it was.'

'What if the Israelis are in the wrong?' I asked.

'You become a PR man for Al Fatah. Good-bye.'

Ianelli and Jill? It was all a plot to get me, I decided as I got dressed. Ianelli was a seventy-three-year-old photographer who stuck stubbornly to his thirty-pound Graflex, the kind you see in the old movies, which I always ended up carrying for him at the end of a long story. He had covered ship news for the old New York *Graphic* and liked to say that he had gotten more actresses to hoist their skirts than Errol Flynn. He still went around, asking everybody from Miss America to Margaret Mead for a little 'cheese-cake, darling'. He worked the early shift and always fell asleep about ten o'clock in the morning. Sleeping was his only talent; he could do it anywhere. I'd seen him doze off while standing in the corner of the crowded press room at City Hall, even sitting in a wheelbarrow, waiting for Mrs Javits to dedicate a hemlock forest in the Bronx.

Jill Potosky was the newest addition to the paper. She was one of those Ivy League Jewesses – God should forgive me for my spiteful words – who could outWasp Eleanor Roosevelt. She was a tall, braless blonde, very regal of bearing and feminist of demeanor. But she didn't mind balling our sexist editor to advance her career. I knew she was just creaming to go on a big story like this, and that the boss had happily assigned her, maybe even while she was lying there in lascivious sheets with him. That thought made my teeth grind and my razor slip, so I concentrated on more pleasant things, like the big, fat overtime and expense sheet I was going to submit at the end of the day. The phone rang as I was leaving.

'Hello, partner.' It was Jill. 'You awake?'

'No, I'm having a wet dream and you're the star.'

'I hope you're wearing your Pampers,' she said.

'I am. Why don't you come up and snap them for me?'

'Yes, well before you further expose your infantile personality, I'd like you to pick me up on your way downtown. I'm afraid my old Jag just won't be able to make it. . . .'

'Oh, it won't,' I sneered. 'Will you deign to sit in my Chevy II?'

There was a silence, then a bored sigh. 'University and Eleventh, Mr Krales.'

'Fifteen minutes, Ms Potosky,' I said, accenting the 'Ms' I filled my Gucci hip flask (a birthday present to myself) with cognac and then poured myself a shot to start the day off.

Downstairs, the ice winter was in the air. A dove had been trapped in my windshield wipers and was flapping its white wings desperately. As I drew closer, the dove turned into a parking ticket, my third of the week. I've got my heap decorated with every antiticket talisman extant – the press plates, the honorary memberships in the Patrolmen's Benevolent Association and the Order of Hibernian Firemen, the City Hall press card, a Funeral Director On Call card, and a Bureau of Water Supply Emergency Service sticker. Any one of these could have gotten me a parking space in the third pew at St Patrick's Cathedral a few years ago. But since then, the cops have become honest. They still take payoffs from pimps, pushers, and gamblers, but they've really cracked down on motorists.

It took me a half-hour to get to the Village. The streets were empty, but my car stalled at every light. Potosky was waiting on the corner. She had on a fleece-lined ski jacket, a New York Rangers stocking cap, jeans – of course, faded – with little floral patches and two embroidered butterflies on each buttock. Her press card was pinned rakishly to her jacket. Add to that the legal pad, khaki shoulder bag, the clipboard, the portable tape recorder, the street directory, and the little black telephone book, and you have *Seventeen* magazine's ideal of the liberated reporter. She reminded me of those little girls in the third grade who always had neat little pencil cases with rulers and little sharpeners. Girls are always better prepared than boys. I had a few pieces of monogrammed stationery left over from my married days, and a Bic Banana pen that was almost out of ink. What the hell, I was going to make the whole thing up, anyway.

'Get lost?' Jill asked, getting into the car. She looked fresh and cheerful. No make-up or bleach, just billows of real blonde hair, which she shook out as she took her cap off, and a pair of legs that ended someplace under her chin. Nice, frank blue eyes too, without a shot of blood in them.

'You don't look very enthused,' she said.

'I don't relish the prospect of freezing my ass off on some pier in Brooklyn all day.'

She took a thermos out of her shoulder bag. 'Coffee?'

'Sure.' I proffered my flask. 'Courage?'

'Not that kind, thank you.' She poured the coffee and handed me the cup.

'Very domestic,' I said. The coffee had a pleasant mocha aftertaste. Of course, she would know some esoteric trick, like putting carbon paper in the grounds. 'It's like we spent the night together.'

'You wouldn't want to,' she said. 'I'm not very good in bed.'

'That's all right, neither am I,' I said.

'Then I wouldn't want to,' she said. 'So let's keep it professional. Tell me you're not excited about covering a collision at sea.'

'Seen one, you seen 'em all,' I said.

'Oh, I forget.' She said, 'You covered the sinking of the "Titanic".'

'All disaster stories end up exactly the same,' I said.

'Really,' she said, arching one eyebrow, the other too utterly bored to make the trip. 'And how is that?'

'I'll tell you,' I said. 'And you see if I'm wrong. First, we'll spend half of our time freezing and seeing nothing because the authorities will have the site closed, and the other half we'll be drinking coffee in some kind of waiting room, or in a hospital, a police station – it doesn't matter because they all look alike and the coffee tastes like monkey shit. Some guy will come out and give us hourly bulletins – *x* number killed, *x* dollars' worth of damage. We'll get the famous oversight explanation.'

'Which is. . . .'

'Which is the pilot was deaf, or the inspectors hadn't checked that part of the mine, or the night watchman fell asleep with his cigarette burning. The families will show up – some of them hysterical, but most looking as if they wanted to get back to the bowling alley. You'll hear that the pretty young thing was just finishing her junior year in Europe, or Grandpa was visiting the old country after sixty years of working as a shoemaker, or the happy couple were on their honeymoon. Then there'll be the dead fireman who had premonitions of doom that morning; the policeman who filled in for his sick friend, and a burning beam fell on his head – did he have an appointment in Samarra kind of thing? All the media get the same stuff because there's only one source. Once in a million you'll get some guy who comes up and points a finger and says the company was too cheap to fill the fire extinguishers, and you get yourself a controversy. But the news-eating public isn't interested in those angles. They want the bloody statistics, the eyewitness shit. You know, "And then Mr Goldberg caught fire, and the only thing left was his belt buckle." That kind of stuff. That's what they want.'

'Fashionably jaded and bitter,' Jill Potosky said.

'You see if I'm wrong. See if you come up with anything new. Anything that doesn't sound like every disaster story since Noah's Ark.'

We drove over the Brooklyn Bridge in silence. To the left lay Brooklyn, my ancestral home. Unlike the debauched quarter we had just left, the Borough of Churches was quiet at night as all the good honest folk slept stolidly in their beds, visions of sixpacks and drumsticks lighting up their slumbers. Little did they know that they would have a bona fide disaster to gulp down with their turkey that day. A little existential cranberry sauce for the holiday drudgery. For the first time in years the big Thanksgiving story wouldn't be the Macy's parade. That was something to give thanks for right there.

CHAPTER TWO

Like I said: seen one disaster, and you've seen 'em all.

It was barely six o'clock, but the pier was crowded with more than the necessary number of cops, ambulances and official hangers-on. A few customs men had come in their station wagon, and the mayor had sent his flunky Farbner to hold the fort while hizzoner had his morning cup of

Postum and prepared to interrupt his Thanksgiving dinner to visit the scene. There would probably be a bunch of noisy ghetto kids at Gracie Mansion anyway, so he'd be happy to leave, and let his wife hand out the turkey wings and the tacky presents.

I looked around at the assembled journalists. None of the first-stringers was in attendance. Even the stations had sent out their minor-league crews. It would just be a matter of waiting for the crippled craft to come chugging in, and that wouldn't be for hours. I got that hysterical feeling that always comes when I'm on a breaking story and nothing's happening. There were no big Coast Guard guys there. The Israelis were handing out coffee and *oy vay*'s to the assembled relatives. No scrambled eggs, no Swedes. All the action had to be down at Coast Guard headquarters in lower Manhattan.

I left Potosky and drove back over the Prospect Expressway looking over the drab two family houses of Red Hook. The sun was rising over Battery Park, the oldest area in the city – a good place to be on Thanksgiving. It was here that Peter Minuit bought Manhattan from the Indians, and peg-legged Peter Stuyvesant defied the Duke of York. The area was loaded with cannon balls and statues, and it made me think of that picture in everybody's textbook, of the noble Indians standing in single file, confronting the pious Pilgrims, while in the background sailing ships ply the azure Hudson. Those colorful days of yore, when the air was clean, the only muggers were disgruntled Iroquois, and you could pull sturgeon out of the river with your big toe.

The Coast Guard building is a big, dirty brown brick affair on Whitehall Street, a little way down from the infamous draft board. The conference room was a jumble of wires and cursing technicians. On the long oak table were the inevitable coffee urns. There was also a silver tray of Danish pastry to attest to the class of Coast Guard. It was this goddamn coffee again. Every time there was a disaster, the coffee companies got rich. If there could be an air crash, an earthquake or mine disaster every day, Maxwell House would soon be outgrossing General Motors.

I had my third cup. My stomach was starting to rumble, so I quieted it with a Danish filled with Elmer's Glue. Bill Morrissey, the police reporter for the *News*, was in a corner talking to an elderly chap with a lot of gold braid, and Marty Appelbaum, a *Times* man just back from Southeast Asia, had another officer boxed in.

I sidled up to Appelbaum's kaffeeklatsch. His officer was a beardless youth with the cropped sideburns and elaborate pompadour of a mod military type, the type that puts a wig and a false mustache on every weekend and haunts the singles bars, telling people he's a stockbroker. It said De Forrest on his name plate; a real old Coast Guard family, I was sure.

'She was a tall blonde,' he was saying. 'I think her name started with an *L* or a *J*, I don't remember which.'

Appelbaum shook his head. 'Don't know her.'

'Kind of an Ivy League type. Real nice bod, really put together. Lisa or Lenore. I met her at this UN party, like I say, for the International Geophysical Conference or UNESCO – one of those operations. I go 'cause there's always a lot of nice pussy. And this one was really heavy. She said she worked for the *Times*, but I got bombed and couldn't remember her name the next morning. But I remember that bod. It just didn't quit. . . .'

Appelbaum looked bored. He hadn't shaved, and a glob of toothpaste had clotted in his mustache. 'Krales here might know her. He's fucked every newspaperwoman in the metropolitan area.'

'You see, there was this girl I met at this UN party for the International Geophysical Conference or UNESCO,' De Forrest said.

'I heard it all,' I said. 'I think I know who you're talking about.'

'You do?' He looked at me with terrifying enthusiasm and blew a cloud of Listerine in my face.

'Yeah, a chick named Jill Potosky.'

'That's it, holy shit, that's it,' he said grabbing my arm. 'Do you know her?'

'Yeah, she works for the *Times*. Appelbaum's going out with her. That's why he wouldn't let on.'

'Oh, I see. I guess I made a booboo.' He didn't look at all perturbed that he had. In fact, he was positively porcine with glee.

'If you want to meet her. . . .'

'I do, I do.'

'Okay,' I said, disengaging from his sweaty grasp. 'Get me some inside information about this collision. Stuff other newspapers don't have. You know, about who's really to blame, and what the Coast Guard is going to do about it. About what, if any, radio messages between the two ships before the collision.'

'But I can't do that,' the De Forrest said. 'I'm in the mess.'

'I don't care about your personal life. I just want the information.'

'The mess, the mess,' he shrieked. 'Don't you know what that is? I'm the one who brought the coffee and stuff in. I don't have anything to do with operations. I couldn't get that kind of info if I wanted to.'

'Then you'll just have to beat your meat, my friend,' I said, and moved quickly away, leaping nimbly over kneeling technicians and crossing wires.

Everybody was jockeying for position for the 'briefing' that was finally about to occur. The media people overwhelmed the writing press by sheer force of numbers. There were only three of us, with a combined audience of maybe three million, tops. Counting reporters, cameramen, soundmen and the nuclear physicists who make four bills a week for holding a spotlight, there must have been thirty of them, with at least ten radio guys toting their little equipages. Their audience was close to twenty million, but we were the nobility, and they all knew it. We got it down on paper; they stood there, holding their electric dildoes. There was a link, however tenuous, between us and Leo Tolstoy. The only forebears they could claim were Norman Brokenshire and H. V. Kaltenborn. We were the lowest-paid people in the room, which added to our cachet. Our poverty automatically conferred greater integrity upon us than they could claim for themselves. They resented us, fallen aristocrats that we were, and rejoiced at our dwindling numbers.

The Coast Guard PR officer was another young man, close of crop and gleaming of cheek, with the pendulous lower lip of a crybaby. 'I'm Lieutenant junior grade Paul Goldburg,' he said. 'That's spelled with a *u*, not an *e*, if you want attribution, although in most cases I prefer to have myself referred to simply as a Coast Guard spokesman.'

Before he could issue more guidelines, the room was an inferno of light as all the TV cameras started turning. Goldburg squinted and sweated and tried to pull himself together.

'Are you rolling?' he asked, swaggering a bit with his use of the jargon.

'Please tell us what happened,' one of the media heroes called. 'Use the pointer and the map.'

'Well, that's what I had intended to do,' Lieutenant Goldburg said stiffly.

Wielding the pointer, he showed us how one ship had been coming from one direction and the other ship from another one, and how they had bumped into each other. He repeated this about ten times for the various media, and looked bushed, but happy, when I approached him.

'Lieutenant, I'm Josh Krales of the *Event*. . . .'

He nodded. 'I've seen your by-line.'

I was flattered in spite of myself, 'PR officer for the Coast Guard,' I mused. 'Funny kind of job for a Jew, isn't it?' I spoke in that jocular, intimate way designed to extract confidences.

The lieutenant shook his head. 'I'm not Jewish, Mr Krales.' He spoke with dull resignation, as if he had repeated that line hundreds of times.

'My mistake,' I said, shrugging and nodding and trying to make it seem as if I made the same mistake every day. Shmuck, I told myself. Goldburg with a *u*, he had made a point of that. Anybody named Goldburg who isn't a Jew doesn't like being taken for one.

'There are many non-Jewish Goldburgs in this country,' the lieutenant said.

'Millions,' I gushed. I could imagine how many nice Jewish girls had run a marriage trip on him, how many *kvelling* Jewish mamas he had met, how much chopped liver he had forced down his gullet when all he wanted was a little nooky, which he could have gotten with no questions asked if his name was Ferguson. Or De Forrest.

'In point of fact I came from a Mennonite family,' he said. 'Steubenville, Ohio. My father's a minister there.'

'Well,' I said, 'that's as far away from a Jew as you can get without being the *Gauleiter* of Bavaria.'

'That's right,' Lieutenant Goldburg said, nodding emphatically.

'I don't suppose you'd care to give me the Coast Guard thinking on this little accident,' I said, half turning to go as if I didn't expect anything.

'The Coast Guard thinking is that two boats collided at sea, Mr Krales,' Lieutenant Goldburg said.

'You know, they call the Coast Guard the Jewish Navy,' I said, and left him to ponder his choice of career.

The Checker radio car of the *Daily News* was parked in front of the building. I gained admission by waving my flask, and discovered a pint of blackberry brandy and another of Southern Comfort already in circulation. In ten minutes the car was SRO. The AP guy had shown up with Ianelli and O'Malley, the *News* photographer. Morrissey had collared some garrulous old patrolman friend of his, and Appelbaum had coaxed the young sentry at the door in for a few. We drank, smoked, belched, farted and blasphemed for the better part of an hour. The car filled with stuporous fumes, and all would have expired if the news hadn't come over the police radio that the crew of the 'Charles XII' had debarked and been taken to Beekman Downtown. So, with many a bibulous 'tally ho' we sped off.

There were so many media cars parked haphazardly around the hospital that the ambulances couldn't get through.

The TV guys were coiffed and cosmetized for their second go-round in front of the cameras. They stood in a tight circle like the hookers at a bachelor party, smoking and talking intently. The radio guys were whispering, 'Testing' and 'Mary had a little lamb', into their mikes to see if their machines were working; their rumpled, harried appearances contrasted with the calmness of their stentorian voices.

A grim-faced intern with sandy hair, blue eyes and the cleanest white coat I'd ever seen, looked with distaste at the fourth-estaters cluttering up his emergency room.

'Any serious injuries, Doc?' someone called.

'The men are suffering from shock and exposure,' he said. 'They've been put to bed. Some have been sedated. Absolutely under no circumstances will I permit. . . .'

'Excuse me, Doctor,' I said, 'but Mr Bergstrom said that I would be permitted a short interview with the captain.'

'I know nothing about that,' he said. 'Who is Mr Bergstrom?'

'He's the Swedish ambassador,' I said. 'I called him in Washington, and he asked if I would act as his sort of unofficial representative until he arrived. . . .'

The doctor looked at me as if I were Mao Tse-tung's appendix. 'Who are you, sir?'

'Gunnar Lindstrom from the *Event*, sir,' I replied brightly, flashing my press card. 'I'm of Swedish parentage and I speak Swedish. . . .'

Somebody groaned in back of me.

I turned to face the traitorous throng. Arthur Miller, the token black at ABC, a clenched fist in a Cardin sleeve, laughed in my face.

'Say something in Swedish, Mr Lindstrom,' he said.

'Svenskfilm industri, motherfucker,' I shouted.

'His name's not Lindstrom, it's Humperdinck,' Appelbaum said.

'Well, I've had enough of this asinine comedy,' the intern snapped. 'There'll be no visitors, no interviews, by order of the administrator of this hospital. . . .'

'What's he trying to hide?' somebody shouted.

'The appalling conditions in this hospital,' I shouted. 'And don't think the public won't be apprised. . . .'

'And if you gentlemen are not out of here with all your

paraphernalia in fifteen minutes, I'll have you ejected by the hospital security personnel.'

I wandered into a phone booth, took out a bent paper clip, stuck both ends through the holes in the receiver, and tried to raise a dial tone. After a few fruitless minutes I settled with Ma Bell and deposited a slug. I called the office first and told them I had nothing. Kalmenson, a twenty-one-year-old day assistant city editor, suggested I used my ingenuity. I offered him a suggestion in return.

Next I called my wife's apartment. My son answered the phone on the first ring.

'Thought you were comin' over, Dad,' he said. He didn't sound concerned. After spending his infancy watching his parents fight, he was shellshocked at six.

'I was, Quentin, but I had to go to work. What's goin' on?'

'Oh, we're havin' a party. Mom's cookin' and I'm not allowed in the kitchen. . . .'

There was a commotion at the other end of the line, and my wife got on. 'Too hungover to keep your promise?' she asked with a sarcastic drawing-room-comedy lilt to her voice.

'I don't want to talk to you,' I said.

'Of course you don't, Joshua.' She always calls me that when I owe her money. 'But there is this little matter of the missing check. Today is the twenty-eighth, and it's due on the first. . . .'

'I sent it by pony express,' I said. 'Down the Chisholm Trail, the Northwest Passage. What are you, anti-American?'

'Do they have alimony jail on the Chisholm Trail?'

'Having a party over there?' I demanded.

'Yes, and you're not invited.' I could almost see her sticking her tongue out.

'Will there be any children there?' I asked. 'Will my son be able to interact with members of his peer group? . . .'

'There are children coming. Now, about the check. . . .'

'What are you cooking?'

'A duck.'

'In honor of your new boy friend, the quack.' She's going

out with a gynecologist. Every night I pray he'll either marry her, or push her off the stirrups.

'Yes, and when you come for dinner I'll make a capon. Now. . . .'

'I'll bring it tomorrow night. Now, can I speak to my son, please?'

'No, I'm afraid that thirty seconds of conversation with you have already overexcited him.'

'Can't say the same about you, can I?'

'No darling, I'm afraid your charm is strictly confined to six-year-old boys. So I'll look for you tomorrow night. Come after the c..h..i..l..d has retired, because it's not your visiting night, and we don't want further overstimulation.'

She hung up, leaving me with an ear full of dead air, and the usual homicidal fantasies I have after our exchanges. In the space of a few hours I had been awakened by a spiteful editor, patronized by a Vassar bitch, manhandled by assorted video technicians, rebuffed by a Mennonite, betrayed by my colleagues, threatened by an intern, reproved by my son, and one-upped by my wife. The world was making it increasingly clear to me that I was a pariah. Well, I had two words for the world, and they weren't 'Happy Thanksgiving'.

CHAPTER THREE

The New York *Event* is the product of three mergers, two acquisitions and a spin-off. In the last round, Hearst dickered for it, Newhouse took a gander, but it finally fell into the hands of the Pritchard Group, a chain of rural weeklies and small-town ad sheets that wanted a big-city front so its executives would have an excuse to come into the city and act like conventioneers. Old man Pritchard – if there ever was one – is supposed to have been a sage, pickle-barrel old typesetter who sent out copies of his first newspaper with tobacco-juice stains on the editorial page. His epigones are a bunch of Midwestern cost-cutters, the types with the denim suits, the short-sleeved white shirts with sweat shadows under the arms, and the short haircuts shaven at the sides. They all look, dress and talk alike, from the executive vice-president right down to the junior accountants, so I can never tell who the boss is. They come in twice a year, a whole army of them, and make camp in the grand old executive offices which were once the sumptuous province of the original owner, Mrs Dotty von Fliess, now banished to her philanthropies somewhere in the East Seventies. Teams of them prowl around the various departments of the paper; when they leave, they take fifteen or twenty jobs with them.

Their strategy is simple: the *Wall Street Journal*, bless its conniving heart, laid it out for everybody a couple of years ago. Big-city papers are the graveyards of the moribund industry. You make your money in the suburbans and the rurals, then you pour it into the urban dailies, and call it a loss. In the meantime, just to keep your hand in, you cut staffs, eliminate sections, and practice other little economies that earn you the admiration of the brokers and the epithets 'hardboiled' or 'unsentimental' from the business sections of the news-weeklies. Slowly, you drive the paper into the ground. Then, after a couple of years in the much-publicized red, you announce with regret that this newspaper, this landmark of American journalism, has to be closed because of rising costs, greedy labor unions, and general public apathy. And then you declare a whopping hundred-million-dollar loss; your stock soars; you earn the epithet 'canny corporate manipulator', among others; and everything works out fine. Of course, you've put another brick in New York's mausoleum, but that couldn't be helped. It's inevitable, you say. The centralized urban areas are becoming obsolete. California is the key to the future: little towns connected by freeways and shopping centers; cheap little dailies that take the news off the wire-service tickers and suck up to the retail advertisers. The death of the cities is unavoidable. After all, you say, we tried to stay in business, we tried to keep the great newspaper tradition alive.

The hell you did. You tried to kill New York. For the last fifty years all these rubes with their purple carbuncles have been trying to level the Big Apple. They hate it. They hate the mockies and niggers and guineas and all the other heterogeneous scum that run the big towns. They also hate the regal Yankees, the real moneyed elite who float along on top of this smelly ethnic goulash on their yachts. They hate the concentrations of financial power where they have had to seek their sustenance, Stetsons in hand. They hate the opera, the theater, all that highbrow crap; the big buildings, the way some sweaty cab-driver or garlicky waiter can give them lip – the help never talks back where they come from. They hate it, and they've been after it all along. First, they dumped their poor and dispossessed on the cities. No unions in their bailiwicks, no welfare, no chance, so the people flowed into the city which hugged millions to its ample bosom until it withered. Then they sucked all the factories down to their red neck of the woods by promising to keep the unions and the wages in line. Now their oil and timber and commodities money looks better and better as the industrial and financial satrapies are taking big beatings. So they're going to come in and milk New York, kick the bound urban Gulliver in the teeth, and turn it into a wasteland, a big parking lot, patrolled at its perimeters to keep the junkies out.

As I drove back through downtown Manhattan, I could see all those towering Wall Street edifices crumbling to the ground and being replaced by fast-food operations where millionaires with pig snouts and string ties sat, feeding their faces, and occasionally stuck out a cloven hoof to kick a passing Hasid down the stairs. That's what booze does to me. It makes me apocalyptic. By the time I got to my office, I was ready to throw the first grenade.

The *Event* is in the old *World* building on Barclay Street. There are still pictures of Pulitzer, Broun, Messrs Scripps and Howard, and other, now-obscure luminaries in the lobby, all smiling out of their wooden frames and sepia backgrounds. There was something puckish, even a little evil about these historic visages. You wouldn't blink if you saw the same photos on a post office wall. A greater collection of dissolute, conniving brigands never existed, not even in political clubhouses or on death row. Reporters really were a slimy lot in those days: boozers, womanizers, plagiarists – in short, a terrific bunch of guys. I had fallen prey to their legend and had become a newspaper man in the hopes of being just like them. So here I was, a boozer, a womanizer, a plagiarist. No wonder I was alone and friendless on Thanksgiving.

Because of the abbreviated schedule, most of the staff had gone home early. A new shift would come on at eight to start work on tomorrow's edition. In the meantime, there was a skeleton crew: a copy boy to watch the wire room, and old Sam Rafferty, once a great rewrite man for International News, who had, single-handed, written every word on the Lindberg kidnaping and trial that INS transmitted, now a broken-down old drunk who did the obits and alerted the editors at home in case of national emergency.

Jill Potosky was also there, sitting at her typewriter, legs crossed, a cigarette dangling, a 3H pencil stuck in her hair.

'You were right about this story,' she said. 'The people said almost exactly what you said they'd say. I guess that's how you can get away with writing most of your stories from a bar stool.'

'This isn't your kind of story anyway. You should be writing about lady bricklayers for the women's page of the *Times*.'

She smiled sweetly, taking a leaf out of Dorothy Parker's book; all the new ladies were smart enough to do that. 'And you should be the diplomatic correspondent for *Screw*.'

'Krales,' Rafferty croaked. 'Phone for you.'

'We'll continue this later,' I said.

'We certainly will not,' Jill said.

'We certainly will,' I said, jamming on the headpiece. 'Who is this?' I shouted.

'Some phone manner, Mr Krales.' The voice was soft and conspiratorial.

'Who the fuck is this?'

'Take it easy. This is Bill De Forrest. Remember, from Coast Guard GHQ this morning. Remember me?'

'Yeah, the horny sailor.'

'Don't knock it, Krales. It's getting you what you want. Not that you deserve it. I called the *Times* to get this girl Potosky, and they said they never heard of her. . . .'

'You've got to know her extension to get connected,' I said. 'Otherwise they think you're a crank caller.'

'Oh yeah?' He sounded skeptical. 'Do you know her extension?'

'I know her home number, Admiral.'

'Oh wow. Look, I'm sorry if I sounded snotty, but I thought you were laying the old okie-doke on me, and. . . .'

'Talk,' I said.

'Well. . . .' His voice was low and hesitant. 'Ah, fuck it, what can they do to me anyway? The guy you wanna talk to is Captain Olson, the guy who ran the rescue operations. I sailed with him once. A regular Captain Queeg, and a boozer to boot. Three sheets to the wind at ten o'clock in the morning. Well, he spoke to the brass here on the ship-to-shore. He's blasted already, I can tell. Says the Israelis violated starboard right-of-way laws. Says it was their fault.'

'Where is he now?' I asked.

'Steamin' back with the "Ben-Gurion". After that, he'll go over to the base in Staten Island. Should be back there at about four or five at the latest. You can just call the base and ask if the "Rensselaer" is in.'

'Hold on a second,' I said. I went over to the address wheel on Rafferty's desk and looked up Potosky's address. She was typing away, busy as a bee. It was a beautiful setup. I copied her address and phone number down and gave them to De Forrest.

'Gee, thanks, Krales,' he said. 'Well, you know, let's keep in touch.'

'Sure,' I said. 'The next time there's a ship collision, I'll give you a buzz.' I smirked at Potosky on my way out. Little did she know. . . .

I had a few hours to kill, and the libraries were closed, so

I figured I'd have a drink. I drove around lower Manhattan, looking for some joint, any joint, to kill time in. The place was a ghost town. The bums had come out of the doorways and the subway men's rooms to air their tatters on the steps of our venerable financial institutions. Two cops were cooping in a patrol car on Church Street. A jammed burglar alarm jangled its warning to the indifferent streets.

I drove up to the Howard Johnson's on Broadway and Forty-sixth. Two old ladies in veiled bonnets, with rouge spots lighting up their yellow cheeks, sat at the bar, drinking Manhattans. I joined them and ordered the same. The bartender was a chubby little homosexual who oozed sympathy with every gesture. He knew what it meant to sit at a Howard Johnson's bar on Thanksgiving, and he wanted to help. He put cherries in the ladies' drinks, a twist in mine. I took this as an obscure tribute to my masculinity, and was grateful, even though I really wanted the cherry.

A bunch of tourists were sitting at a round table, silently consuming the Howard Johnson's special Thanksgiving dinner. It looked perversely appetizing in its portion-controlled neatness, so I ordered one. The bartender set a doily with a map of Cape Cod in front of me, and a minute later there was my dinner. It was good; even those starchy little dinner rolls and the tired little tossed salad were good. I had a piece of pumpkin pie with a scoop of rum raisin ice cream for dessert. And then two more Manhattans. I was starting to have fun, but a call to the Coast Guard base confirmed that the 'Rensselaer' had floated in, so it was off across the Brooklyn Bridge again, this time over the Gowanus Parkway, to the Belt, a circular highway that girdles Brooklyn. I took the scenic route, which runs parallel to the Narrows, or South Bay, as the Pilgrims called it. Across the bay stood the docks, barges and warehouses of dismal New Jersey. Ahead, the Verrazano Bridge, my Rubicon, rose like a golden, celestial transport between two cloud kingdoms.

The 'Rensselaer' was snuggling in its berth, hardly winded from its exertions. A guard stood at the gangway and saluted. Another took me below-decks, hopping over all sorts of nautical impedimenta that had been put out for repair.

Captain Olson's quarters were at the end of a long, narrow corridor. The guard knocked at a rusty metal door and stepped back with an ironic bow as he ushered me into the room.

The room was small, not at all the kind of layout Captain Bligh had. Captain Olson got up from behind his desk and offered me a hand as hard as a grappling hook. There was a half-empty bottle of Early Times Bourbon on his desk.

'Didn't get your name or your affiliation, sir,' he said.

I searched desperately for a publication that might find favor.

'Kilkenny, sir, *US News and World Report.*'

Captain Olson nodded and sat down. He was a trim little man in his late forties with a pinched, crimson visage and short sandy-gray hair. There was that boozer's glitter in his smile and that overprecision in his movements – he had to concentrate more on lighting a cigarette than Einstein did on $e=mc^2$ – that always gives the lushes away. Most drunks his age are either bloated or emaciated. But he looked lithe and muscular, and was probably still living off the legacy of an active youth, which would be played out in a few years, and would leave him suddenly quite old and incapable. They say the body is a fragile thing, but when you realize how long it bears up under our suicidal assaults, you have to wonder. This man probably hadn't had a square meal in ten years, and probably wouldn't until he got it at a Salvation Army shelter. But here he was running a ship and drinking enough to sink it.

'What can I do for you, sir?' he asked.

'We're interested in a little information about the collision today.'

'Ah yes.' His tight mouth widened a millimeter into his version of an expansive smile. I still hadn't seen his teeth. Drunks also have this thing about keeping their mouths and chins very tight, lest they fall off. 'That unfortunate occurrence at the Verrazano Bridge, if I may make a literary reference.'

'A very apt one, I might add,' I said.

'Well, sir, we sailors are not totally illiterate, you know,' the captain said. 'We know a bit about the world.' He produced a plastic glass and gave me a sly look. 'For example, we know that journalists are known to be serious drinkers.'

' "Dedicated" might be a better description, sir,' I said.

He filled the glass with bourbon and pushed it across the desk to me.

'To the Coast Guard,' I said, lifting the glass.

The captain mumbled something in Latin and took a healthy swig, which I, in turn, feeling the depravity of the profession at stake, imitated. The bourbon went down like a sack of hot nettles. Sweat broke out on my forehead; tears rose in my eyes. The captain dissolved in a hot blur, and I had trouble bringing him into focus again. I had been drinking all day, but I knew this interlude was going to push me over the edge.

'Well, Mr Kilkenny, what can I do for you that our information mill on Whitehall Street hasn't?' the captain asked.

'To put it bluntly, sir, you can tell me who was at fault in this incident,' I said with all earnestness of a callow midshipman. 'I don't feel that that is an unreasonable request, but your Lieutenant Goldburg. . . .'

'My Lieutenant who? . . .'

'Goldburg, sir, the PIO officer, I guess you'd call him. He just won't tell us anything beyond the very routine facts about the collision.'

'Well, isn't it obvious why he won't?' the captain asked with an avuncular smile for my naïveté.

I batted my baby browns at him. 'No, sir, I'm afraid it isn't. We're just reporters after a true version of the. . . .'

'This Lieutenant Goldburg' – he pronounced the name as if he were describing a peculiarly loathesome type of vermin – 'may have stronger loyalties and obligations to other parties, if you know what I mean. You see, I don't know this Goldburg . . .' he lingered over the name again, '. . . but I've met officers like him. Not very many of course, but enough to know just what kind of bird I'm dealing with. Or burg, if you like. You'll notice that they always have soft shore jobs. No sea duty for them, or just the minimum, anyway. And it's just as well too.' He leaned forward and whispered confidentially, 'These Jews don't make very good sailors, you know.'

'But, sir,' I protested, 'there was a whole boatload of Jewish sailors on the "Ben-Gurion" and....'

'Exactly my point. You see, I'm of Scandinavian extraction. Vikings, Mr Kilkenny, a natural bent for the sea. We never lose our headings, and we don't violate simple traffic rules. I spoke to that Swedish captain, and I agree that the little incident with the crew aboard the "Charles XII" was still not enough to cause them to veer off course the way the Israelis claim.'

'A mutiny is a serious matter, sir,' I said, taking a stab.

'Yes, but a couple of drunken deck hands is not, Mr Kilkenny. Grog is as natural to seafaring men as ink to printers. It keeps the salt out of the lungs. Why, it's part of the mythology of the sea.' He emptied his glass and looked pointedly at mine, which I promptly drained.

'So to sum up, sir, the Israelis were at fault,' I said. 'They were off course, and they refused to correct themselves.'

'Refused or were just plain incapable of doing so,' Captain Olson said.

I struggled to my feet. The light, almost imperceptible, rocking of the boat was making me sick. 'Anyplace here where a man can void his spleen?' I asked with seaman-like heartiness.

'Head's right out in the hall, two doors to the left,' Captain Olson said, refilling both our glasses.

The captain was settling in for the night, but I had other plans. I sneaked through the corridor, slinked off the gangway, and ran to my car. I figured the odds were even money that the captain wouldn't notice my absence until he was too drunk to remember I'd even been there.

It was after seven when I got back to the office. I put in a courtesy call to the Israeli consul and told him what Captain Olson had said.

'Any rebuttal?' I asked.

'They blame us for killing their Messiah, so what should we expect from a shipwreck?' he said. 'Print your story. We'll have our day in court.'

I hung up and put a page in the typewriter. Hunching over with the excitement I always feel when I have an exclusive, I wrote: 'A Coast Guard captain charged today that the Israeli boat "Ben-Gurion" was at fault in the collision at sea that destroyed the Swedish freighter "Charles XII" and killed one of its sailors while crippling the "Ben-Gurion" and injuring. . . .'

'How many people were injured?' I asked Rafferty. He always knows these things.

'Thirty-three,' he said.

'. . . thirty-three passengers,' I wrote, and then slammed back the carriage for a new paragraph.

'Captain Charles Olson, who commanded rescue operations aboard the cutter "Rensselaer", said that the Israelis were off course and "refused or were unable" to correct themselves.'

'According to Captain Olson, the mutiny of drunken sailors aboard the "Charles XII" before the collision was not a contributing factor.

' "Grog is as natural to seafaring men as ink to printers", he said, and added that "a couple of drunken deck hands" was "not a serious matter." ' Further details on the mutiny were not available.

'Of more consequence, according to Captain Olson, were the errors made on the Israeli boat. He would not specify what these errors were, but said, "These Jews don't make very good sailors."

I ripped the copy out of the typewriter and showed it to Rafferty.

'There's one guy who's going to be commanding a dinghy at the South Pole, thanks to you,' he said.

'Fuck him,' I said.

After the lead, the story wasn't much fun to write. It was just a tiresome rehash of details I'd been carrying around in my head all day. I put in a few purple patches about the rescue at sea, which I knew the dyspeptic philistines on the copy desk would cross out, and made up an eyewitness quote from a sailor on the 'Ben-Gurion', something about the Red Sea or Noah's Ark, a nice biblical reference that tied the story with a blue and white ribbon. After all, we are the people of the Book.

'Better stay off the Staten Island ferry,' Rafferty croaked. He got up and staggered over to pick up my story. I was immensely flattered that anything I did could pique the pickled interest of this profoundly uninterested drunk, and left with celebration on my mind.

By now all the bars would be swinging. Everybody would be sharing anecdotes about their bittersweet days with the family. There'd be a lot of loose women around. They come out on holidays, looking for relationships. It's easy to get a lonely woman into bed on a holiday, but it's almost always a waste. All she wants to do is talk about her parents or ex-husband. She shows you the scars, physical and mental. The sex is always perfunctory, the fee she pays for a shoulder to cry on. I decided to go home.

My apartment was cold. I undressed with the lights out. After a day of too much drinking, smoking and aggravation, the mirror wouldn't understand. I lit the last Camel and tried to remember if this was the second or third pack I'd been through. My throat was scratchy. With every drag I took, my lungs acted like a bellows, fanning the blaze in my sternum. The room stood on its head and whirled around when I closed my eyes. The Chinese army was on maneuvers in my mouth. But I was okay. I would have a good night's sleep. In the morning I would take two thousand milligrams of Vitamin C, a thousand of E, one Vitamin B complex and twenty protein pills, and they would neutralize the fifth column of terminal microbes lurking and conniving within me.

In some distant apartment on my plumbing line, somebody flushed the toilet. The sound acted like a mating call to my toilet, which responded with a forlorn grunt and a poignant spritz of its own. The sink groaned and trembled in sympathy, and the shower emitted a noisy drop or two. The whole bathroom was a quivering mass of unrequited passion. The apartment squeaked and cracked like a marshmallow in heat.

Morpheus was giving me the cold shoulder. I considered

Tuinal, but that didn't mix with booze. Some teenybopper had left a joint in my drawer a few months before, but I was too lazy to get up and light it. The only solution was masturbation; that got me to sleep faster than an Antonioni movie. But my pecker was as cold as a dog's nose. The only woman I could focus on with any consistency was the Potosky bitch, and I wouldn't give her the satisfaction – not even with Mary Fivefingers.

There was nothing to do but wait until whiskey's sodden wakefulness subsided. Well, at least there was one consolation.

'You're good at your job,' I said to the darkness.

A little voice came out of the closet: 'Big deal.'

'It is a big deal,' I insisted. 'It's a big deal to be good at your job. If you're good at your job, eventually you get everything you want out of life. God sees the truth, but waits.'

And comforted by that thought, I collapsed on my unmade bed and fell into a fitful, drunken doze.

CHAPTER FOUR

The story held up through the morning. They put it in big headlines on the front page, with their 'EXCLUSIVE' banner running across the top: 'COAST GUARD CAPT SAYS ISRAELIS ERRED'. As the day went by, it improved. Other reporters running down my leads discovered that the Swedish ship had been virtually helmless at the time of the crash because of an insurrection by the largely Chinese crew. The Israeli captain, it turned out, had been showing some representatives of Hadassah around the engine room. Later in the day it became one representative – the regional vice-president for the Midwest, of all places. And the locale of the little tour became increasingly vague.

Captain Olson caught it pretty good from everybody too. The other papers hit him at eight in the morning, when the *Event*'s first edition went to press. He was hungover and confused. Nobody from the *Event* had been up there, as far as he could remember. Just some very nice fellow from one of the magazines. An Irish fellow, as far as he could remember. When the truth dawned on him, he went berserk. He threatened to have my job in the first edition; in the second edition he was going to walk into the *Event* city room and blow me away with a flame thrower; in the late editions he had decided to chug up the Narrows in a destroyer and bombard the *Event* building. All of his quotes got into the running stories about the disaster until reporters calling his quarters in early evening got a polite PR officer who said that Captain Olson was being transferred to a top-secret assignment and was unavailable for further comment.

I slept late. The clock radio woke me with a news spot on the collision. My story was quoted: 'The New York *Event* reports. . . .' It gave me a warm, triumphant feeling.

I took a hot, leisurely shower. The bathroom got all fogged up, and Jill Potosky walked out of the mist, wearing a sombrero and nothing else.

'Ha,' I told her. 'I get hallucinations instead of hangovers, so don't expect me to honor you with a hello.' She turned around and disappeared without a word. 'Smart girl,' I hollered after her.

I had a bachelor's breakfast of cold meat loaf I had taken home from my mother three weeks before and the last flat dregs of a bottle of quinine water, and then sat down to the almost carnally pleasant task of figuring out my overtime. Adding it all up, I arrived at a total of $344.15.

It was a magnificent sum, eccentric and apt in its asymmetry. There was something honest and workmanlike about it, like a laborer's check or a tax refund. I contemplated it with pride and decided that my authorship proved that my years in the newspaper business had not been entirely wasted. I only hoped that management could brush away their bourgeois inhibitions and appreciate this document in the manner it deserved.

They couldn't. Fifteen minutes after I dropped it on the desk of Kettle, the city editor, it came flying back at me in the shape of a paper plane launched by my redoubtable editor, Stanley P. Grissom.

But first, a few words about that worthy. Stanley Grissom is the type of newspaperman who calls women 'gals' and lunch 'chow'. He's one of the group of aging Broadwayites who went into mourning when Toots Shor's closed. Stanley Grissom likes his 'sauce', as he puts it. He's been working on papers in New York since the thirties, has done every job on a newspaper, and has been mediocre at all of them.

Stanley P. Grissom hasn't used a pencil – except to pick his nose – in years. He is a large man with that booze-breadth to his chest and shoulders. He has short gray hair and a purple face with little white eyes that rove like prison spotlights in his head. Tufts of iron-gray hair coil out of his shirt collar. He has a loud, hectoring bass voice, a frown which he thinks is menacing, and a smile which he flashes with great confidence whenever he wants to charm someone. But I don't get any of his histrionics; just a poker face when he's putting it to me. As he was at that moment.

'Very amusing document,' Stanley P. Grisson said. 'It gave me a chuckle.'

'I so hoped you'd be diverted,' I said.

'Yes, well, if you want to hand in a realistic statement, maybe you'll get some money for yesterday's sterling endeavors.'

'Realistic?' I simulated indignation. Retrieving the slip, I shook it in his face. 'Do you want to challenge this? I've submitted proof of all my expenses.'

'I can't clear a statement like that,' he said. 'Management will jump down my throat. . . .'

'Why? You got a good story out of it. You sold papers with it.'

'We'd sell papers if we put the crossword puzzle on the front page.'

'May I quote you on that?'

A muscle twitched in Mr Grissom's cheek. That was the

distress signal I had come to know so well. It meant that he was struggling to control himself, that a fresh vat of hydrochloric acid had been dumped into his stomach.

'Give me something between ninety and a hundred dollars, and I'll clear it,' Grissom said. 'Otherwise, float it down your anal canal.'

I stood up and glared in his face. 'Grievance,' I shouted. 'You're trying to intimidate me into changing a legitimate overtime statement.' I turned and faced the city room, which had stilled its buzz and clatter to witness the confrontation. 'That's a grievance. I've done everything with perfect propriety, according to the letter of the contract between the Newspaper Guild and the *Event.* If you don't clear this statement, I'll have the shop steward bring an arbitration hearing. I'll call a chapel meeting and close the whole goddamn paper down. Then how will you explain *that* to management?'

Grissom shook his head. His expression was superior, but that little panic muscle was twitching a mile a minute. 'You have delusions of grandeur. You couldn't close. . . .'

'I gave you an honest day's work yesterday,' I said.

'How touching,' Mr Grissom said. 'And how unusual.' He took the statement out of my hand and held it at arm's length as if it were a dead rat. 'Nevertheless, we'll clear this odious piece of perjury, and take steps' – he favored me with a malign smile – 'to see that this never happens again.'

And that's how I got to Brooklyn police headquarters.

Brooklyn headquarters is known as 'Siberia' in the trade. Anybody over twenty or under sixty who is sent there is being banished for conduct unbecoming a humble scribe. Mr Grissom uses the silent threat of Brooklyn headquarters to keep reporters from handing in exorbitant expense sheets or claiming too much overtime. When a reporter has broken a big story and bids fair to become a celebrity in his own right, Grissom dispatches him to Brooklyn headquarters for a few weeks of monkish anonymity.

The Brooklyn police press shack is located on Bergen Street, just off Flatbush Avenue, across the street, fittingly enough, from Brooklyn police headquarters. It's a runty, rodent-prone, two-story taxpayer built fifty years ago to accommodate the scores of papers then in operation; now it's practically deserted. Downstairs, where the afternoon papers once held sway, is a catacomb of dusty, deserted offices, little rooms which have been picked clean by thieves, except for magnificent roll-top desks – one in every office – which were once nailed firmly to the floor and have resisted all attempts at surreptitious removal.

As the representative of the last afternoon paper in New York, I'm alone downstairs. The *Event* office is in front of the building. You can sit by the window and watch the paddy wagons pull up with their full complement of junkies, purse-snatchers, and muggers. You can always tell them apart. The junkies wobble, rubber-legged, up the stairs; the purse-snatchers are wearing sneakers, or 'felony shoes', as the cops call them; the muggers seem removed from it all. They look around with absent gazes. They don't swoon like the junkies or jive and argue like the thieves. They are unregenerate criminals, and they take arrest and imprisonment as natural concomitants of their work. You can see them every day, four or five manacled together, or only two handcuffed in casual intimacy.

I spent a week sitting at that window. I became a cop-watcher. I saw the patrolmen – paunchy, red-faced and jocular – bouncing up and down the steps; the robbery detectives in work clothes and windbreakers; homicide detectives in those soiled, creased suits and run-down shoes, their thick necks and angry eyes sticking out like neon signs reading 'COP.' It's weird how cops unconsciously take on the coloration of their quarry. The gambling and rackets guys with their tans and suits and pinkie rings looked like button men; some of them probably were. The vice squad guys wore long hair and hip-huggers, sunglasses and platform shoes. They're the happiest cops of all. They really get off, busting hookers and fags. They're fulfilled.

Occasionally, I'd see a skinny hippie with long hair, faded jeans, zodiac necklace, army surplus – the whole trip – bounding up the steps, or a young black with the Afro and the beads bopping around. You do a take and look twice and then three times, until you see that the kid isn't so skinny; he's got thick strength-tendons running up and down his arms, and the black isn't spaced out at all, but has a peculiar lucidity to his gaze, a core of sanity to his insane regalia. These are the undercover narcs, the undetectables. They set up middle-class kids for busts and domestic tragedies, infiltrating, balling the chicks, smoking or snorting the dope, and then, when the time comes, closing the party down. These guys have fun too. For every Cuban with three pounds of coke and a submachine gun that they bust, they collar fifteen kids with an ounce of pot and a ton of mouth. A great bunch of guys.

I spent a week doing nothing. The shift begins at five o'clock, three hours before the first edition goes to press. I'd arrive, and sweep the junkies off the doorstep. Upstairs, the lights would be on in the *News* office. Old Teddy Ryan, the *News* night man, would be up there, playing solitaire.

'Seven less niggers in the world,' he announced cheerfully as I entered one morning.

He had the stories all laid out for me. A couple of shootings, a stabbing or two, one bludgeon death, a jumper, and a wino who had been set ablaze by person or persons unknown.

'Nothing here for me,' I said.

'What do you mean?' Teddy asked indignantly. He's from the old school that flourished in the days when there was one murder a week in Brooklyn, and that was always page one. To Teddy, homicide is still an event.

'Just an average Thursday night in the Borough of Churches,' I said. 'Now, if all seven had been killed by the same maniac, you know, a mass murder. . . . But this shit isn't even news to their neighbors. And besides' – the dormant liberal in me rose – 'how do you know they're black?'

'Lookit the names and addresses,' Teddy said.

I looked. Okay, I'd give him Washington on Gates Avenue. Green on Blake Avenue could be a Jew – it wasn't impossible; a landlord who made an evening collection or something. He was the one who'd gone out of the window, which was a method of egress used occasionally by ghetto proprietors.

'How about Griffin of St John's Place?' I asked. 'That's not necessarily a black name, and there are a lot of young white people living in the brownstones around there.'

Teddy shook his head in disdainful condescension. 'In Fargo, North Dakota, Griffin's not a black name, but on St John's Place it is. Besides, white people don't get moidered this way, and you know it. They don't get it in the streets. They get shot by their wives or put away by some off-duty cop in a saloon. They get it out in their ranch houses by the ex-husband with the antique fowling piece or in the office from holdup guys; they get their balls sliced in hotel elevators by hookers or their heads broken by collectors, you know what I mean, kid. There's no use pullin' that bleedin'-heart shit on someone who knows the route. These are all niggers, and you know it. Seven in one night has gotta be worth something.'

Teddy was wrong. I went back down to my office in a blue funk. Seven murders, and the paper would only take a few paragraphs.

'What do I do to get this shit?' I asked Leventhal, the assistant city editor.

'Well, you can kill a cop,' Leventhal said. 'Or, if you're the suicidal type, take a walk down Flatbush Avenue with a ten-dollar bill stuck to your forehead.'

'I can't make any overtime or expenses on this beat, Murray,' I pleaded.

'I know. That's why you're there. Grissom's got a hardon for you like I've never seen before. He wants you to leave or be fired or drop dead – he don't care which. The only thing you can do is luck into a story so big and exclusive that only you can handle it. Oh, by the way, your overtime check came in.'

A lot of good that would do. Grissom would make sure I would never see another one again. I sat back and watched day break over the ghetto, which is not the most esthetic experience in the world. I needed a story, a good one with a lot of leg time, so I could get back on the overtime train. A nice, juicy coed rape, a Mafia rubout, a seventy-seven-million-dollar drug bust, a milquetoast schoolteacher who decapitates his wife and runs off with the maid. I needed a biggie now, as big as the collision, or I'd never leave the shack.

I waited until eleven, but nothing came. I called Amalfitano, my connection at headquarters. He's always good for a nice, sexy story. He picks them up from all over the city and then tells them to his wife at night as a prelude. But Amalfitano was dry.

'I don't know,' he complained, 'people don't fuck any more, they just kill. We had a slasher in the seven-four yesterday. Three nice-lookin' broads on Parkside Avenue. He just took their purses and give them a little nick, so they now all look like Al Capone. I was sayin', "Jeez, if you're gonna do that, why don't you at least fuck 'em first, you know." '

I called Garfinkle at the Brooklyn DA's office. 'Mafia is the key word,' I told him.

'No indictment, no new crimes, no bodies,' Garfinkle said. 'Not even a floater we can lay off on the wise guys. Nothin'.'

That was it for me. I was sick and dispirited. It was eleven-fifteen. An hour and a half later I called in for a good night. Another unproductive day. My name hadn't been in the paper in a week, and that was bad. My mother would start to worry, my wife would gloat, my son would forget who I was, I wouldn't be able to impress women with my by-line. There was absolutely nothing I could do about it. So I decided to get drunk.

CHAPTER FIVE

In countries where alcohol is the operative vice of the administering classes, one taboo has always been rigidly enforced. Military men are warned against taking a drink before 'the sun is over the flagstaff' or 'the yardarm', depending upon your branch. Mad dogs and Englishmen may very well go out in the noonday sun, but only barbarians take their gin and bitters before twilight. Men measure their sanity by their ability to keep up a good appearance, freshly shaven and clothed, and to keep away from the sauce in the afternoon. You can be a drooling alcoholic when the sun goes down, but take one drink in the afternoon, and you've hit the skids, brother, for the duration.

It's a shame, really. Life is too short for such spartan self-denial. A coated tongue has no clock. The larynx of a drinking man starts to dry and tighten like a piece of raw-hide in the sun at about eleven in the morning. A beer or a silly little *apéritif* at lunch won't do the trick. We can sit there, dunking breadsticks in our Dubonnet, but what we really need is a very dry martini to fortify our lagging spirits. Why has society mobilized its massive moral bulk against our harmless little habit?

Because afternoon drinking is a dangerous thing, that's why. It is a more potent de-civilizer than hemp leaves or Nubian slave girls. If everyone drank in the afternoon, our postindustrial society would grind to a halt. The day which began with such martinal briskness would drift off like an unfinished pronouncement, a squiggle from a stilled pen of Adam Smith's Invisible Hand. The streets would be filled with mildly inebriated people, giggling and goofing off. For every brawl or violent death, seven lovely courtships would be born. Afternoon drinking would open the flood-gates to every kind of promiscuity of thought and deed. Its interdiction is the only thing that holds our world together in these parlous times.

So I would advise the revolutionaries: lay down your Molotov cocktails in favor of the more potable kind consumed by the light of the sun. To those sinister lechers who are seeking a taboo sweeter than incest: there is no better way to thumb your nose at two thousand years of Western culture, four centuries of the Protestant Ethic, and three decades of your parent's admonitions than to skulk into a saloon of an afternoon.

The virtues of postprandial and nocturnal drinking cannot be compared. At night the bars are dim, or vaporous and violent. When they are crowded, one has a feeling of discomfort; when they are empty, one feels despair. Night-time drinking is an anxious business. There are women to seduce, colleagues to best in argument, strangers to impress, brawlers to defeat. This condition just does not apply during the day. The bar is always half-empty – you expect it to be so. There are absolutely no pressures on the tipplers to excel or be witty or seductive or supermasculine. No one gets drunk or abusive; voices are raised in jocularity alone. It is recognized that the exclusive goal of the afternoon drinker is to kill time as pleasantly and anonymously as possible, and no one wishes to impede him in attaining this lofty goal.

I went to the Albany Nightboat in the Village in a state of anticipatory tranquillity. The whole afternoon lay before me like a patient about to be etherized on a table. I took a small corner table and contemplated the first dose of anesthetic – a glass of white wine.

The bar was peopled with characters of my acquaintance, none of whom was put out by my aloofness. Afternoon drinking is a solitary pursuit best carried out in, but not among, a crowd – or vice versa. A few slender men in ornate clothing stationed themselves at the corner of the bar nearest to me. They spoke softly and seriously in proper afternoon manner, and threw me anxious side glances in violation of the afternoon code, which expressly forbids deviant explorations. I made a tactical switch to martinis. The management brought out a free buffet – chicken wings, cocktail franks, toast wedges with glutinous smears of various types, and garlicky little shrimps. My waitress, sensing my immobility, brought me a plate with my first martini. I was beginning to enjoy myself in that abstract manner that does not include other people except as objects of fantasy. This meant that I was getting drunk, and that was all to the good.

Light drained from the day, like white wine from a dark bottle. The afternoon people left. I also noticed that my waitress had gone off without collecting the check. Two bartenders now stood behind the stick, staring with bleak hostility at the gathering crowd. The night shift. It was time to leave.

They say the first stage of alcoholism occurs when the drinker blacks out and cannot remember anything the morning after. In my case these lapses are always providential: I don't want to remember. It's very convenient to leave one place, and then, seemingly a split second later, find oneself in another, transported through time, space, and any number of indiscretions, with no residue of guilt or resentment. To awake blissfully unaware of the source of the bruise, the hickey, the scrawled phone-number-cum-endearments, with no need to cringe the morning after over the gaucheries of the night before – that is indeed a state we should all aspire to. However, it has its disadvantages.

I came to my senses on a bench in the pocket park on Sheridan Square. It took me several seconds to realize that the hand feeling so gently around in my breast pocket was not mine, but belonged to a young black entrepreneur, who good-naturedly relinquished his claim when I complained. Reality came upon me in retroactive epiphanies. I shivered and realized that I had lost my coat. It was the eleventh I'd lost in two years. I buy cheap ones now, and didn't mourn for it.

I looked at my watch and noticed that the back of my hand was scraped and bloody. Immediately I experienced intense pain in that area. The knuckles on my right hand were cut, and the wrist was stiff. Had I hit somebody? If I had, then I had to be maimed or dead. I tenderly groped my body for further injuries. My legs seemed all right. Change and keys jingled in my pockets. My shirt was stickily moist, but not with blood. Some other clotty substance. It felt like semen. I couldn't have come while in this coma. The only possible explanation was that someone had come upon me, as it were. While lying in my stupor, I had acquired an anonymous swain. Just another illustration of the perils of passing out on the permissive streets of New York. In the old days all you had to worry about was getting your pockets picked. Now your virtue is compromised as well.

A careful search of my person revealed all fiduciary assets intact, with the exception of the thirty bucks I had spent on the night's entertainment. There was a tiny marble on my eyebrow, which I soon realized was an injury. My lips were caked with some substance which I now hoped was blood.

And it was four-thirty. In a half-hour the phone would start ringing at Brooklyn police headquarters, and if I wasn't there to answer it, Stanley P. Grissom would put another note in the voluminous dossier he was, no doubt, compiling on me.

I staggered to my feet. I would have no choice but to appear at work in this bespattered, bespermed state. I could only hope that no major disaster would occur to compel my attendance. I turned down Bedford Street in search of my Chevy II. It's a wagon, a relic of domestic days when I spent Sundays in the country with wife, infant son, and other similarly-burdened couples. Bedford is a well-known mob street. It was dark and quiet, with all the numbers runners and loan sharks lolling in their righteous slumbers. There was a slight splash of light from the half-open door of an apartment house. It spread out into the street and licked at the feet of a girl who was standing in the shadows.

She was slouching against the open door of another building in a peculiarly provocative position, her head thrown back, pelvis thrust forward. I knew better than to accost girls on this street, and pressed on, but, oh damnable parallax, as I changed my position, the light fell on her face. Her eye to be exact. One staring, challenging eye. It burned into me, inviting, daring, throwing down the gauntlet. I surveyed the area. Halfway down the block there was an Italian bakery, Skivoso and Iboopa's. The lights were on, and there seemed to be a lot of activity inside. Still, they were busy. They wouldn't notice, nobody would. Jockey into the doorway, exchange a few pleasantries, remove all hindering articles of clothing, go in, pull out; a perfectly satisfactory erotic adventure. I rushed across the street to my beloved. She seemed to smile at my approach. Her lips were parted for my embrace, her arms hung limply, submissively, at her sides. There was only one serious drawback: she was dead.

An instrument that looked like a shishkabob skewer had been inserted between her breasts, pinning her to the door. She didn't seem at all alarmed about this state of affairs. No grimacing death mask here, but rather a dim, relaxed look.

She was a nice-looking girl – tall, with shoulder-length brown hair. Rings glittered on each of her slim fingers, and there was a rhinestone star on her blouse. Her skin was soft and cool. She was wearing the dark lipstick and the forties rouge favored by the younger sybarites. A Vuitton pocketbook lay unopened at her feet. Blood seeped from around her wound, but the body was otherwise unmarked and intact.

I tiptoed a few steps down to the other open door. It had one of those tiny vestibules with just room enough for a mailbox. Lying on his stomach was a tall, expensively-dressed black man. Most of his head was oozing off the wall under the mailbox, although he had kept enough of it to have a positively horrified look on the side of his face that confronted me. There was a story here, I decided. A double murder, an interracial romance thwarted in Little Italy.

I stepped over the corpse and pushed open the door that led directly to the stairway. A pair of platform heels peeked out from the first landing. A trickle of blood was inching a trail down the tattered stair carpets. Its source was the chest of another tall, expensively-dressed black man, who was sitting against the wall outside an apartment with his head in his hands, gurgling his last. Now it was a triple murder.

The story was getting more complicated, the headlines bigger, the overtime more lavish.

The apartment was cramped and meagerly furnished. There was a horsehair sofa, a greasy blue rug, a huge color TV with the tube kicked in, and a stereo system. The smell of incense and cordite was in the air. The faucet was dripping in the bathroom. Another tall black man was there, standing over the toilet, his forehead pressed against the wall; it looked like he had gotten his while urinating. Quadruple murder? The massacre of the Grambling basketball team?

The bedroom turned up two corpses who killed the sports angle. One, a fat man with a beard and a chef's cap, was lying on the bed, staring at a poster of Jimi Hendrix on the opposite wall; and the other, a young girl very much in the mold of the girl downstairs, dressed in jeans and a halter, was lying face down next to the bed, her long hair matted with blood.

Six motley cadavers in Greenwich Village, on a street which I was sure hadn't seen a murder in fifty years. I poked around the apartment a little bit, being careful not to disturb anything or leave my prints. The closets were empty, and so was the refrigerator. Whoever lived here had obviously put the place to very special use. Stepping gingerly over and around the corpses, I went downstairs. My girl friend was still there, a little droopier than when we had first met, but still placid.

The street was quiet. There had to have been shots and screams, but no one had been curious enough to take a look. Nobody would leave his house until the bodies were discovered. And nobody would know 'nuttin'' when asked.

There was a phone booth on the corner. I called the office and spoke to Persky.

'Look, the damnedest thing just happened. I just discovered six corpses in an apartment in the Village.'

'Is one of them Judge Crater?' Persky asked.

'Pay attention, this is your lead story – I haven't called the cops yet. I've got no information at all, other than. . . .'

'I'll put you on with a rewrite man. . . .'

'You take it, you lazy bastard. Have you forgotten how to write? Two girls, attractive late teens, early twenties; three well-dressed black men, late twenties, early thirties; one stocky white man, early forties, wearing a chef's cap. One girl stabbed with a shishkabob skewer, the others shot.'

'You been whackin' off to Julia Child? A shishkabob skewer, a chef's cap.'

'Send a photographer over. You'll get pictures that'll make the whole city throw up. The address is 1797 Bedford. I'll give you a five-minute jump, then I'll call the cops. You can start the first edition with a bold paragraph on Page One. You'll have the whole story for the next edition. I'll stick around here, so you'd better send someone to cover Brooklyn headquarters.'

Persky laughed. 'You sonofabitch. You pulled a Manson just to get out of Brooklyn, didn't you? You killed those people. . . . Jesus, are you lucky. They had you boxed for life out there.'

'Mass murder in the Village,' I said. 'Send a photographer.'

I hung up, counted to thirty, then ran down the street to the bakery and banged on the door. A swarthy little guy in a white apron came to investigate.

'There's been a murder!' I hollered through the door.

He opened it up a crack. 'Oh yeah?'

'Let me use your phone,' I said.

The man let me in and gestured at a pay phone in the corner. The front of the bakery was still dark; only the back was lit. About a half-dozen people in white aprons and shirts were moving slowly about. The little guy didn't even tell them what I had said.

'Did anybody hear any screams?' I called as I dialed my home number.

'What are you, a cop?' the little guy said.

'Yeah. Farinacio, Manhattan South Homicide.'

'We didn't hear no screams,' he said.

'We didn't hear nuttin',' a fat man with a huge, round face said. Dark trousers and black shoes showed from under his white apron. Like the telltale shoes under the curtains in all those thirties movies, they alerted me. I was too exhilarated to be frightened. Persky was right: I had lucked into another one. Only this time, the overtime was going to hit the thousand mark.

'Would you believe my office doesn't answer,' I said. 'Not even a cop can find a cop when he needs one. I'll just have to try again.'

The bakers, sallow and sepulchral in the fluorescent light, stared at me with their arms folded as I dialed 911.

CHAPTER SIX

The cops arrived on the scene as if it were a riot. Patrol cars flashing and shrieking, doors opening, flashlights, tense voices: all this for a handful of silent stiffs who posed no danger to the populace. They woke the whole neighborhood up, and if the murderer was lurking in the woodwork, he had ample time and warning to make his getaway.

The first thing the cops do is close off the area. This is done, presumably, to keep it pristine for the lab men and investigators. The next thing the cops do is 'check out' the scene, dropping prints everywhere, trampling evidence underfoot, leaving the general impression that the crime had been perpetrated by a horde of elephants. The 'check out' procedure is like a scavenger hunt. Ten or fifteen cops spread out, looking for loose money, jewelry, or anything spendable, hockable, or wearable. They have to move fast, before sergeants and detectives arrive for their turn. The cops know that huge sums can sometimes be found in tenement apartments. They know that millionaire shylocks and bookies live in these run-down Italian buildings, men who'd sooner stash their money in a coffee can under the bed than a bank, for obvious reasons. One of the tacit rules of the hunt is that the area can't be too badly mauled, and the bodies have to be left tranquil. This doesn't mean that you can't go through closets and drawers, or slip watches off dead wrists, but only that your disruption can't be too obvious. The cops look for a pattern. If they find a dollar bill in a book, then that means that every book has to be opened, and the bindings torn to shreds. This comes under the heading of acceptable disruption of the premises. It is, however, unacceptable to turn bodies upside down, or try to pry gold fillings out of teeth. Also, taking the shoes and socks off decedents in search of hidden cash is considered in the worst taste.

By the time I returned to the scene of the crime, the treasure hunt had begun. A noncommittal patrolman standing at the door next to my dead girl friend looked at my press card and informed me that I couldn't go upstairs.

'But I'm the one who discovered the bodies,' I said.

'Nothin's changed since your first visit,' he said.

McCarthy, the coke-head who works the lobster shift at the *Event*, was snapping away furiously at the girl from all angles.

'Did you get upstairs at all?' I asked him.

'Only to that dead spade in the hall,' he said. 'The pigs threw me out.'

The patrolman at the door blinked at McCarthy, like a camera recording his face. McCarthy's eyes glittered like costume jewelry.

'Every one of these shots is gonna make me a hundred bucks,' he said. 'You know who that broad is?'

'No.'

'That's 'cause you didn't get around as much as you think,' McCarthy said. 'She's. . . .' He stopped, looked at the cop at the door, then beckoned me back a few steps.

'You're sure making a friend,' I said.

'Fuck him,' McCarthy whispered. 'I got enough white powder in my pocket to send me away for life. I gotta worry about him?'

I was momentarily derailed by McCarthy's logic. 'Anyway, tell me who she is,' I said.

'She's Pamela Sue McClough, the daughter of Arnold

McClough, who's Ambassador to Germany and heir to the Bramble tobacco fortune,' McCarthy said. 'She's hot shit, I'll tell ya. That's the billion-dollar class. I covered her coming-out last June at the Pierre. Man, I'll never forget it. I'm standin' there in line with the rest of the dudes, clickin' away at all these little chickies in white dresses, and here comes this mama. Tall and together, man. She's really got that long, high-class stride down. And she's got a great bod, and she's got jugs for the whole world to see. But she ain't got no pupils, man. Dig it, she's like Little Orphan Annie in a D cup. . . .' McCarthy grasped my shoulder and wheezed with silent laughter.

'And she's whacked out of her gourd, man. I mean, I pin her right away as a stone freak, you know. Okay, so I do my clickety-click, and I catch up to her a little later, and you know, I tell her I know where she's comin' from. . . .'

'So?' I asked, waiting for the lubricious denouement.

'So she's got that kind of Southern accent that gets you off when she says hello.'

'So?'

'So, so, what are you a tailor?' McCarthy said. 'So nothin'. She went away, and I put her picture in the paper, and now every rag in the country's gonna buy these shots. The dead debutante, can you dig it?'

Pamela Sue McClough. Now that I knew the stiff was a debutante, I noticed things I had missed. That Anglo-Saxon curve to the cheekbones, you didn't see too much of that in New York; the long, supple fingers strengthened by grasping bridles and tennis racquets. And the bizarre composure. Sure. These women never lost their poise, even when they were about to be skewered. Whatever they felt, they kept out of their faces and voices. Even the prodigal daughters like this poor girl knew how to do that.

A heavy hand interrupted my reflections. It belonged to a swarthy sergeant with a clipboard. 'Are you the gentleman who discovered the body?' he asked, accenting the word 'gentleman' so I would understand that he thought I was anything but.

The sergeant took me upstairs. There was a crowd of

cops on the landing and in the apartment, all doing nothing but looking. We sat down on the couch to wait for the detectives. One cop was snapping pictures of the bodies with an Instamatic, obviously for his private collection.

'You know any of these people?' the sergeant asked me.

I shook my head, trying to look as nonchalant as possible. He stared hard at me for several seconds, and then, satisfied that my guilty demeanor was more Oedipal than circumstantial, turned away.

Lieutenant John Duffy, a honcho in the Manhattan South Homicide Police Squad, entered with his huge black henchman, Detective Silas Gray, and a horde of photographers and technicians. He looked at me and scowled.

'What's he doing here?' he asked the sergeant.

'He discovered the bodies.'

'That's great,' Duffy said. 'We gotta deal with this big mouth now.'

'That's great,' Detective Gray said, shaking his head sadly.

Lieutenant John Duffy looks like a cherub with a bellyache. He is short and roly-poly, with pudgy red hands, and a shock of blond hair falling over a pale, downy brow. In his youth he might have been said to have apples in his cheeks. But the apples have long since fermented; the flush in the cheeks is purple and angry. Duffy doesn't look like he could knock down a cockroach, but he's the youngest lieutenant in the detective bureau and is supposed to be the gutsiest. In any case, he has Gray along to take care of the cockroaches.

Gray looks like a WPA mural of John Henry. He is at least six feet eight inches tall, and so perfectly proportioned that it's always a surprise to learn that he's close to three hundred pounds. Gray's arms dangle to his knees, and rumor has it that he wears an eighteen shoe. He has the look of faraway nobility that one always associates with field slaves who rush through the burning plantation to save little Missy and her poodle. He never loses his temper, never seems to undergo any emotional changes at all, aside from an occasional laugh at one of Duffy's infrequent witticisms.

He is devoted to Duffy, functions as his door-breaker, head-knocker, area-clearer, and general all-round physical handy-man. He is content to exist without an identity, as Duffy's spare body.

Duffy's altar-boy blue eyes roamed coldly over me. 'You had quite a night, didn't you? Got drunk, got into a fight, got laid too, did you?'

'You're the detective,' I said. 'You find out.'

'You look half dead,' Detective Gray said. 'Sure they weren't trying to get you too?'

'They were, but I ducked.'

'Did you kill them yourself?' Duffy asked.

'Let's see,' I said, 'I know I killed somebody last night. What's today, Monday or Tuesday?'

A technician came out of the bedroom with a disgusted expression. 'Jesus, they're all over the place,' he said. 'This joint's gonna stink to the high heavens in about an hour.'

Another came out, bearing a wad of blood-soaked bills. 'Found 'em underneath the chef on the bed,' he said, offering the wad to Duffy.

'Count the money,' Duffy told Gray.

Gray went off in a corner and counted the bills, his lips moving. Duffy wrote down my statement in a smudgy little notebook.

'See anybody on the street?' he asked.

I shook my head.

'Notice anything suspicious?'

'Everything was nice and quiet. Too quiet, as they say in the movies.'

Gray came back. 'Three hundred hundred-dollar bills,' he said.

'A nice, round number,' Duffy said. 'Go down to the car and get a voucher slip,' he told Gray. 'Mr Krales here will be our civilian witness to the recovery of this money.'

'Why don't we just? . . .' I made a dealing motion.

'Do you realize you just committed a felony?' Duffy asked. 'Attempted bribery. Just for that I'm going to make you count the money to verify our number.'

The bills were new, and syrupy with half-dried blood.

Some were stuck together in clumps, and I had to peel them back to count them.

'Serpico a friend of yours?' I grumbled.

'Did you ever try to spend bloody hundred-dollar bills?' Duffy asked. 'Not even hookers'll take 'em.'

I signed the voucher, and Duffy told me I could leave.

'I gotta get a comment from you,' I said.

'Okay,' Duffy said. 'No comment. I don't talk to the press. I don't want my name in the paper, and I ain't runnin' for anything. I got six bodies here, and I don't know who they are. With three' – he looked over his shoulder at Gray and lowered his voice – 'niggers from nowhere, two teeny-boppers, and a small-time guinea, I've got my day all organized, wouldn't you say? The last thing I need is a wise-ass like you hanging around. So go back to your paper. From now on, all the news on this squeal will come out of the deputy commissioner's office.'

He turned away from me, and Detective Gray moved over between us. Gray's hands swung like twin pedulums at his sides. They seemed to be coming closer to me with every swing. Even a glancing blow from one of those grabbers would have left permanent brain damage. I went downstairs, picking my way through the welter of lab guys, who were spraying, powdering, or just gaping. The scene reminded me of a Hollywood première, all those forensic flashbulbs popping, the bustle and excitement. The corpses grinned and goggled obligingly. Everyone seemed happy enough.

CHAPTER SEVEN

Death sells papers. The grim reaper is the best circulation booster. Put 'FIFTY DIE' in front of any headline from 'IN FRISCO FIRE' to 'IN HEMORRHOID EPIDEMIC', and they'll be grabbing those papers off the stands. Give them a couple of mutilated bodies, and they'll read that eight-point type until their eyeballs ache.

And so in tribute to their provenance, newspaper people have sprinkled the lexicon of their craft with morbid allusions. Clippings are kept in a 'morgue', a story is 'killed' when it is proved false or obsolete, type in a composing room is 'dead', editions run on a 'deadline'. A newspaper is like a vampire, sucking enough sustenance out of the world's misery to survive (unions and advertisers permitting). It is also like a butterfly, living for twelve glorious hours before it tumbles earthward, its wings graying and crumbling. A vampire butterfly. If there is such a creature, it should be called *Lepidoptera periodica.*

Nothing more resembles the Mummy's Tomb than the *Event* city room on the graveyard shift. Here a skeleton staff of zombies, who have slept à la Dracula during the day, prowl the premises, pumping ghastly nourishment into the withered corpse of yesterday's paper. Under the sputtering fluorescents they sit, as brittle and yellowed as the clippings that pass through their fingers. They slouch and sigh like willows in a cemetery. They evince as much enthusiasm as cadavers, and don't say a hell of a lot more, either. That is, until they find a proper butt for their moribund humor, I, in my bedraggled condition, obligingly provided it.

From the door to my desk I ran a gauntlet of witless gibes.

'Whyn't you shave before you come to work?'

'You oughta stay away from those gay bars, Krales.'

'I guess it's the valet's night off.'

Persky called me over to the city desk. Lichtenstein, the city editor, looked up briefly and then went back to his crossword puzzle. He is an ex-Communist who stayed with the party through the show trials, the non-aggression pact, the Doctors' Plot, and the invasion of Hungary; and finally quit because the *Daily Worker* wouldn't give him a raise. Lichtenstein is a wispy man with a silent, superior smirk. He eats six bananas a night, and no one has ever had the nerve to ask him why. Like all ex-Communists, he has a reputation for absolute brilliance – training in dialectics and all that. He never speaks to subordinates, and he can pronounce Stalin's real name, which seem to be only apparatchik qualities that remain after thirty years under the hammer and sickle.

Persky was on the phone to the art department. He made a face and waved me away. 'Lookin' that bad, you must stink too,' he said. 'Hope you didn't shoot this deb with her pussy up in the air,' he shouted into the phone. Then, cupping the receiver in his hand, he whispered confidentially to Lichtenstein. 'He says they got good shots of the girl and the guys in the vestibule and on the stairs. A lotta tripe and ketchup.'

Lichtenstein peeled a banana and shook his head. 'No pulp-magazine stuff,' he said.

'Okay, forget the cheesecake,' Persky hollered. 'We'll run the usual pictures of the backs of cops' heads.' He looked pointedly at Lichtenstein. 'And if you've got a Currier and Ives of Washington Square Park, we'll run that too.'

Lichtenstein pondered his crossword puzzle and nuzzled his banana. Persky got angrier.

'We're callin' this broad an heiress,' he said to me. 'Is she?'

'I don't know,' I said.

'Whaddya mean you don't know?' Persky said.

'Whaddya mean what do I mean I don't know?' I replied. 'Wanna go around again?'

'We get sued for libel, and you go around and out,' Persky said.

Lichtenstein permitted one eye to stray from the puzzle and graze me briefly. 'We've got a few hours before the story has to be written,' he said with irritating calmness. 'Let him stay around and keep on the police for a positive identification.'

'So sit around for a while,' Persky said, 'and maybe you can pick up a positive ID.'

'It's your dime,' I said, heading for my desk.

Lichtenstein whispered something to Persky.

'Krales,' Persky called, 'while you're waiting, why don't

you go back to the neighborhood and pick up a little background?'

'For the same reason you don't take your finger out of your ass and fly to Honolulu,' I said. 'I like it here.'

Somewhere in that massive mausoleum I heard a giggle. But it faded, like the rustle of dead leaves, into the cricket chatter of typewriters and wire-service machines.

I called Abe Breitel, an ex-rackets cop who hadn't made an arrest in his last ten years on the force and who retired with enough money to open a detective agency. The phone rang at least ten times before a dying rhinoceros croaked into it.

'Who is this?'

'Krales,' I said. 'Don't you keep a phone by the bed?'

'Yeah, but you caught me in the middle of a little unfinished business,' Breitel said.

'And it took you ten rings to finish it?' I said. 'Either you're in love, or you can't get it up.'

'Whaddya want, Krales?'

'How would you like me to owe you a favor?' I said.

'What? Listen, it's too early in the morning to. . . .'

'I found six stiffs in a crash pad on Bedford Street tonight,' I said. 'One of them was a debutante. Pamela Sue McClough. Ever heard of her?'

I heard a scratch as Breitel lit a cigarette. He exhaled into the phone. 'I don't get around in those circles too much,' he said.

'She was a little out of her element too,' I said. 'Anyway, this all happened down the street from a bakery called Skivoso and Iboopa's. When I went over there to use the phone, I caught a coupla wise guys without their rolling pins. So I'm curious.'

'About Skivoso and Iboopa?'

'Yeah.'

'Who's on this squeal?' he asked.

'Duffy.'

'Didja tell him about this?'

'No.'

'Don't. Okay? And I'll get a run-down on the case for you, right from Homicide.'

'Fair enough,' I said.

It took Breitel forty-five minutes to call back, and when he did he sounded out of breath.

'Did you run to headquarters?' I asked.

He groaned.

'Are you balling again?' I demanded like an outraged citizen.

'Better,' he said.

A great melancholy enveloped me. 'What's her name?'

'Joey.'

That did it. Girls with cute nicknames are always built like locomotives.

'Put her on the phone,' I said.

'I can't, she's already on the extension. Hah, hah. . . .'

There was the sound of a slap, then a voice that sounded like Zasu Pitts imitating Marilyn Monroe. 'Who is this?'

'Just an ordinary guy with a million bucks and a ten-inch extension,' I said.

There was a shriek and a giggle, and Breitel repatriated the phone. 'Talkin' dirty to my old lady?' he growled.

'Your what? I'll give you a hundred bucks if you can tell me her last name,' I said. 'Your real old lady's out in Roslyn walkin' her fur coats and wearing lace panties for the milkman. Your kids are shooting skag under the ping-pong table, and the maid's drinking up all your booze. . . .'

'Hah, eat your heart out, Krales,' he answered. 'You wish you had a setup like that.'

He was right. 'I'm working on it,' I said. 'Meanwhile, you got anything for me?'

'Did I ever let you down? First, it was a deb. A wallet full of credit cards and fancy ID, and then the old man came down and made her.'

'The Ambassador?' I asked.

'Yeah. Right down to Bellevue morgue. No tears and didn't look surprised, say the murmuring pines and hemlock. . . .'

'Wasps don't display emotion in front of the lower ethnic forms,' I said.

'Well, tootsy was the one and only Wasp in this epidemic,' Breitel said. 'The rest of them just came out of the trees. You writing?'

'If you're talking.'

'The niggers were heavy dope dealers in Harlem. Arrests and no convictions, that kind of thing. Alex Robinson, thirty-four, nicknamed Poontang. Emmet Rand, thirty, a k a Slim the Stick. . . .'

'What's this, *Guys and Dolls*?' I asked.

'Just take this down, I got things to do. The third one is Dean Tyler, twenty-three. The broad's Olivia Bernazzo a k a – oh, you're gonna cream over this – Zarita Durand. Only twenty-two and she had a book. Drugs, prostitution, zip to two at Bedford Hills Women's Prison. Was she a good-lookin' head?'

'Yeah, but she just laid there, you know. No personality.'

'God's gonna punish you for talking like that.'

'Who was the guy in the chef's cap?' I asked.

'A neighborhood *goombah*. Vern Palucci, forty-six, twenty arrests on gambling, extortion. Oh, and that's a baker's cap you dig?'

'Uh huh.'

'He works for Skivoso and Iboopa. He's a master baker.'

'I'm not interested in his sex life.'

'And I got more,' Breitel said. 'Everybody was shot. No wild bullet holes, which means the hitter had some practice.'

'Same gun?'

'They don't know yet, but from the size of the holes, they don't think so. . . . Now our debutante. . . .'

'Our debutante? Since when are you a partner?'

'Be possessive, see if I care,' Breitel said. 'She was killed with a trocar, a sharp instrument used by undertakers to puncture the stomach so blood can be drained, fluid pumped in. Got the picture?'

'Very efficient,' I said. 'They embalmed her before she was dead.'

'Is nothing sacred with you, Krales?' Breitel said. 'There's one guy, believe it or not, with an MO that could fit this little hit. Name of Gaetano Albino, nicknamed Trocar. An old-timer from Brooklyn, looks like Frankenstein. Could probably kill you with his breath. Over eighty hits on his plate. Took a seven-year manslaughter flop at Attica. Just out a coupla months ago. Workin' as an embalmer. Lieutenant Duffy has summoned him for interrogation. Now you know everything the cops do.'

'And I can print it?'

'Sure, knock yourself out. Be a hero. Maybe you'll even get some pussy.'

'The stuff's not that good,' I said. 'You gonna make Skivoso and Iboopa for me?'

'What's to make?' Breitel said. ' A coupla junior button men. A little of this, a little of that. Arrest sheets on both of them long enough to wipe a giraffe's ass. What can I tell ya?'

'You've said enough. Now what can I do for you?'

'You come and shovel my driveway when it snows. Maybe you wanna walk my wife's fur coat for a while.'

'You got guys to do that, don't you?'

'What I'm sayin' is that you be there whenever I call.' Breitel suddenly got dead serious. 'And you do whatever I ask you to. I did good by you, and you do the same.'

'But nò details,' I said.

'When you need 'em, you'll get 'em. Okay?'

'A deal's a deal,' I said.

'You better believe it,' Breitel said. And he clicked off, leaving me with the ominous feeling that I'd been suckered. I'd asked him to fix a ticket, and now he'd want me to kill my grandmother. One of my guiding principles is, don't take favors from cops or hoods. It's too sage a maxim to live by.

I sent a copy boy to the morgue to check the clippings on all the names that Breitel had given me, and called Duffy. I read him everything Breitel had told me. He listened without interrupting, his short, angry breaths exploding at regular intervals like depth charges.

'Where'd you get this?' he asked when I had finished.

'A source,' I said. 'You know I can't tell you.'

'It's garbage,' Duffy said. 'I hope you didn't shell out too much.'

'Don't jerk me around, Duffy,' I said. 'I've got a job to do.'

'I don't give a rusty fuck about your job,' he said.

'And I don't give a squirrel's turd about yours, okay? Printing the names of the decedents isn't going to hurt your investigation, and you know it. You're just holding out because you're a sonofabitch. And that's not a good enough reason.'

'You went over my head,' Duffy said.

'No, I didn't,' I said.

'You print this, and you won't be able to walk into any precinct in this city. Not even to use the crapper.'

'Which is the last thing I would want to do in a precinct house,' I said. 'But you come down on me, and you'll never find out who fed me. You do want to know who screwed you, don't you?'

'And if I do?' Duffy said.

'So be nice. Give me a hand on this story, and when it's over from my end, I'll tell you.'

'You know I've got you on tape,' Duffy said.

'I hope you delete all the expletives,' I said, trying to sound casual, while the sweat spurted out of me like blood from Caesar's wounds. 'C'mon, Duffy, let's work together.'

'Okay, Krales, your names are good,' Duffy said. 'And we're talkin' to Mr Albino, but I'm sure his alibi'll check out. Two guns were used, and they look like a Walther and another kind of thirty-eight.'

'No other names or ideas to give me?'

'None. We're trying to trace the money, but you know we won't.'

'Okay, then, thanks, Duffy. Now, ain't it nice to be nice?'

'You've got an end to hold up too,' he said.

'I'll come through,' I said.

'Uh huh. You'll be hearing from me.'

I dropped the phone like a hot potato. That malign instrument had really been my undoing so far. It had seduced me into two deals with two hard guys that neither they nor I intended to honor. Only they were dangerous guys and carried guns; I was curious and yellow.

I started writing the story:

'The bodies of six people, among them the debutante daughter of a prominent diplomat, were discovered in a Greenwich Village apartment early today, the apparent victims of a gangland execution.

'Police identified one of the victims as Pamela Sue McClough, 19, the debutante daughter of Arnold McClough, Ambassador to Germany, and heir to the Bramble tobacco fortune. She had been stabbed once with an undertaker's implement known as a trocar, the point going through her body and pinning her to the outside door of a three-story apartment building at 1797 Bedford Street, where the bodies were discovered. The other victims, four men and a woman, were linked with a Harlem narcotics ring. Police theorize that they were shot while trying to escape from their assailants.

'The murders were discovered at 5:00 AM by this reporter, who was in the area working on an investigative series about organized crime. His attention was drawn to the body of Miss McClough. Upon investigating further, he found the body of. . . .'

It was beautiful. It would give Grissom apoplexy and make me rich. Krales, I told myself, since nobody else is going to say it, I will: You're beautiful, Krales. You play those typewriter keys like Horowitz doing the 'Hungarian Rhapsody'. You've got a rotten, calculating brain on you like no one else. But if you're so smart, how come you're always broke and in trouble? Reporters always ask good questions, don't they?

CHAPTER EIGHT

I waited until the first edition rolled, and then I started to go uptown in search of my car. But before leaving, put in my usual precautionary call to the tow-away pound. My old pal Sergeant Ginley was on.

'We gotcha, Mr Krales,' he said. 'Soon as I came in this morning, I saw the heap. But don't worry, I got it stashed for you.'

'Sarge,' I said, near tears, 'thank goodness there are still men like you on the police force.'

'Hey, what a nice sentiment, Mr Krales,' Sergeant Ginley said. 'Usual rates?'

'Usual rates, and God bless you, Sergeant Ginley,' I said.

I wedged myself into the uptown express. The place was a sensory riot, a panorama of two thousand years of cultural mishaps. On either side of me stood two massive Hasidic Jews, complete with coats, caps, beards, and the kind of holy halitosis that comes from eating fried herring and onions after the morning services. On my left was a shabby black youth with yellow eyeballs who glared balefully at me, having decided that I was the only person on the train who was in worse shape than he was, and therefore a fit object for his contempt. In front of me three Spanish girls chirped happily. One had braces and a rump that nudged me at every turn. I told myself it was innocent, and concentrated on my newspaper. But as we were brought closer together in the crush, the contact became more intimate. I sneaked a look over the top of the paper. My secret lover was prattling on, oblivious to the lustful poignard poised at her delicate parts. She was carrying a Spanish confession magazine with the page opened to a story entitled '*Mi Vida, Mi Amor*'. You bet it is, sweetheart, I thought. I hadn't kissed a girl with braces in fifteen years. My God, she was only a child. So what: they grew up fast in the tropics. The thoughts and images came faster now as we hurtled through the darkness. I pressed home under the cunning pretense of swaying with the movement of the train. She leaned back, ostensibly to read her magazine. Was that a quick, apprehensive look she gave me? Why was she gnawing her lips? The lights went out for a blessed moment. Then on. We had reached Times Square, crossroads of the world. There's a broken heart for every light on Broadway. Without even a toss of the curls, a snap of the proud black eyes, a click of the castanets, she was gone. And I was left alone with my receding hopes, leaning against the pole, panting inwardly, a dirty old man with a newspaper.

At home I stood under a hot shower until the pipes squawked and the water ran brown. My suit was such an obvious testament to my activities that I was ashamed to give it to the tailor. There were spots of dried blood on my shoes. That was something to tell the grandchildren.

I chased the cockroaches off a piece of Brie I had been aging on top of the refrigerator, and ate it with a couple of rubber saltines. The phone began ringing. Four rings a friend, five to seven some girl, seven to eleven the office, eleven to infinity my wife. I shaved, brushed my teeth, got dressed, and left while it was still ringing.

Skivoso and Iboopa's was open for business. A little guy with a big nose and horn-rimmed glasses was leaning against the counter, dunking a bagel into a container of coffee.

'I didn't know they made bagels here,' I said.

'They don't,' he said. 'I got it across the street.'

'Hey,' I said, leaning forward confidentially. 'These are pretty mean guys. They might not like that, you know, bringing a bagel into their bakery.'

He nodded. 'Thanks for the warning.'

A massive creature in white waddled out to the counter. His face looked like it had been put together with five raisins and a lump of dough.

'You Mr Skivoso?' I asked.

'Iboopa,' he rasped.

'I was here last night,' I said. 'Remember? Farinacio, Manhattan South Homicide.'

It took him about two minutes to shake his head. 'I don't remember,' he said.

'Well, anyway, I wanted to talk about Vern Palucci,' I said. 'You remember him, don't you?'

The raisins turned into capers, and Iboopa raised a forearm that could have caused an eclipse of the sun. 'Get outta heah.'

'Listen, Iboopa,' I said with a swagger. 'you wanna talk here, or you wanna come downtown?'

The little guy with the bagel laughed. 'Farinacio, that's funny. It's a good thing for a reporter to do, you know, make believe he's a cop. This is Josh Krales, Augie, 'famous reporter for the New York *Event*.'

'Never hoid a him,' Iboopa said.

'He's trying to fool you into givin' out some information,' the little guy said.

'Dat I know,' the behemoth said.

'Yeah, well, at least I don't bring a strange bagel into your bakery,' I said.

'That's funny, ain't it, Augie,' the little guy said. 'This guy's a pisser, right?'

'Get him outta heah,' Iboopa rumbled, and waddled back where he'd come from.

'Uh, Mr Krales,' the little guy said, scuffing his sneakers in embarrassment.

'I know, I know,' I said.

The little guy followed me out into the street and tugged at my sleeve. 'That was a pretty ballsy trick, Mr Krales.' He sounded sincere, but he was a little guy with butter glistening on his upper lip and holes in his windbreaker, so who cared? Still, I looked him over before getting too obnoxious. His hands were pretty big for a little guy, and his shoulders were thicker than they should have been. As a matter of fact he was built like a Sicilian laborer, so in lieu of kneeing him in the groin, I crossed the street. And he tagged along.

'What are you so mad about?' he said. 'This guy knew

you weren't a cop. I just tried to make a joke out of it, so he wouldn't trow you tru the window.'

'Oh, you mean you were looking out for me,' I said.

'Yeah, that's right.'

'Why?'

The little guy shrugged. 'I'm a fan of yours. I read your stories in the paper, okay?'

'No, not okay,' I said. 'I don't have any fans. My mother isn't even sure she likes me. And only people I owe money to are looking out for me.'

The little guy shook his head. 'Jeez, you're a pisser, you really are. I'll prove my good feelings. Ask me to do something. Anything.'

Never take favors from cops or hoods, I told myself. So I took one.

'Tell me where Vern Palucci lives,' I said.

'Hey, that's easy,' my unexpected benefactor said. 'I'll even take you to the door.'

The little guy walked me around the block to a tenement next to a fish market. 'You walk up the stairs. It's on the second landing,' he said. 'The shmuck lived with his mother. He wasn't a hundred per cent up here, you know what I mean?'

He opened the door and ushered me into a dark hallway that smelled of cats and rotten *baccala*. The steps creaked, and it was so dark I didn't see the three guys in dark suits sitting on the landing until I almost stepped on them.

'Yeah?' one of them said.

'Mrs Palucci home?' I asked.

'Who are you?'

'I'm from the Veterans Administration. We want to arrange for her son's benefits and see if she wishes him to be buried in a military cemetery with full honors, seventeen-gun salute, all befitting. . . .'

'Palooch wasn't in the army,' Second Dark Suit said.

First Dark Suit got up and squeezed my face between his thumb and forefinger. 'Whaddya talkin' about?' he asked rhetorically.

'Trow him down the stairs,' Third Dark Suit said.

First Dark Suit grunted and slammed my head against the wall. A fire engine roared through my brain and was wiped out by a tidal wave. Plaster rained down from the ceiling. First Dark Suit, who had suddenly acquired a twin brother, gently brushed it off my shoulder. 'Get outta heah,' he said softly, as if reluctant to wake me up.

I wobbled up an endless flight of stairs, but somehow ended up in the street. Then I was pushing against a stone wall, which I realized, after seeing all the shoes around me, was the sidewalk. Waving away solicitous passers-by, I crawled over to a garbage can and sat against it, repeating my name, address and phone number until my head cleared and began to hurt. Then I staggered to a phone booth. I had left all the slugs in my other suit, but I called the office anyway. Switchboard passed me to Kettle, the City Editor.

'Where the hell are you?' he asked. 'You're supposed to be at the Brooklyn shack.'

'I'm working,' I said. 'Remember that inconsequential little story I got for you last night?'

'That was last night,' Kettle said. 'What are you doing for me today?'

'Plenty,' I said. 'I'm gonna keep this thing alive for weeks. You won't be able to get it out of the paper with a shoehorn.'

'You get your ass over to Brooklyn shack, or you're out of a job,' Kettle said. 'I'm onto your overtime dodges.'

'You mean you'd turn down a big circulation-boosting story, one that only I have the inside track on, just to screw me?'

'Something like that, yes,' Kettle said.

'You'd screw the bosses just to screw me.'

'You're getting the idea,' Kettle said.

'You know, I've got you on tape now,' I said, borrowing Duffy's dirty trick.

'What do you mean?' he asked angrily.

'Get ready for San Clemente, boss. Only in your case it'll be a nursing home in St Petersburg with the toilet down the hall.'

'You're lying, Krales,' Kettle said. 'Play it back.'

'Why should I? I don't have to prove anything to you. The boys at Pritchard Communications, Inc, will tell you that it says you'll be happy to screw them just to screw me.'

'You're bluffing, Krales. . . . ' There was less conviction in his voice.

'Stock up on those shirts with the alligators and the mermaids and the beach balls, Kettle. Maybe they'll make you support-hose editor of the Large-Type Gazette.'

'What are you pullin' on me, you crud?' Kettle shrieked. I could imagine every face in the city room turning toward him. 'Now you're on my shit list for keeps.'

'Oh gosh, does that mean no more cement fruitcakes for Christmas?'

'I'll get you for this.'

'Would you mind speaking a little louder? The traffic noise. . . .'

'All right, what are you after?'

'I want to work, that's all. I don't want to vegetate in some shit hole just because you don't like me. I want to work, and I want to get paid for the work I do. Eight years I've been bumpin' heads with you idiots. And all I ever wanted to do was work.'

'All right, hero,' Kettle said. 'Knock yourself out. Only get something good, real good. You fall out of the front of the paper one time, and. . . .'

'Yes, speak up, Mr Kettle.'

Mr Kettle hung up, and I looked in the phone book for the New York address of the Honorable Arnold McClough.

McClough lived on Sutton Place in a moneyed building staffed exclusively by ancient Irishmen with white and pink Peter Rabbit faces. They were the residue of the original servant class of the 1860's in New York, the sedate ethnics of the Gilded Age – happy throwbacks to indentured servants: polite, snobbish, and very hard to get around. Dressed in blue uniforms with gold braid and shiny gold buttons, the doorman and the hall man blocked the entrance, their puffy, hieratic hands clasped at their bellies, primed for a bow or a dismissing gesture.

'Help you, sir?' the doorman asked in an unctuous brogue with a tinge of menace.

'Why, yes,' I said. 'I'm here to see Ambassador McClough.'

'May I say who's calling?'

'Yes, you may,' I said, assuming my best patrician manner. 'Steven Swarthmore of the State Department, in regard to the tragic events of yesterday evening.'

He waddled to the house phone, whispered into it, then waddled back. 'This way, sir.'

He took me to a tiny elevator where a simpering leprechaun awaited, his eyes aglow at the prospect of transporting my honored person.

'Penthouse, sir, yes sir. Terrible thing, sir, young Miss McClough.'

'Oh, did you know her?' I asked loftily.

'Oh yes, sir,' he said in the hushed, reverential tones one reserves for the dead. 'She lived here while the Ambassador was in Germany. Quite a nice girl while her nanny was with her. You know, her mother died when the girl was only fifteen. Drinking problem, the poor woman.'

I thanked God for the slow, stately elevators of the rich. 'You said she was a nice girl. What happened when this nanny left?'

'Well, sir, eighteen is a bit young to be livin' alone. Especially when you don't have to worry about feedin' or clothin' yourself. You've got a lot of time for mischief, don't you?'

He slid the elevator door open to a foyer where a dumpy gray lady in a gray uniform awaited.

'Mr Swarthmore?'

'Ummm,' I mumbled, nodding portentously.

She led me through a gloomy, thickly-carpeted hallway, past a sunken living room with a huge aquarium glowing and bubbling and full of brightly-colored tropical fish. Scores of abstract paintings battled for space on the walls, and the furniture was done in black and white. It was the kind of room for cocktail parties and magazine spreads, but not for watching TV with your shoes off.

The gray lady paused at an oaken door with a wrought-iron handle. I heard the growl of controlled, angry voices. She knocked, and the growls stopped. The door was opened by a dark man in a sleek gray suit. Gold glinted all over the man, on his cuffs, his wrists, his fingers, probably in his mouth too.

'How do you do, sir,' he said. 'I'm Peter Nardo, Ambassador McClough's attorney.'

'How do you do,' I said, taking his hand.

He stepped back and let me pass into a den all done in brown leather. There were paintings of sailboats in stained pine frames, a portrait of a severe middle-aged man (McClough, Senior?), a phony fireplace with a gas flame, an old oaken desk that took up half the room. Books in old bindings stood in neat, unread formation on the shelves, and Ambassador McClough, in an old silk dressing gown, slouched in a corner with his hand over his mouth, like a little boy caught eating candy.

'Mr Swarthmore?' he said, coming forward with his hand extended. His voice was carefully stentorian, his manner desperately brisk. But Arnold McClough wasn't fooling anyone. He didn't have the look of a conqueror, rather that of the spoiled son who knocks up the maid, drinks too much and runs down the gardener's crippled son. He exuded a sense of softness, from the neat little paunch that rose roundly over his belt, to his soft, hairless hands, the fingers fidgeting, clutching at the empty air. He had an ingrown chin, over which hung a lachrymose lip. Beads of sweat lubricated the hollows under his eyes; his gray, viscous eyes squinted plaintively. He would be a whining drunk, a premature ejaculator, a hopeless bore. In short, he was a dangerous man. For there is no one more dangerous than a weakling with power.

I took his hand with a blank look. 'Sorry? Swarthmore?'

The Ambassador looked puzzled. 'From State?'

'No sir,' I said. 'My name is Krales, sir.'

'But they announced a Mr Swarthmore,' the Ambassador said.

'Oh, that must have been the gentleman I rode up with.

Perhaps they assumed that we were together because we entered simultaneously, as it were. Is there another person in the diplomatic service in this building?'

'Warburton on the eighth floor was commercial attaché in Luxembourg. . . .'

I flashed my charming smile. 'Oh yes, the eighth floor is where this gentleman disembarked.'

'Well, what's your business, Mr Krales?' the attorney said.

'I'm with the New York *Event*, sir, and I was. . . .'

'You don't really think we're going to give you a story, do you?' the attorney asked, feigning patrician amusement to cover the rage of a street kid who's been had.

I turned to the Ambassador. 'Sir, I was the one who discovered your daughter's. . . . Now, I don't claim that my efforts to save her entitle me to any special considerations, but I. . . .'

'Was she still alive when you got to her?' the Ambassador asked.

Stanislavsky taught that the easiest way to project sorrow on stage was to look at your shoes. I looked at my shoes. 'Barely,' I whispered.

'Did she say anything?' he asked.

I averted my eyes from his and shook my head, then looked at my shoes again. 'I know this is a painful moment, Ambassador. I'm only here because I know many people will wonder how a girl from such a distinguished family could get herself involved in such a tragic situation. People with daughters her age will want to know what can be done. . . .'

'I'm in no position to give anyone advice on child-rearing,' the Ambassador said. He moved behind the oaken desk and came up with a pack of cigarettes.

'He wants to get some juicy quotes from you,' his attorney warned. 'He wants to dress up his story.'

I turned and gave him a long look of reproof. 'Mr Nardo, I take that as an unsolicited insult. I'm sure the Ambassador understands the necessity of going on the record. I'm only here to help him.'

'Will you have some coffee, Mr Krales?' the Ambassador asked, pulling a rope.

'Yes, thank you, sir.'

The gray lady appeared. The Ambassador said, 'Coffee', and she disappeared.

'You're quite right that I would be expected to make some kind of statement,' the Ambassador said. 'Unfortunately, in my daughter's case I would be speaking in total ignorance.'

'Oh,' I said sliding uninvited into a large oaken armchair in front of the desk. The Ambassador blinked at me and sat down.

'I hadn't seen too much of Pammie Sue over the last several years,' he said. 'I was away in Europe, and she was in school here at Blodgett, or,' he smiled ruefully, 'let's say I thought she was.'

'Arnold,' Nardo said, stepping around behind the desk, 'don't get into all of this.'

'Quite right, Peter. Mr Krales, I'm afraid nothing I would have to say about my daughter would be very inspirational.'

'I understand,' I said, looking at my shoes for the third time, and extruding as much unction as my throat could bear. 'I imagine – correct me if I'm wrong – that she dropped out of school and became something of a hippie or a flower child.'

'I wouldn't know what she became because I didn't see her for a year until . . .' – the Ambassador blushed like a pregnant nun – 'until we heard the news this morning.'

'I see,' I said. 'She was kind of a runaway.'

'From time to time I'd get little tidbits,' the Ambassador said, making a face. 'The last I heard she was living on the Upper West Side with a Negro musician.'

'Where did your family originate, Ambassador?' I asked gently.

'Scotch-Irish salt of the earth,' he said. 'South Carolina, Mr Krales. When I was a boy, my father bragged that a camel could die of thirst trying to cross his tobacco fields. Naturally, we've diversified quite a bit since then. A camel would die of thirst trying to walk across our tax returns at this point. Pammie Sue lived on in Pulham after her mother died. I should have kept her there, even though she was scandalizing the whole town. It would have been better.'

'Yes,' I said. 'New York can be a dangerous place for a young girl without supervision.'

'Pammie Sue was my only child,' the Ambassador said. 'Her mother had a drinking problem, and I was never the most attentive of fathers. Perhaps because she came late in life to me I lacked the patience. . . .'

'You said she was scandalizing Pulham?' I suggested, hoping he'd fill in the blank. But Nardo was too fast for me.

'Arnold,' he said, grabbing the Ambassador's shoulder hard enough to make his knuckles whiten and his client wince.

McClough shook his head. 'Regional peccadilloes, Mr Krales,' he said. 'Nothing that could translate across the Mason-Dixon Line.'

'Have you any idea who could have been responsible for this?' I asked as a matter of course.

'None,' the Ambassador said. 'Lieutenant Duffy said it looked like she might have witnessed something, and had to be killed herself.'

'She didn't know Zarita Durand, I assume.'

'Oh, I don't know,' the Ambassador said, showing his teeth, letting his diplomatic patience wear thin. 'But in any case that's the kind of question we should leave to the police, don't you think?'

'Quite right, sir, I'm sorry.' I leaned across the desk and offered my hand. 'Again, sir, my apologies and condolences. And, of course, my heartfelt thanks.'

Nardo showed me to the door. We passed the gray lady sitting in the living room, smoking a cigarette. Nardo cleared his throat, and she jumped up and looked for something to do. I realized that she had never brought the coffee.

'You pulled that little maneuver to get in here, didn't you?' he said.

'What law firm are you with, Counselor?' I asked.

'Any sleazy trick to take advantage of a man in his

grief. A real example of yellow journalism in my book, Krales.'

'Practicing your rhetorical technique, Mr Nardo? I mean, there's no jury here, so there's really no need to make a speech. Why don't you write a letter to the *Times*?'

'Just don't come back here for seconds, you understand. You've had your shot, and now McClough's off limits.' Nardo squared his shoulders and blocked the doorway like a bouncer.

'Nardo,' I mused aloud. 'Odd name in a way. You'd expect a lawyer for the McCloughs to have some Wasp name like P Chilton Dingleberry.'

The elevator door opened, and the servile leprechaun pulled back the door. 'Yes, sir, Mr Swarthmore,' he said, happy to display his excellent memory for names.

Nardo made a noise. It began in his diaphragm where the alluvial sludge of his early days on the streets still percolated. It was the roar of a schoolyard fighter, a kid who resolves everything with his hands. But by the time it ascended through the layers of repressions, credentials, and ambitions, it came out a confused squeak. He stood there, a headbuster with a law degree and a four-hundred-dollar suit. We watched the elevator slide shut on each other's faces.

CHAPTER NINE

Page Two of the New York *Event* belonged to me that afternoon. Leading it, with a six-column headline across the top of the page, was my by-lined story about the murders. Squared off at the bottom was the feature I had phoned in for the afternoon editions after my visit with McClough.

The two lead paragraphs were a triumph of yellow journalism: ' "Unfortunately, nothing I have to say about my daughter would be very inspirational."

'In this way Ambassador Arnold McClough summed up the melancholy life of his nineteen-year-old daughter Pamela Sue, a life which came to an abrupt and savage end in Greenwich Village early today.'

I had altered the quote a bit, but kept the sense. In the next three paragraphs I told Pammie Sue's story, from drunken Mom, the nonattendance at posh schools, the début, and the débâcle with the 'Negro' musician. The art department got my drift, and ran a photo of Pammie Sue's coming-out on one side of the story, and one of her skewered form on the other. After demolishing the McCloughs, I made a Shakespearean descent through the levels of society, mentioning the taciturn Iboopa and the three goons on Palucci's doorstep.

It was a classical job – neat, restrained, and modest. I left out the manhandling I had gotten. In print it would have seemed self-serving, even though it had really happened. The story nestled under a head set in severe roman type: 'THE DEAD DEBUTANTE'. Everything had been done with taste. Naturally, my by-line had not been appended. The same by-line appearing twice on the same page would make *Event* look like a country weekly. To remedy this, I made everyone read the story, and then I told them that I had written it.

My audience was small and disappointing, made up as it was of the population of the squad room of the Tenth Street Precinct, a few blocks from the murder scene, where Lieutenant Duffy had set up temporary headquarters. I absorbed a few overtime hours playing gin and listening to the lurid reminiscences of my companions. To hear them tell it, all women, with the exception of their female relatives (they don't even include yours), are nymphomaniacs and fetishists. And cops are their prime targets. It just seems that there's something about a beer bell and a billy club that sends women of astronomical proportions into a frenzy. Every cop I know has a story about a rich or famous personage ('It wouldn't be right to mention the broad's name.') who begged to be handcuffed and diddled with a police special. The city streets are a lush preserve of ravenous widows, divorcées, social workers and young mothers who lie in wait for New York's finest, scrub, feed, service, and gush all over them, and then remain on twenty-four-hour call in perpetuity.

Maybe it's all true. Maybe our wives and mistresses do languish in our arms, dreaming of violation by the Tactical Patrol Force. For that matter, maybe every ribald adventure I've ever heard was true, which would make me the only liar in the world, a condition I began to doubt after a two-hour survey of the wet dreams of the assembled civil servants.

When Duffy entered, all such conversation stopped. You can curse in front of him, but you can't talk dirty. Duffy wades in degradation right up to his short hairs five days a week, but believes that the sinfulness of the world must be kept a policeman's secret, so that no one else will demand a piece of the action.

'Give me two minutes, Lieutenant?' I called.

He nodded and waved me into a private office. Gray came along and closed the door.

'I need a little something for tomorrow's first edition,' I said. 'Just routine-type stuff. Like how many detectives you've got working on the case.'

'Five,' Duffy said. I wrote, 'twenty-five.'

'What, if any, leads you have.'

'None,' Duffy said. I wrote, 'Gangland angle.'

'What organized crime figures you've questioned.'

'Albino,' Duffy said.

'That's yesterday's godfather,' I said. 'Got one for me today?'

Duffy shook his head.

'C'mon, Duffy. You Catholic schoolboys can never lie. Tell me, or I'll get the sisters to rap your knuckles.'

Duffy's Tiny Tim face turned a bright pink. 'You're a cagey guy, but what does it get you?' he said.

'It gets me the name of the wise guy you questioned today.'

Duffy shrugged. 'Ah, big deal, I'll tell you. A courtesy call was paid on Victor Lupo.'

'The Don of the Village, huh. I bet he wasn't too enthused.'

'Well, this thing went down in his territory,' Duffy said. 'He had to be tossed.'

'And?'

'Nothin',' Duffy said. 'What did you expect, a confession? He didn't know any of the people and couldn't tell us what they were up to, and I believe him for the simple reason that he don't shit where he eats. When Victor Lupo orders a hit, it's done in Nutley, New Jersey.'

'But he did make Skivoso and Iboopa for you,' I persisted.

'Not necessarily.'

'Duffy, I've been there, understand? Old Don Vittorio stands on his dignity and says he knows nothin'. You mention Skivoso and Iboopa, who have *omerta* written all over them. He disclaims them. You ask what they're doing in his territory. At this point he realizes they've been put on the map, and even if they are in his family, he gives them away. Right?'

'You don't need me,' Duffy said. 'You can write your own stories.'

'I do, but I have to put the words in your mouth. Anyway, I can't print anything about those guys right now. So whatever you give me is strictly a backgrounder.'

'Okay, it's dope,' Duffy said. 'Seems like they're freelancers, but they got big friends. Otherwise they wouldn't set up shop in Lupo's turf. The old bastard hates them, and he says he wishes somebody would put them away.'

'So they wholesale for the metropolitan area, and they're covered by Lupo's protection money,' I said.

'No matter what the squeal is, you people always bring police corruption into it,' Duffy said.

'You trying to tell me Victor Lupo is running gambling, shylocking, hijacking, bootlegging, extortion, and probably narcotics in a fifteen-block area, and the cops don't know about it? That would make them awfully incompetent.'

'He says he's not into dope,' Duffy said in a subdued tone.

'Sure. He'd drown his grandchildren for a dime, but he's

too principled to sell heroin to a bunch of boots and spics a hundred miles away. Maybe you think he's Marlon Brando.'

'Look, Krales, I'm in Homicide,' Duffy said. 'Nailin' Lupo ain't my department. You got rackets guys, strike force, FBI, who knows who else sneakin' around him. All I know is he didn't hit those people, and he's gonna know who did before I do. So my thing is to get him to tell me. Or, if they belong to him, like you say, then he's gotta give them away. Meanwhile, I ain't takin' a nickel from him or anybody else.'

'I know you're not,' I said. 'I just don't want you to make believe nobody else is. Even if Don Vittorio drew the line at heroin, he'd still be a piece of shit.'

Duffy nodded solemnly. 'Agreed.'

'And just 'cause you're kissin' his ass, it don't make you a bad person.'

I heard the door click open in back of me.

'You go too far, Joshua.' It was Silas Gray's courtly bass. He was standing by the open door, shaking his head sadly. 'If the conversation continues in this vein, I'll probably have to eject you physically from Lieutenant Duffy's presence. So let's anticipate that unpleasant moment.'

'Who could argue with such an articulate person as yourself,' I said.

'Before you go,' Duffy said. He came around from behind the desk. He was smaller than me, and he didn't look like much, but here he was measuring me for a punch. 'I'm glad you don't think I'm a bad person,' he said, favoring me with the fastest, shortest smile I'd ever seen. 'I kinda like you too. I'm gonna hate to bury you.'

The *Daily News* radio car was in front of the precinct, and McGuane, the *News* night police man, was in the front seat, reading the *Event*.

'Improving your vocabulary?' I asked.

McGuane squinted up at me suspiciously. 'How'd you get so close to the choir boy?' he asked.

'Who? And you'd better not let him hear you call him that.'

'He's one strait-laced cop, I'll tell ya.'

'Now just because a cop isn't on the *News* payroll doesn't necessarily mean he's honest,' I said.

'What do you mean?'

'If you let me listen to your radio calls, I'll tell you everything.'

We drove a few blocks north on Seventh Avenue to the Hyena. It was cocktail time: the place was packed to the rafters with eager, shouting people; the jukebox was going full blast; everything that the species had yet contrived to assuage depression was on display, but to no avail. The place still had the feel of a Bowery gin mill at two o'clock in the morning.

The Hyena is sunk below street level like a former speakeasy, and had one window, which affords an unedifying view of the lower torsos of passers-by. It is lit like the lobby of a Bronx tenement with a couple of bulbs blown out. The bar and walls are fashioned of spiritless, splintering wood. In sum, the place is so determinedly lacking in pretension, so scrupulously disdainful of the amenities, that only a masochist could patronize it. Needless to say, it is packed every night.

The Hyena is known as a 'literary bar'. In addition to newspaper people, you can find PR flacks, political hacks, ladies'-magazine editors, talky graduate students, one-book novelists, and a goodly number of aspirants to the above-mentioned fields. You'll also find literary mascots – cops, prizefighters, deracinated proletarians who have been apprised of their characterhood by some literary type, and now think that everything they do, from throwing up to telling pointless anecdotes, is in the best novelistic tradition.

The Hyena also gets an occasional biggie, a writer who was a regular before hitting with a big book. These luminaries make contrite pilgrimages to maintain their stock with the 'real' (read 'poor') people. They have graduated to the paperback and movie sales, the talk shows, the second wives. They are the stars of innumerable 'I knew him when' stories retailed with vicious relish in their absence. They know how vindictive the underside of their little world can be, and seek to mollify it with good fellowship. Bellying up to the bar, they look their former friends in the eyes with counterfeit frankness and try to make believe nothing has changed – a pathetic try doomed to discomfiture. Fitzgerald was right: the rich are different, even the *nouveau riche.*

McGuane got me a martini and disappeared in the crush. I looked around at the hundred-odd people in the room and realized I knew every one of them. Horrified, I gulped down my drink and made my way to the bar for a refill.

McGuane was talking to a large, shapeless lady wearing leather pants. After one and a half drinks he was out to lunch. He gave me a stage wink that they could see in Hoboken. 'Krales, c'mere f'r a second. I want you to meet, uh . . . Cary Grant.'

She smiled and tweaked his little red nose. 'I think you've got me confused with another of your fantasy objects. I'm Cora Grahame,' she said to me, 'and who might you be?'

'He might be your Aunt Tilly, but he's only Krales, a pencil-pusher with the *Event.*' McGuane giggled and dropped a lit match on his pants.

'Oh, another reporter.' She turned full-face to me. She was wearing a button that said, 'MY PLACE OR YOURS'. She licked her lips, and looked me over as if I were a cocktail frankfurter. She had the biggest incisors I'd ever seen off a walrus.

'Cora's doing PR for this new prostitute's union out on the Coast,' McGuane said.

'GASH,' she said. 'Glendale Association of Street Hustlers. Like it?'

'It scans,' I said, and waved my empty glass frantically at the bartender. 'Somebody knocked over my drink.'

'I see they knocked a few drops onto your chin,' he said sourly.

'I got it, Mike,' chirped a familiar voice at my elbow. It was the little guy from the bakery, pushing his way through, waving a ten-dollar bill. 'Whatever Mr Krales here wants and a glass of sherry for me.' He was wearing a gray suit with faint golden stripes, a blue shirt, and a fat shocking-yellow tie.

'You're not buying me a drink,' I hollered.

The little guy handed me a drink and waved to the bartender. 'I don't take change, Mike. It makes bulges.'

The bartender's surly visage softened and became positively worshipful. 'Thank you, Mr Carbonaro.'

'I don't want your drink, buddy,' I said.

McGuane got off his stool and grabbed my arm. 'Hey, shmuck, cool it,' he whispered.

The little guy shook his head and looked at me with admiration. 'Boy, you're a pisser, you know that? Take the drink, what do you care?'

'I don't like your act,' I said. 'You're full of shit. And I don't want your booze.'

A local Tammany type named Ferrara shoved his way through to us and glared at me. 'What's goin' on, Frankie?' he asked the little guy.

'This drink is goin' on your friend's new suit if he don't get the hell outta here,' I said. I raised my hand, and was immediately overpowered and pushed back against the wall by a mob of well-wishers who ripped my jacket and really did spill my drink.

'Know who that is, you asshole?' McGuane hissed. 'That's Frankie Carbonaro. He's a wise guy. He's a stone killer.'

'I don't care who he is,' I shouted. 'He got me into a jackpot this morning, and I don't want his goddamn booze.'

The little guy looked hurt. 'Okay, I screwed up,' he said. 'I gotta sit in purgatory forever? Don't you see I'm tryin' to apologize? Can't I make it up to you?'

'Bang your head against the wall, and fall down a flight of stairs,' I whispered back. 'Then we'll be even.'

Carbonaro threw back his head and laughed. I looked down his throat; he even had scary tonsils. 'Hey,' he said, addressing the crowd, 'this guy's a pisser, right?' He grabbed my arm, his eyes shining with some undefinable emotion. 'Hey, listen, I'm gonna buy you a drink.' His grip strengthened, his eyes narrowed a millimeter; to mock him now could be dangerous.

'Sure,' I said. I let him move me out of the bar to a big black Mercedes double-parked at the curb. A thin, gray-haired man with a tic sat twitching at the wheel.

'This is my Uncle Al,' Carbonaro said. 'This is Mr Krales, Uncle Al. Any time you see him around, you take him where he wants to go.'

'Okay, Frankie,' Uncle Al said. A glass partition rose silently from the back of the front seat.

'Hey, Uncle Al,' Carbonaro said. 'You don't have to do that.' But it was too late. The big car rumbled healthily and inched into traffic. Carbonaro tricked a little lever, and a bar slid smoothly out.

'You were drinking martinis, huh?' He mixed one with Tanqueray Gin, and poured himself a glass of Harvey's Bristol Cream. 'I'm not much of a drinker,' he apologized. 'Just a little something sweet before dinner, and afterward, you know, something for the digestion.' He hoisted his glass. 'Here's to a free press.'

We clicked glasses and drank. Carbonaro smacked his lips. 'You hungry? You look like you don't get much time at the supper table. Divorced guys like you don't take care of yourselves.'

'I'm separated,' I corrected. 'But how did you know?'

'How do you know I'm married?' he said. 'We're about the same age, huh? Thirty-two. Only you're Jewish, I'm Italian. You married some broad, and after a coupla years she started breakin' your balls. You don't make enough money, you don't fuck so good, you ain't nice to her parents. So finally, you couldn't take it and got out. And now she's got you payin' through the asshole, right?'

'Right,' I said.

'But me,' he said bitterly. 'I get married when I'm nineteen. My wife's an Italian girl. When she's eighteen, she looks like Sophia Loren. Now she looks like Carlo Ponti. Only she's got a mustache too. With the Italians, you get married, your bite your lip, you stick it out. We don't get no shit from our wives, and sometimes you'll hear the *paisans* braggin' about how they run their houses, how tough they are. Sure, their wives don't run around – who would want 'em? Sure, they stay home with the kids – they don't know nothin' else. I don't think I've had a conversation with my wife in ten years. If I don't wanna eat or fuck, she can't help me. But don't get me wrong. . . .'

'I love my wife,' I said, finishing his sentence for him.

He smiled sadly. 'You've heard it, huh? If I wanna be your friend, I'm gonna have to tell you things you've never heard.'

'That you'll never do,' I said. 'Just tell me things I want to hear.'

He nodded. 'I got your drift. You know I like having a little intelligent conversation. It's worth a lot to me, given the atmosphere I spend most of my time in.'

'Which is. . . .'

'Sullivan Street, the Social Athletic Club.' He made a face. 'With the black windows and the *goombahs* hangin' out front, you wouldn't mistake it for the Bloomsbury group. If you like to play pinochle and talk about your girl friend's tits, you'd be happy there. Unfortunately, that's where I do a lot of my business.'

'Which is. . . .'

Carbonaro shrugged and threw up his hands. 'I'm a botanist.'

'And your Uncle Al's a petunia,' I said.

'Yeah, that's right.' He leaned forward and mixed me another drink. 'What can I do? I tried it the other way.' He flashed his ruby pinkie ring at me. 'You see, Georgetown 1964. I was with the brothers, but it seemed stupid, you know. Guys I graduated with are breakin' their humps to make twenty K a year. I do it in a month, tax-free.'

'There are other things aside from money,' I said half-heartedly.

'Lemme say this. There are and there aren't. You know what I mean?'

'Exactly,' I said.

He flushed with pleasure. 'We agree. So let's eat.'

We drove down to Elizabeth Street. The street was narrow, and Uncle Al parked the car on the sidewalk to keep it from being sideswiped. The restaurant was a few doors down from the Fifth Precinct, but nobody seemed to object.

The restaurant was called Solo's. It had a neon Schaefer sign in the window, which is usually a bad omen. The television blaring over the bar also boded no good. A sweaty, worried fat man in a greasy apron came out of the kitchen.

'Frankie, I gotta talk to you.'

'After dinner, Tony. For now say hello to my friend Mr Krales of the New York *Event*. You read the papers, don't you?'

I squeezed a quart of olive oil out of the fat man's palm. 'Any friend of Frankie's is welcome here, Mr Kroll,' he said.

'What can you give us to eat, Tony?'

'I'll make you a nice *fritto misto* with the fish and the vegetables. Got a nice baby lamb, some fried potatoes.'

'Okay, and start us off with a little macaroni and sauce.'

'Right, Frankie.'

'And bring Mr Krales a Tanqueray martini, and me a glass of Harveys.'

'Right, Frankie.'

We sat in a circular booth meant for six. Our waitress was a low-slung crone with rage lines around her eyes. She slammed the settings down in front of us. Frankie poked her in the behind.

'Hey, *fatchim*, you're gonna spoil my appetite with an ugly face like that. Here.' He threw her a twenty. 'Go get yourself a permanent. Hey, Tony,' he hollered into the kitchen. 'Ain'tcha takin' good enough care of your wife? Can't stand a sourpuss broad when I'm eatin',' he confided to me.

The woman came back with the drinks. 'I'm sorry, Frankie,' she said. 'But you know, with Angie in jail and everything. . . .'

Carbonaro wedged another twenty between the buttons of her blouse. 'If this don't cheer you up, then I'm gonna hafta get personal,' he said.

She straightened up, raising her flaccid bosom, and pushed back her hair. When she smiled, she looked like a teen-age girl. 'Any time, Frankie, you know that,' she said softly, and ran away into the kitchen.

'That's what I mean about Italian broads,' he said. 'You give 'em a chance, and they go, married or not. Whew.' He shook his head. 'You see how my finger sunk into her ass? She's got some pair of knockers too. That slob don't give her nothin'. Whew.' He shook his head again. 'She'd kill ya, a broad like that.'

The food was fat and greasy, like the chef. After a while I began feeling as if a diving bell was sinking into my stomach. Carbonaro ate with great appetite, throwing down glasses of vinegary red wine, prodding me to eat, to 'enjoy' myself. Our table was visited by one heavy set, unshaven classical scholar after another, all of whom had a hearty greeting for Carbonaro and a 'How are ya' for me. I looked around the room and realized there wasn't a man there I could beat up. And that probably covered some of the women too. For dessert the by now lovesick waitress set down a pot of espresso and a bottle of anisette. I understood why espresso is drunk in small cups – it's too foul to be consumed in normal amounts. Carbonaro emitted a volcanic belch and beamed at me. I lit a cigarette and prayed for a Gelusil.

'Good, huh?' he demanded. 'I like it here. The guy owes me money, and he can't pay.'

'So he's trying to poison you to wipe out the debt,' I said.

Carbonaro gaped at me, then broke into hysterics. 'Oh, that's beautiful. Beautiful. Hey, Tony,' he called to the chef, who had been hovering around us. 'He says you're tryin' to poison me to wipe out the debt.'

The chef wiped his face and laughed nervously. 'That's funny, Frankie. . . . Funny.'

Carbonaro dipped into his endless supply of twenties and shoved one in the chef's shirt pocket.

'Here, that's twenty-four more dollars you owe me,' he said, and turned purple with hilarity, wheezing and pounding on the table. 'We're havin' a good time, huh?'

'Great,' I said. 'I'd enjoy myself even more if I knew why you were wining and dining me.'

Carbonaro tried a wide-eyed, innocent expression. 'Does there have to be a reason? Can't it just be that I'm a guy who's desperate for a little intelligent conversation?'

I shook my head and waited.

He nodded, his expression wary. 'Answer me this,' he said. 'What do you think of a guy like me?'

'They told me back at the Hyena that you were a killer,' I said.

Carbonaro raised his hand solemnly. 'I swear I never hurt anybody in my life. I swear on my mother's grave.'

'So you're just a button man,' I said. 'You take people's money.'

'Wait a second,' he cautioned. 'I dispense a necessary service, just like you do. A guy wants to gamble, I cover his action. Sports, horses, numbers, maybe he wants to play cards or dice somewhere where he knows he won't get cheated or knocked on the head if he wins. You put a dime on a number and you hit, I give you forty-seven fifty. That's a little better than the market, ain't it? Suppose you need money to buy a house. Who trusts you when the banks throw you out? Me, that's who. Sure, I take a big vig, but why shouldn't I? A guy's obviously a risk. Otherwise he wouldn't come to me.'

'And if he can't pay back?' I asked.

'Hey, if I beat up everybody who's defaulted on me, I wouldn't have time to take a shit,' Carbonaro protested. 'A guy owes me money, I talk to him and make other arrangements. I've gotten into some nice businesses that way. As soon as I get my equity out of it, I turn the business right back. That's what I do. Just like Chase Manhattan, I can afford a couple of deadbeats.'

'Why are you telling me all this?' I asked. 'If you're doing PR work for the Mafia, that's really a waste of time. If you're trying to impress me, the way you do it is with money and muscles, the two things I don't have. Humanity I'm overstocked with.'

'I'm just trying' to show you that money doesn't always take first place with us, that's all,' Carbonaro said. 'Now you take my Uncle Victor. Victor Lupo.'

'Never heard of him,' I said.

'He don't like having his name in the papers, and since you put it there. . . .'

'The paper's not even on the street yet,' I said. 'How does he know?'

Carbonaro shrugged. 'How does anybody know anything? Somebody tells 'em. Anyway, he don't like being associated with these guys, especially since it's gonna come out that they're into dope.' He looked at me carefully.

'That is going to come out,' I said.

'Yeah, and Uncle Victor don't like that. You know these guys were forced down his throat, I won't tell ya by who, and he don't like havin' them in the Village. Dealers bring junkies, and junkies are a waste. They don't gamble, and you can't lend them money. If you got a coupla restaurants, or you're runnin' a festival, you sure don't want them around. . . .'

'Except if their trade is worth more to you than all the book joints and shylocks and restaurants you've got.'

'There you go, thinkin' we do everything for money,' Carbonaro said. 'Now, if you wait a second, I'll show you how we turn easy money down. Iboopa over there had a guy workin' for him, a nigger named Artis Pettibone. In the middle of everything this afternoon he turns around and tells me that this Pettibone knocked up his niece. I could care, right? Iboopa and the other greaseball there were layin' for him, but he never showed up for work this morning. Maybe he was tipped, or maybe he was comin' down the block and he saw the shit hittin' the fan, 'cause three o'clock is when he's due in.'

'Do the police know about this guy?' I asked.

'Who's gonna tell those stiffs anything?' Carbonaro said. 'Anyhow, here's the point. Iboopa tells me to tell my uncle that he'll pay ten grand to anybody who finds this kid and brings him back alive. Imagine that. Ten grand. I got guys in this joint who'll turn a nigger upside down just for expenses, and this *buffone* is offering ten grand. He even gives me the kid's address, says he's afraid to go over there himself 'cause he'll scare the kid away.'

'So?'

'Lemme put it this way,' Carbonaro said. 'Anybody ever makes an ethnic slur about the Italians, I'll kill him, understand? But these guys. . . . I'll tell ya what they are. Greaseballs, you know what I mean? Swamp guineas. You got no idea what goes on in the brain of a clown like Iboopa. If he offers ten grand, that means at least' – Carbonaro gave me a significant look – 'I don't know, let's say five hundred thousand dollars.'

Pettibone, half a million, they were all key words, and Carbonaro was giving them to me because in some way they had something to do with the McClough killing.

'Where does this Pettibone live?' I asked casually.

'Jeez, I don't remember. Who pays attention? Maybe he said 1597 Gates Avenue. That's in Brooklyn, ain't it?'

'Bedford Stuyvesant,' I said.

'Oh, is that where?' Carbonaro mused. 'I guess it figures, him bein' a nigger. He's a pretty valuable nigger now.' Suddenly he awoke pointedly from his reverie. 'Hey, I'm sittin' here havin' a good time, and the joint's fulla guys who got things to talk about.'

'And I'm supposed to be out looking for the love of my life,' I said.

'But the love of your night will do, huh?' Carbonaro gave out with an Opera Buffo sigh. 'It's great to be single. Just for once I'd like to screw a broad and sleep over.'

'Get a live-in maid,' I said. I got up. 'Thanks for the heartburn.'

'Hey, don't be a stranger now,' he said. 'Say hello now and then.'

'Be seein' you,' I said. I sauntered through the door and broke into a run as soon as I hit the street.

CHAPTER TEN

Three cab-drivers passed me up; the fourth asked me where I was going, and flashed his off-duty sign when I told him. The fifth, an older man, said his doctor had expressly forbidden him to take passengers to Harlem, the South Bronx, or Bedford Stuyvesant. 'I get palpitations in those neighborhoods,' he explained. When I refused to get out of the sixth cab, the driver turned the car off, took the keys, and left, suggesting that I push the cab to my destination. The seventh was kinder: he threw me the keys and said I should bring the cab back to the garage when I was finished. The eighth told me to take the subway and offered to notify my next of kin in twenty-four hours. The ninth, a hysterical Puerto Rican, held the gun he presumably carried for protection to his head, and threatened to shoot himself if I insisted he take me to Gates Avenue.

By this time I had walked to the foot of the Manhattan Bridge, which crosses the East River into Brooklyn. A private car with the sign 'South Brothers Transportation Service' approached, and I jumped in front of it, waving my arms. The car screeched and skidded to a halt.

I ran to the window, shouting, 'This is an emergency. I must get to 1597 Gates Avenue.'

The driver, a massive black man with a shaven head and a gold earring, looked me over calmly, oblivious to the honks and protests behind him.

'Ain't never seen nobody in a hurry to get to Gates Avenue,' he said. 'I seen 'em in a hurry to get away, though.'

He peeled out, and we crossed the East River into the nether regions of Brooklyn.

Brooklyn is the Casbah of New York, a jungle of ethnic satrapies spreading like Roschach blots on either side of its main thoroughfares. Brooklyn goes on forever. Once you depart from the comforting logic of its main arteries, you are lost in a maze of twisting byways, cul-de-sacs, obscure corners; even the numbered streets and avenues begin, are interrupted and retrieved with no discernible order. If Mr Kurtz is alive, he is stationed in a grocery store on one of Brooklyn's murky backwaters.

Coming off the bridge, we drove down Flatbush Avenue, through the ruins of what was once the business district of a proud borough. The stately old Paramount Theatre with its Art Deco façade stood in semi-abandonment; further down the famous Brooklyn Fox, once the home of first-run vaudeville attractions, was draped with a banner proclaiming the advent of an evangelist, Reverend Herb, who promised to instruct his flock in 'Making the Almighty Dollar and Making the Almighty Happy.'

We turned left off Flatbush Avenue. The streets were broad here and well lighted, but they narrowed and darkened perceptibly as we drove further west, and the gloom of Bedford Stuyvesant slowly engulfed us.

Gates Avenue is a spacious street lined with brownstones and small apartment buildings. It was dark, the few intact lamp posts casting forlorn splashes of light. Occasional bloodshot flashes of neon announced a bar; a lone police car prowled the area.

We stopped in front of a neat three-story brownstone.

'This is it, my man,' the driver said.

'How much?' I asked.

'Three dollars'll do,' he said.

'What if I gave you ten, and you waited until I came out?'

'If you don't come out, that ten'll be awful short bread.'

I gave him a five-dollar bill for his candor, and stepped out. There wasn't a soul on the streets. The light bulb had been knocked out of the entrance vestibule. I struck a match to check out the mailboxes. The door opened, and a small, very black man with a big and very shiny butcher knife emerged.

'You a social worker?' he asked, tickling my thorax with the tip of the blade.

'Who me?' I gulped and laughed as if this was the silliest idea in the world. The man was probably a maniac with a homicidal grudge against social workers. 'Absolutely not. Far from it. I. . . .' I stopped. My voice was getting shrill and flighty, like a Noel Coward heroine's.

'Well, in that case, I can rip you off,' the mugger said. He made a tiny incision in my jugular. 'Better step into my office.'

We moved in a rather stilted lock step into a dark hallway. The mugger pushed me face first against the wall, and fumbled around in my pockets. He threw my wallet down in disgust.

'Thirty-two bucks. Is that all you got, you jiveass honky?'

'Yes,' I laughed, 'isn't that absurd, a grown honky, I mean, man . . . I'd be happy to give you a check, and I give you my word it will be good.'

'Motherfucker come around here with a suit on and no money,' the mugger mumbled. 'I'm gonna cut you now, baby, deep, wide, and many times. . . .'

I flailed desperately at the knife, and caught something fleshy with my forearm. The mugger cursed, and a rush of wind told me he was swinging at me. I ducked and swung out again, hoping to catch him in the groin, and made contact with something. There was a yelp, and the mugger came flying by and slammed into the wall. A family of rats scurried away squealing. The mugger slid down the wall and sat on the floor, looking up at me in semi-comatose astonishment. I examined the back of my hand, marveling at the wonder it had wrought. Someone lifted me rudely by the armpits.

'You all right?'

It was Breitel. He was wearing an electric-blue ski jacket, his kinky red hair rose in neat ledges off his freckled forehead. A blackjack dangled, spent, from his fat wrist.

'What are you doing here?' I asked.

'Do you care? I would say my presence was fortuitous, wouldn't you?'

While feeling myself gingerly for perforations, I repeated the question.

'I came here to find Artis Pettibone,' he said. 'What about you?'

'Me? Oh, I just like to browse through dark hallways in Bed Stuy,' I said. 'You never know when you might come across a first edition or a Queen Anne chair. I thought the police didn't know about Pettibone.'

'You thought wrong,' Breitel said. He kicked the semi-conscious mugger in the ribs. 'Okay, Einstein, where does Artis Pettibone live?'

'Who?' the dark form croaked.

Breitel kicked him again. 'Go ahead, play hard to get. Your ribs'll wear out before my shoe does.'

'Top floor rear,' the form complained.

Breitel kicked him a little higher. There was a sound like walnuts cracking. The mugger mumbled something and turned over onto his stomach. We proceeded up the stairs.

Light oozed from under a rickety wooden door at the top floor back, and canned laughter cracked from a television. Breitel banged on the door like a Gestapo chief.

'Who is it?' requested a timid female voice.

'Police,' Breitel hollered. 'Open up.'

'A little tact,' I whispered.

He shook his head. 'It's the only way.'

There ensued a symphony of clicking locks, all protecting a door that could have been kicked in by a paraplegic. Finally, the door opened a crack, and a blustery male voice, choked with fright, demanded identification. Breitel flashed a Texaco credit card. The door opened on to a tidy little room, which was taken up almost completely by the biggest, most vivid color television I had ever seen. A thin, elderly black woman wearing a man's woolen sweater stood back to let us pass. An elderly black man with a cane was rummaging in a closet. Breitel dashed through the room and pushed him away. 'What you got there, Pop?'

'Nothin',' the old man whined.

Breitel came out of the closet with a shotgun. 'Kinda heavy for you, ain't it, Pop?' he said, hefting the gun.

'I could still shoot the eyeteeth off a squirrel at fifty yards,' the old man said, straightening up.

'Sure you could, Pop,' Breitel said. 'So where's your son?'

Puzzled, the old man looked at his wife. 'He's dead. Killed in Korea in 1952.'

'They probably mean Artis,' the old lady said. 'He's my nephew. I hope he's not in trouble. . . .' She stopped herself before saying 'again.'

'No, of course not,' I said. 'We just want to talk to him.'

'Well,' she said, 'he left for work last night, and he hasn't been back. We been waitin' for him. He does all our food shoppin' for us. It ain't safe goin' out day or night, you know. Got some treacherous people around here.'

'Does he usually stay away like this?' I asked.

'Sometimes on weekends,' she said. 'But he should be home by now. It ain't like him to be out durin' the week.' She shivered and pulled her sweater around her.

'Artis is a good boy,' her husband piped up. He dragged painfully over to us. 'See that TV? He give it to us, and the toaster too. When I got sick, he took me over to the hospital. I had bleedin' piles and ulcers so bad I. . . .'

'Aw, shut it,' the old woman said to him without malice. 'These gentlemen's don't wanna hear nothin' about your miseries.' It was odd how her speech became more heavily inflected when she spoke to him, while she pronounced perfectly, in courtly Southern tones, when addressing us. 'Would you gentlemen like some tea?'

'No thanks, Mom,' Breitel said impatiently. 'Listen, maybe you know some friends he might be staying with.'

The old lady shook her head and looked regretful. 'No, I don't think he has any particular friends. . . .'

'A girl maybe?' I suggested.

'I can't think of any special girls, I'm afraid,' she said.

'Where are his folks?'

'If you know, tell me,' she said. 'His daddy went one way, and his mama, she's my sister, went the other. That was fifteen years ago, and I been raisin' the boy ever since. His sister's in New York. She just kinda popped up last year, and he been seein' a good bit of her.' She took a matchbook out of a drawer. 'Serena's her name. I don't know where she's livin', but she works in this here nightclub.'

There were a top hat, a cane, and a set of drums on the cover. It said, 'The Nirvana – Dining, Dancing, Private Parties.' The address was on Lenox Avenue, in the middle of Harlem.

'Last I heard, Serena was studyin' to be a nurse,' the old lady said. 'Guess she quit.'

'Maybe she's working her way through college,' I said. 'We'll look her up and see.'

Breitel slipped a bill into the old man's vest pocket. 'Buy yourself some buckshot, Pop,' he said.

'If Artis isn't back by tomorrow, call the Welfare Department to send somebody to do your shopping for you,' I said.

'He'll be back,' she said.

Breitel and I felt our way down the stairs. My erstwhile mugger bestirred himself at the sound of the front door opening, and got his blade in striking position. Through the smoked glass we could see someone lighting a match and looking at the mailboxes. The mugger slipped open the door.

'Step into my office,' he said.

There was a grunt and the mugger came flying back as if he'd been shot from a cannon. A big man in a black overcoat and Homburg, with a round saffron-colored face came after him.

'Stupid bastard,' he said matter-of-factly. He threw the mugger in the corner like a bag full of dirty laundry, and continued up the stairs. Breitel and I flattened against the wall, and he passed within a garlicky breath of us. It was the same man I'd seen in the bakery the morning of the killings.

'If that's Trocar Albino,' I whispered to Breitel, 'he's gonna kill them.'

'Nah,' Breitel said, 'only if he was paid for it. And if he was paid, it wouldn't be ethical for us to interfere.'

We heard a polite knock on the Pettibone door. 'A friend of your nephew's,' Albino responded to a muffled query.

'Maybe he'll scare' em into tippin' on the kid,' Breitel said. 'We'll tail him when he comes out.'

We waited a few minutes. A door opened, and Albino's

voice said, 'Thank you, ma'am, and please accept this contribution. . . .'

'They're doin' pretty well tonight,' Breitel whispered.

We started down the stairs again, just in time to see the indefatigable mugger, muttering a bit to himself, getting ready for a third shot.

Albino had also begun his descent, but stopped at the sound of voices. The mugger had found his knife and had gotten his nerve up. Another figure was playing a flashlight around the mailbox. The mugger inched the door open.

'Step into my office,' he said, seemingly determined to use that phrase until it worked.

A huge shadow darkened the doorway. The mugger, shaking his head in disbelief, backed away and took a lukewarm swipe at it. The shadow swooped, lifted him high in the air, and threw him through the door. The glass popped from the force of the impact, leaving a clean, head-size hole. Lieutenant John Duffy walked in over the debris. The shadow leaned into the light, and was revealed as Detective Silas Gray.

'We can deal with him later,' Gray said.

The two started up the stairs. I thought of Albino on the third floor, us in the middle. The devil and the deep blue sea. I squeezed back against the wall and felt for Breitel. He was stretched out on the floor, and advised me with a sharp rap on the shin to join him. I came down knees first on his chest, my mouth glued to his neck, and we stayed that way until Duffy and Gray trudged past to the third floor, and announced themselves.

'You're givin' me a goddamn hickey,' Breitel whispered vehemently. 'Get up.'

'I don't want to,' I whispered back.

'You gotta kid around?' he said. 'Let's get the hell outta here.'

Our unlucky mugger was sprawled across the stoop, blowing bloody bubbles through his broken nose. Glass splinters glittered in his Afro, and he had one hand raised supplicatingly to the heavens, no doubt wondering what he had done to deserve such a visitation of unmuggables.

A black El Dorado was parked across the street.

'That's Trocar's,' Breitel said.

Further down, in front of a fire hydrant, was a dusty green Plymouth. Breitel went over and let the air out of the front tires. 'Gives ourselves a head start on Duffy.'

'Why don't you do the same on the Caddy?' I asked.

'Because Trocar found a way to get out,' Breitel said. 'Probably a stairway to the roof, where he'd be standin' right now, watchin' us, you understand?'

'You have a certain animal cunning that's very rare in Jewish men,' I said.

'That sounds like a putdown for a guy who just saved you from gettin' slashed and robbed by a nigger, beat up by a guinea, and locked up by a mick. That I don't call gratitude.'

'Why did you come out here, anyway?' I asked.

'What if I just left you to find your way out of here alone?' Breitel asked.

'I withdraw the question,' I said.

'Okay,' he said. 'Now let's go see sister Serena.'

CHAPTER ELEVEN

The Nirvana announced itself to Lenox Avenue with an electric-blue neon mixed metaphor depicting a slave girl contorting around a seated Buddha. At least ten million dollars' worth of vehicular hardware was parked in a glistening row in front of the club. I saw Cadillacs – 'Pimpillacs' in the trade jargon – equipped with vinyl roofs, bubble tops, porthole windows, and wire wheels. There were four black Rolls Royces, a stark white Bentley with gold door handles and a red leather interior, a metallic-silver Jensen, a forest-green Ferrari with a modish dent in the front left fender, and a group of shiny Detroit confections that stood off to the side like poor relations.

'I'm surprised nobody rips these cars off,' I said.

'Who's gonna fence a Rolls Royce?' Breitel said, scowling at my ignorance. 'Besides, these guys are heroes in the neighborhood. They add a little class, give the kids something to shoot for. If Harlem ain't complaining, why should you?'

'Yeah, but they're bleeding their own people. . . .'

'Who would you rather hate, the Jew landlord who doesn't give you any heat, or the dude in the custom hog who gives you a bag of smack to keep you warm?'

'All right,' I said, 'I'm a phony liberal, and you know the score. Do you know this joint?'

'I achieved Nirvana about once a week when I was on the Gambling Squad,' Breitel said.

'Make a lot of arrests?'

Another dyspeptic grimace for my naiveté. 'Kojak makes arrests; I made money. Also made some enemies, so I'm takin' a rain check.'

'You mean you're sending me into that bucket of blood alone?' I asked.

Breitel reached around and opened my door. 'C'mon, I got a heavy date.' He opened his glove compartment and took out a traveling case full of small aerosol cans. He sprayed himself under the arms, on top of the head, in the mouth and on the backs of his hands.

'I'm reporting you to the Pollution Control Bureau,' I said.

'I got a spray for my balls too, but the way you were kissin' me back there, I ain't takin' no chances. C'mon, before I turn out your pockets and cuff you to a fire hydrant.'

That would be a fate akin to staking a missionary out in red-ant country. I got out of the car on the off chance that he wasn't kidding.

'You ever going to tell me why you're interested in this kid?' I asked.

'When you find him for me,' Breitel said. 'In the meantime, I'll give you a hint. What can't buy happiness?'

He rolled away from the curb, shaking his head and looking at me in his side-view mirror. I gave him the finger.

He gunned the motor, and the car seemed to rear up on its back wheels before zooming away.

A group of blacks, dressed in the motley of the procurer's trade, stood around the entrance of the Nirvana. They looked like the corpses on Bedford Street.

'He goin in?' one of them asked in mock astonishment.

'Question is, is he comin' out?' another asked, provoking an uproarious burst of laughter.

I sidled my way through without looking anyone in the eye. Darkness and soul music whooshed up at me. I headed for the bar, but a Yield Right of Way sign loomed in front of me. A little intense squinting, and the Yield sign turned into a tall, very black man in a yellow velour jumpsuit.

'Sure you're in the right place, sir?' The accent on the 'sir' was predictably contemptuous.

'This is the Christian Science Reading Room, isn't it?' I said. 'I'm looking for Serena Pettibone.'

'She don't work here,' he said.

'Is that a fact or a criticism?' I asked.

One crack too many. I had perplexed him, which meant he was about to get angry.

'You in the wrong place, man,' he said. 'You can take your kinda business out on the street.'

I found an old cleaning ticket in my pants pocket, folded it, and pressed it into his hand. 'Serena around?' I whispered.

Without looking, he slipped it into his pocket. 'Who are you, man?'

'Do I have to show a résumé just to see one strung-out hooker?' I asked.

I saw two rows of feral white teeth, which I assumed meant he was smiling. 'Go sit at the bar,' he said. 'I'll bring her over.'

I sauntered toward the bar, marring my insouciance a bit by tripping over a step. There was much muttering and scraping of chairs. My fellow revelers looked at me as if I were a dead leper. The bartender, showing commendable neatness, polished a cocktail glass until it squeaked, and then went to work on another, ignoring my presence.

I felt like an ugly white duckling in a crowd of festooned

black swans. The men seemed to favor wide-brimmed hats and outfits with deliberately clashing colors – green shirts, tapered orange pants, blue clogs, or variations thereof. Leather was popular, as were heavy gold African bracelets and necklaces, which clinked and dangled from their disembodied wearers. Rings glittered off rhythmically flailing hands, sweat lay in sequined trails on dark skin, cigarettes glowed like tiny beacons. I was the only white man in the room, but a great deal more than race separated me from these people.

There wasn't an ugly woman in the place, as far as I could see. The white girls seemed to be having the best time of all. They dressed and acted with more abandon than their black sisters, who were stylish but subdued. It made sense. The white girls were there by choice. This was the realm of their fantasies given flesh, the jungle wherein they were worshiped and violated at the same time. They shrieked and clutched at their amused escorts. They seemed to be trying to shake their bodies loose from their clothes, their inhibitions loose from their bodies, determined to lose control, to dissolve their stubborn superegos in music and booze and dark embraces.

My attention was drawn to a blonde girl who was shaking with frenetic, arhythmic defiance to the music. She had her back to me, but there was something familiar in that cascade of blonde hair, those long legs. Her partner moved easily from the waist, making suave little circles with his fingers. They were a perfect match – instinct seeking repression, repression seeking release. At the end of the tune, the girl did an awkward pirouette and fell backward into her partner's hands. She was wearing jeans with floral patches, and she almost jumped out of them when she saw me. It was Jill Potosky.

She detached herself and walked toward me. I tried to wave her away, but she kept coming. Breathing hard from exertion and indignation, she brushed a wet strand of hair off her face.

'Having a good time?' she said loudly, and all the hostile faces that had just turned away from me, turned back. 'Do you come here often, or just when you're told to spy on me?'

'Go away, please,' I whispered. 'I'm working on something.'

'Did our esteemed superior put you up to this?' she asked, contriving to raise her voice a few decibels. 'Were you the only one in the office low enough to do his bidding?'

'Will you go away, please,' I said.

'Johnny,' she called. Her dancing partner heeled obediently. He was wearing a leather vest and purple shades. Potosky grabbed him by the back of the head and thrust her face into his in the most strenuously passionless kiss I'd ever seen. After an acceptable interval she pulled away triumphantly. 'There,' she said. 'Now you can tell everyone in the office that you saw me and my lover in a coke dealer's hangout in Harlem. And you can tell them he's one of the biggest dealers in the city.'

'Uh, baby,' her boy friend said, looking around nervously.

'Let's go, Johnny,' Potosky said, with a defiant look at me. 'He's got enough for a memo.'

'Stick around, and we'll have a seminar on the myth of the vaginal orgasm,' I said.

'It would be a myth to any woman who slept with you,' she said.

'And then you can give a talk on the manifestation of the collective unconscious in *Guess Who's Coming to Dinner*.'

Potosky moved in on me, hands on hips. 'You'd like to think this was a social thing, wouldn't you? Then you wouldn't have to be confronted by your own' – her voice skittered out of control – 'inadequacy.'

This debate threatened to go on all night. The patrons encircled us like spectators at a cock fight. It was unlikely that the Nirvana's languid air had ever been split by such Freudian expletives. I was about to impute hysterical frigidity to Potosky's actions when a smooth tawny arm slipped around my neck.

'Hey, baby, you got a dude, so leave my squeeze alone, y'hear?'

The voice oozed with the musical menace of the Southern drawl. The scent that came with it tickled seductively at my nostrils. It wasn't as coarse as the voice, but its allure branded it as vulgar. The woman that came with the scent and the voice didn't belong with either. There was an Oriental cast to her features: high cheekbones, soft and severe; full lips, sensual and scornful; oval brown eyes that were at once vulnerable and accusing. She was wearing one of those grotesque blonde wigs that does not attempt to imitate hair, but proclaims its own medium. Along with it went a bright orange halter that pressed her breasts into a buttocks shape, and harem pants that billowed at the thigh and clung at the pelvis. Her fingernails and toenails were painted vermilion, and two crimson splotches had been daubed on her cheeks in that girlish incompetent manner affected nowadays by mannered, competent women. All these cosmetic effects were as irrelevant as panties on a lamb chop. There was something going on behind those eyes that intrigued me, something that didn't belong to the outfit, not even with the body that promoted itself so flagrantly against me.

Potosky saw only the surface and was impressed. She looked the lady up and down, getting pointers. This was her image at least for the evening. It was what she would try to become in the arms of her coke dealer.

'Excuse me,' she said archly. 'I guess I was being a little paranoid. I had you figured for a Grissom spy.'

'Don't worry about it,' I said.

There was seduction in Potosky's smile. She was one of those girl-children who start out believing that only their daddies have penises, and in later life have to see or sense the penis in a man before they'll acknowledge he has one. By seeing me with this girl, Potosky had discovered mine. Henceforth, I would emerge from the mass of prickless men who pressed their attentions on her.

'You and your main squeeze been steppin' out, huh, baby?' my benefactress asked.

'She's not my main squeeze,' I said. 'We work together.'

'Welfare Department?'

'Why do black people always take me for a social worker?' I asked.

She smiled, her eyes lyrical with contemplation, reached around, and pinched my cheek. Her breath smelled of sweet liqueur. 'Who told you about me?' she asked.

'If you're Serena Pettibone, it was your Aunt.'

She jumped back as if I were poison ivy. 'Then you *are* a social worker.'

'I'm a reporter for the New York *Event*,' I said. 'I'm looking for your brother.'

'You ain't no reporter,' she said.

I showed her my press card.

'That could be a phony.'

'You'd better hope it's not. Think of what I might be if I'm not a reporter.'

'What do you want Artis for?' she asked.

'I'm covering those murders down in the Village, and his name came up, so. . . .'

'Police think he done it?' she asked.

'I don't know, but they're looking for him, and so are some very mean Italian people, and so's a private detective who'd kill his grandmother for a pastrami sandwich. Of all these folks, I'm the best guy he can talk to, because if I get his name in the paper, I make him immune to some kinds of arrest and most kinds of death.'

'That Bible-bangin' old bitch want money?' Serena asked. She hadn't heard a word I'd said.

'If you mean your aunt, she's worried about Artis,' I said.

'Only thing she worries about is how much she can run her mouth,' Serena grumbled. 'Anyway, I don't know where Artis is. . . .'

'Your aunt said the two of you had gotten pretty close,' I said.

'That don't mean I keep him under my bed,' she said. 'You're movin' too fast for me, my man. . . .'

'All right,' I said, 'I'll slow down. Artis knows something about those killings. If the police get to him, they'll arrest him; if the mob gets to him, they'll kill him; and this private detective will do whatever he has to do to make a little money. That slow enough? Now, I might be the only guy who can protect him.'

She pulled at her lower lip like a little girl about to cry. 'I gotta go take care of somethin',' she said. 'Have a drink. I'll be back.'

'Going to locate Artis?' I asked.

'Only if he's in the john,' she said.

I put my cigarette out in a puddle on the bar. It sizzled and smoked and got the bartender's attention.

'Jack Daniel's,' I ordered.

He piled a mountain of ice into a rocks glass and poured the whiskey out of a thimble-sized jigger.

'Is that a drink or are you drowning your crabs?' I asked.

'Three-seventy-five,' he said, slamming the glass down in front of me.

I threw four singles on the bar. 'Keep the change if you can find it.'

Two weary-looking blacks in tuxedos wandered onto the stage. One went to the piano and toyed with a few blues chords. The other sat at the drums, lit a cigarette, and swiped at the ride cymbal like a cat at a ball of thread. A third man, carrying an electric guitar, came out and turned on his amplifier, filling the room with an electric shriek. He waited a few agonizing seconds, then turned it down.

'Just wanted to see if y'all was payin' attention,' he whispered into the microphone. Then he said something over his shoulder, stamped his foot twice, and they were off. The loose, anarchic feeling was instantly transformed into an alert unity. They swung into up-tempo blues as if they'd been playing for hours, leaning into the music like skiers building up speed, and then slowly pulling back as they gained momentum. In no time they had reached the bottom of the slope. The pianist was meandering through a series of clichés; the sizzle of the cymbal drowned out the beat; the guitarist played the same two chords in the same monotonous rhythm. Still, the room exploded with shouts and applause as they faded into silence.

A very black young lady with a mountainous Afro and an enormous behind came out on stage.

'Candy, I call my sugar Candy,' she sang, performing fellatio on the microphone.

'You've changed,' she lamented.

The microphone was now sliding back and forth in her substantial cleavage. There was a commotion in the back of the room as a swooning redhead and her escort exited hurriedly.

'Take it easy, honey, it won't fall off,' the singer said.

Serena's scent preceded her. A little more of her hard-boiled hooker façade had slid off, and she looked scared.

'Where's my drink?' she asked in mock indignation.

'I'd rather buy it for you someplace else,' I said.

'Uh huh,' she said. 'How much money you got?'

'About $18,' I said. 'I'll give you seventeen-sixty-five, and keep subway fare.'

'No wheels either,' she said.

'Ass 'n' heels beats gas 'n' wheels,' I said.

'No bread, no wheels, no deal,' she said.

'You take American Express?' I asked.

She shook her head. 'You gonna get me in trouble,' she said. I could see her struggling futilely against her own nature. A woman like her would see through all the standard male blandishments of wealth, beauty, virility, but would fall for and be constantly deceived by strays, weaklings, and con artists. In short, she would be unable to resist me. 'I can't tell you where Artis is,' she said.

'Who's Artis?' I said.

'Ain'tcha never balled a black chick before?'

'Sure, but never you.'

'Well, ballin' me ain't gonna change nothin',' she said with a sad smile.

'I hope not.'

'Okay.' She moved away so quickly I had to jump up and follow her. I caught up with her outside, hailing a gypsy cab.

'I didn't want the boss to see me splitting with you,' she said.

'Who owns the place?' I asked.

'I don't know, Whitey Downtown, I suppose. I'm talkin'

about Ronny the manager. He likes to pick my escorts for me.'

She lived on the third floor of a brownstone on a dark street off Convent Avenue. The steps creaked all the way up. Somebody was playing an Elvis Presley record on the second floor.

A cat scurried out into the hall as we entered. He paused at the top of the stairs and meowed balefully.

'That's Tom,' Serena whispered.

'Uncle?' I asked.

'No, cat.' She giggled, and let me press against her as I walked in. 'I gotta put him out when I have a man in, otherwise he jumps up on the bed.'

I stopped and put my lips to her neck. The skin pulsed like jungle drums under my touch. 'That would break my concentration,' I murmured.

She let me nuzzle and explore a bit before pulling away. 'This ain't the senior prom, baby.'

Her apartment was neat and pathetically homey. Framed colored prints of sylvan scenes hung in the kitchen. Woolen throw rugs were scattered over the living room floor, and more pastoral scenes were on the walls. There was another mammoth color TV like Aunt Sarah's, and a stereo-tape console that looked like the instrument panel of a spaceship.

I sat down on a suède young-married-type sofa. She sat next to me and slid an ash tray under my cigarette.

'You wouldn't drop ashes in your mama's house,' she said, sliding her hand under my shirt. Her fingers moved lightly over my nipples, and I felt it all the way down to my big toe. There was, unquestionably, something to be said for professionalism.

'Let's get to it before I drop something that I dropped in my mam's house all the time,' I said.

The bedroom had more throw rugs and pastoral scenes, interspersed on the walls with photos and posters of black movie stars. Poitier and Belafonte stared at me with glossy blandness; Jim Brown dispatched evil whites in a huge color poster. And miracle of miracles, Serena had a single bed.

‘Only nuns have single beds,’ I said. ‘What’s a girl in your, uh, line. . . .’

‘I don’t bring men up here,’ she said. ‘Always go to a room, or somewhere, but never in my home.’

‘What about me?’

She smiled and stretched languidly on her undersized bed.

‘You’re special, honey. Just special, I guess.’

‘I thought you were going to say I wasn’t a man,’ I said.

She lifted her legs over head and slipped her pants off. ‘We’re gonna find that out right now.’

Always ready for feminine challenges, I considered immediate retreat. She turned off the light. Her clothes slid off in silken protest. The wig stood, headless, on the dressing table. I undressed hurriedly, dropping everything in a pile by the bed. She lay under the covers with her hands behind her head, and chuckled.

‘This your first time?’

‘Every time’s my first time,’ I said.

I squeezed in next to her. In that bed there was no place to hide; you were forced into direct intimacy. Touching her was like rubbing your feet on a shag carpet. Sparks flew, and you were stuck. I stroked the insides of her thighs with my fingernails. She shuddered and slammed her belly into mine.

‘That a snake crawlin’ up my leg?’ she whispered. She had that expectant expression that most passionate women have; she looked as if she were waiting for a train. I tried to lick her navel, but only got as far as her rib cage, realizing a major displacement would be necessary to get at her hind quarters. Serena sighed, and stroked my face like a blind woman reading a poem.

‘Okay,’ she said. ‘I don’t get off when it’s for bread. Besides, $18 ain’t sayin’ shit But you gotta do somethin’ for me. Don’t ask me if I came, and don’t ask how big your joint is compared to black dudes.’

‘It’s a deal,’ I said.

For the next few minutes I made love to history. Her face

had the impassive sensuality of an Indian statue. Her breasts were like the gentle slopes of the Fertile Crescent, the hollow in her spine that flowed up from the gentle jut of her buttocks had the timeless wisdom of the Nile Delta. I told her all this, and she said, 'Sheet', and offered another geo-historical area to my speculations.

Traveling down her body was a trip back into time. I left the perfumed and painted cities, descending through terrain where civilization was a memory growing fainter and fainter. Going down until the deep, sure scent of the earth filled my nostrils, the sea roared in my ears, and I was lost.

They say it's like whistling in a spittoon, or yodeling in a herring barrel, or whatever they say. For me it was like calling a question into the sibyl's cave at Delphi, thrusting, shouting into the darkness, and getting no reply. . . .

She moved and muttered, but never lost control. As we rose and fell in unison, she watched me, her eyes unblinking and intense. I felt nothing but curiosity coming out of her. Yet when it was over and I had smoked a cigarette, she came running from the bathroom, smelling of soap and toothpaste, and asked, 'How do you like to be done?'

I told her, and she seemed amused by its simplicity. Nothing complex or racy, just an adolescent's aching, melancholy dream, easy to fulfil.

Afterward, covered with sweat, saliva and sperm, we lay so close that our hearts thumped in each other's chests. Face to face and silent until her warm breath lulled me to sleep.

I awoke with a fiery pain in my arm. Her slumberous head was heavy on my shoulder. I eased myself free and dressed. Jim Brown seemed to be aiming his tommy gun right at me. Suddenly I felt like an intruder. I had to leave. I tiptoed out of the room, holding my shoes.

'You don't have to sneak out,' she said from the bed. She was leaning on her elbow.

'You were sleeping,' I said lamely, knowing she had read my mind in the furtive curve of my flight.

'All you motherfuckers become so jive after you get off,' she said. 'You can't wait to get the hell away.'

'I'll be back,' I said. 'Right now I have to get out and try to find your brother.'

'Maybe the next time you come around, he'll be here too,' she said.

'And when might that be?' I asked.

'Call me in the afternoon,' she said. 'Now let me get my beauty rest.' She closed her eyes stubbornly, like a child feigning sleep, and I made my escape.

A stabbing, icy wind snaked down Harlem's streets. I picked my way through the dawn, looking for a cab with one eye, a mugger with the other, although at this hour Harlem was a profitless desert for both. A black Cadillac dawdled by, probably seeking some hardworking hooker who was still on the job. The memory of Serena's body warmed me all the way down Broadway to the subway station.

I got home a little after six. It was too late to go to sleep, too early for work. I watched the American flag on television until the sunrise semester came on, and hastily shut it off, lest culture trap me in an unguarded moment. Then I listened to the paint peeling off my bedroom ceiling. The building was coming alive. People were farting and retching in their bathrooms, slamming doors, rattling crockery. Toilets flushed, sinks sputtered, the elevator crawled up and down its shaft. The morning pick-me-ups, the amphetamines or the reefers, the Valiums or the gallons of black coffee were being prepared. The physical problems, pimples, nostril hairs, bald spots, menstrual stains were being attended to. At that very moment up and down the Eastern Seaboard, millions of gallons of Right Guard were being discharged into the atmsophere. Millions of grimy soap bubbles were gurgling down billions of drains. A percentage of morning erections were being dealt with, while the rest were left to quiver and fall. So many thoughts, so many words, so much rage, frustration, and sadness. At this moment someone was writing a sonnet, chopping down a tree, eating a grapefruit. I could snap my fingers and a baby would be born, someone would die, and, if I waited a few seconds, a murder would be committed....

A murder. . . . You see so much in New York that you don't see anything. Nothing unusual about a black Cadillac prowling Harlem's streets early in the morning. Coming up behind me and stopping. Stopping. . . . That Cadillac stopped ten times in my mind before I located it in front of Serena Pettibone's house.

I screamed, put my hands to my head, and tore a chunk of hair out from behind my ears. Then the world went by in a blur. There were horrified faces in the elevator. An old Jewish cab-driver with a bald mottled head refused to go to Harlem, and then went, his hands trembling on the wheel from something I said.

The Cadillac was no longer in front of Serena's house. A neat, square hole had been cut out in the glass near the knob of the vestibule door. Serena's tomcat brushed by me on the stairs; he was in a big hurry.

The door was open, but the living room seemed tranquil enough. All the action was in the bedroom. The first thing I saw were the big black spots on the soles of Serena's feet. They looked like beach tar, but beach tar isn't ashy around the edges. The world slowed down to a halt now. Serena had been tied spread-eagle to the bed, very carefully and lovingly by someone who appreciated her beauty as much as I, but had a different way of showing it. There was only a little blood. It dripped from her nose onto the towel that had been jammed into her mouth. Her eyes were past horror and pain; expectant again, this time for the end. There were little black burns up and down her legs and thighs, a small red hole in her stomach a little above the navel. A bullet or a trocar? Her nipples were burnt. He had tied her with belts, towels, pantyhose; a stocking was wound tight around her neck and tied in a grotesque, girlish bow. A piece of paper protruded from between her legs. It was a partially burned photograph which had been lit and inserted. It had been taken around a table in a nightclub. Most of the faces had been obliterated, but Serena was there, and a blonde girl was sitting next to her. It was Pamela Sue McClough, and she had a big, toothy All-American grin on her face.

I went out to the phone in the living room and called Manhattan North Homicide. That wasn't Duffy's voice. Let him find out in the police department's own good time. Then I called the *Event*.

'Back with the plebes again,' Persky gloated. 'All right, go to Siberia, and call in when you get there.'

'Isn't there a way to get out of that goddamn police shack?' I asked.

'Sure,' he said. 'Just find another body.'

'Get your pencil poised,' I said. 'I'm gonna make you a believer.'

CHAPTER TWELVE

Serena's smell was still on my fingertips, her taste was on my mustache, my clothes were fragrant with her perfume. She was very much alive all over me as they draped her body in a white sheet and moved it out of the apartment.

Duffy and Gray had arrived before the district detectives. They ignored me and poked halfheartedly around the bedroom. Serena's photograph – the one that had killed her – was burning in my breast pocket.

Duffy worked his way over to me. He looked angry enough to be mean. 'What's the story on this one?' he asked me. 'Another coincidence?'

'No, I was coming up here to talk to her about her brother,' I said.

'At seven-thirty in the morning?'

'I like to get an early start,' I said.

'You got the lead on her at about ten-thirty last night, though.'

'Don't go fishin' with me, Duffy,' I said.

'And don't stonewall it with me,' he said. 'The old lady gave you her name. You were with the big redheaded guy, all right? We showed up about ten minutes after you. So stop the shit and start talkin' before I lock you up on suspicion.'

'You can't do that,' I said.

'Sure I can. I put the cuffs on you and book you. You make your phone call and you sit for a coupla hours until they spring you. Meanwhile you get fingerprinted, pushed around a little – I'll see to that – and maybe you even stick around for the night and get cornholed by a four-hundred-pound soul brother.'

'You going to arrange that too?' I asked.

'Why not?' Duffy reddened, and took a step toward me, but Gray touched his arm, and he stopped. 'Just to get even for lettin' the air outta my tires. Maybe one of these days I'll let the air outta your head with an unregistered thirty-eight.'

'May I quote you?' I asked.

'Cutie pie,' Duffy said. 'If you hadn't been so cute, maybe we could have saved this broad. Think about that, if you got a conscience. And meanwhile tell me where you were between eleven and seven o'clock.'

'Bouncin' around saloons,' I said, with as much brazen confidence as I could muster.

'Saloons close at four,' Gray said gently.

'I know some that stay open later,' I said. 'And I've got witnesses.'

'And who's this redheaded guy?' Duffy asked.

'His name's Red,' I said, and extended my arms. 'All right, Officer, I'll go quietly.'

'Get outta here,' he rasped. He turned away, and I tried to circumnavigate him, but when I passed within arm's length, he snarled and lashed out at me. It was an awkward punch thrown without proper coplike calculation. But it caught me flush on the cheek and was sharp-knuckled enough to cause instant swelling. I staggered back, determined not to give him the satisfaction of seeing me fall.

'Arrest that man,' I hollered at Gray. 'He just committed a felonious assault upon me, and you're a witness. Arrest him.'

Gray clenched and unclenched his fists. 'If I hit you, then we'll both be defendants. You'll have to make a citizen's arrest.'

'I'm gonna crucify you, Duffy,' I shouted.

'Get outta here before I lock you up,' Duffy said.

'All right, then take that badge off and give me a shot at getting even,' I said.

'Raise your hand to me, and I'll blow your head off,' he said.

'You think you're hot shit, Duffy, but you're just another Cossack,' I said. 'I'm gonna nail you, Duffy.'

Duffy shook his head. 'Give the guy a dime so he can go in a pay toilet and whack off,' he said.

Gray placed his forefinger gently onto my chest, pushing me back a couple of steps. 'You're getting in the way. Be happy we don't hold you as a material witness.'

'You're not holding me because you can't,' I said. I wanted to rush at Duffy and tear his head off, but Gray had his big hand splayed across my chest and was easing me backward. 'Why don't you be a little more cooperative?' Gray said gently. 'People would like you a lot more.'

'It's not in the contract that people have to like me,' I said. 'I don't have to be St Francis. I can do a lot of things, but I'm not allowed to hit people. And neither are you, Duffy.'

'Listen,' Duffy said, shaking his finger at me. 'My life is tough enough without you around breakin' balls. . . .'

'Tough life? You got twenty-five grand plus extras a year. You've got a pension, paid vacation, hospitalization. You've got a gun and a badge. . . . People shit when you walk into the room. You can shake down anybody you want, screw anybody you want. Now you want me to feel sorry for you?'

'Get him outta here,' Duffy said, turning away. 'I'm gettin' nauseous.'

Gray pointed solemnly to the door.

'You won't know whether to puke or have breakfast by the time I finish with you,' I shouted in parting, and shoved my way through a clutch of bulky bluecoats who had gathered at the door.

I wandered around Harlem for a half-hour before I found a pay phone that worked.

'I've got a must replate,' I told Kettle. 'You've got to stop the press run to get this in.'

'Find more bodies?' he asked.

'No, I was just assaulted by Lieutenant John Duffy, who's running the case,' I said.

'So, I know plenty of people who'd like to assault you.'

'I'm getting my Pulitzer for this one,' I said. 'Now get me a body to take this down.'

Kettle put me on with Potosky.

'The great man's going to give me an insert,' she said.

'A story,' I said. 'New lead slay. I'm changing the story I phoned in before. Me and Flaubert. Try not to break your nails keeping up.'

'Oh, I'm all a-twitter.'

'Okay,' I said. 'The sister of a mystery figure in the Greenwich Village massacre in which debutante Pamela Sue McClough was slain was found brutally murdered in her Harlem apartment early today.'

'Such variation,' Potosky said. ' "Murdered, slain, massacre" in the same paragraph. Your mind is full of carnage.'

'Try to be professional,' I said. 'Now to continue. . . . New paragraph. The nude body of Serena Pettibone, 24' (it seemed like a good age for her) 'was found tied to the bed in her Harlem apartment. Burn marks covered her body, indicating that she had been tortured with a lit cigarette before being murdered. Cause of death was as yet unknown, but police surmise she might have been killed with the same weapon that was used on Pamela Sue McClough, an undertaker's implement known as a trocar.'

' "Lit cigarette" is redundant,' Potosky said. 'You couldn't torture her with an unlit cigarette.'

I continued on, undaunted. 'Miss Pettibone was the sister of Artis Pettibone, 21,' (another reasonable age), 'an employee of Skivoso and Iboopa's bakery down the street from the scene of the massacre, who disappeared that night, and is being sought for questioning by the police.'

'You could say, "the Greenwich Village massacre which claimed the life of Pamela Sue McClough",' Potosky suggested.

'In a bizarre coincidence, the body was found by *Event* reporter Josh Krales, who had discovered the bodies in the earlier killings. Krales had gone to Miss Pettibone's apartment to question her about her brother's disappearance when he made the discovery.'

'How about "tortured by being burnt with a cigarette"?' she asked.

'While at the scene Reporter Krales was punched in the face by Homicide Lieutenant John Duffy, who is investigating the case. Duffy threatened Krales with arrest and further injury. His colleagues refused to arrest him on Krale's complaint. No reason was given for the assault.'

'It's disjointed,' she said.

'Like bursts from a machine gun,' I said. 'Short, brutal, devastating sentences following each other with preternatural inevitability.'

'You talk a good game,' she said. 'I guess you think I'm a smartass cunt for correcting you.'

'I think you're a smartass for thinking you're a smartass cunt. Know what I mean?'

I hung up before she could tell me she did.

I loitered in front of the house for a while. Technical cars arrived, and more cops. They roped off the area with signs: 'Police line. Do not cross'. No reporters showed. They wouldn't. The call would hit the ticker in police headquarters. 'Another nigger hooker', one of the resident fascists would say, and that would end it until my story hit the streets. Then they'd all come running up just in time for nothing better than a shmooze with the neighbors. Duffy would disappear to avoid questions about his 'assault' on me, and they would be left with some third-stringer who would give them the same old litany about time and probable cause, pleading ignorance on everything else. I had beaten the bastards again. And I had scored too. Wasn't I lucky.

CHAPTER THIRTEEN

There was no place to go but a bar or the office. Just to vary my routine, I chose the latter. The switchboard had a raft of messages for me. It seemed that every bigwig in the police department had called about Duffy. Most of them probably wanted to buy him out, but I was sure that one or two wanted to bury him. They were the ones who would keep calling, long after the good guys had quit. My wife had called three times and left the same message: 'MONEY'. There were calls from several collection agencies, and one from Dr Sprain, a chiropractor who had rendered me immobile several months before and now wanted $50 for his disservices. And, as always, I found my weekly bulletin from Mr Broigast, the oldest resident at the I.L.G.W.U. Nursing Home, who believed that there was a worldwide conspiracy to put all the Jews in spaceships and resettle them on Mars.

And there was a separate pile devoted to messages from a Mr Nardo, with 'URGENT. MUST RETURN CALL' written on all of them.

I called Nardo's office. When he answered, I said, 'Hello, this is Josh Krales,' and hung up.

I leafed through the paper. The Russians had put three Jewish physicists in insane asylums on the assumption that they were crazy for wanting to emigrate; a French politician charged that the Jews were the secret owners of the Middle East oil fields and were jacking up the prices to turn popular sentiment against the Arabs; the Israeli ambassador had been disqualified from the UN ping-pong tournament after he offered to spot the Chinese ambassador ten points. That's why the rest of the world hates us, I realized. We never let anybody else in the newspapers.

I put Mr Broigast's message aside for future reference, and dialed Nardo's number.

'Hello, Nardo,' I said, 'this is Krales again. Your secretary must have disconnected us,' and hung up.

Potosky passed by, radiant from her ritual ravishment of the night before.

'Quite the lady-killer, aren't you?' she said.

'Now we each have something on the other,' I said. 'You know I'm a murderer, and I know you're not a virgin.'

I dialed Nardo's number again. 'Hello, Nardo, this is Krales. What the hell are you trying to pull?'

'Listen, you sonofabitch,' he said.

'I can't hear you,' I said. 'Speak louder.'

'I've got to talk to you,' he shouted.

'We must have a bad connection,' I said. 'Hang up and call me again.' I hung up.

I called police headquarters and asked for a run-down on all unidentified black males brought in wounded or dead during the past forty-eight hours. While I was waiting, Nardo called.

'Meester Krales isn't here,' I said. 'Dees is his Filipino houseboy. . . .'

'Lemme get one sentence in, Krales,' Nardo said. 'I want to talk to you about Artis Pettibone.'

'Where?'

'Come to McClough's house.'

'See you in fifteen minutes,' I said.

Headquarters had five unidentified black DOA's for the evening. Cause of death on four was listed as 'visceral congestion,' which is the medical examiner's catchball for suicides by excess, whether it be by alcohol, drugs, or barbiturates. Four young lives scraped off the street or dragged out of hallways. The other kid had blown his brains out in the men's room of the Fifty-seventh Street Automat. I got tag numbers on all of them, so I could call back later and get their identities, if they were ever established.

The doormen at the McClough residence pretended they'd never seen me before. The lady in the gray dress was polite. Nardo, who had changed his suit and his jewelry, was almost amorous. He took my hand and led me into the library, where the Ambassador slumped in a leather chair, looking like Lyle Talbot caught embezzling from the family business.

'You're a character, you know that?' Nardo said, making a desperate attempt to be friendly. 'Why'd you give me such a run-around?'

I ignored him, took out the photo, and shoved it under the Ambassador's nose. 'Know this girl?'

'Of course,' he said, 'that's my daughter.'

'I mean the other girl,' I said.

'Let me see that,' Nardo said.

I moved in front of him and threw an elbow in his chest. As long as he was on his best behaviour, I could push him around a little.

'You don't need the advice of counsel,' I said. 'Just tell me if you know her.'

'I don't,' the Ambassador said, shaking his head in sincere puzzlement.

'That's the sister of the man you want to talk to me about,' I said.

'Serena?' Ambassador McClough said, reconsidering the photo.

He said it so naturally it didn't register at first. Then it hit me, and I stared at him, too stunned to talk. I expected a flush, a stammer, a hasty attempt to cover up. But McClough just sat there, looking at the photo and shaking his head.

'Poor girl,' he said. 'I didn't recognize her with that wig. She was always very clean and well-groomed. Her aunt wanted her to become a nurse.'

'Then you do know her,' I said.

'Arnold,' Nardo said.

'Oh, it's all right,' the Ambassador said impatiently. 'We were going to tell him, anyway. I knew Serena as a child. Her aunt and uncle worked in our house. Sarah Pettibone was a wonderful woman. She raised me from an infant, and took charge of Pammie Sue. . . .' The Ambassador gulped. A tear rolled down his cheek. He wiped it away with his finger, leaving a smudge. I could see he'd been a colicky baby. 'She was one of those wonderful black women it's not good form to talk about these days,' he said.

'She's not ready for a "was" yet,' I said. 'She and her husband are still alive.'

'Oh yes, I know,' he said.

'They're living in Bedford Stuyvesant and don't seem to be making out too well.'

The Ambassador looked regretful. His admiration obviously did not extend to solicitude. 'Sarah would be too proud to ask for help in time of need,' he said, thankful for another of the woman's sterling qualities. 'And I wouldn't press it on her.'

'I imagine you know Artis too,' I said.

'I'm going to do the talking about Artis,' Nardo said.

'You're as useless as a fart in an iron lung here, Nardo,' I said. 'Why don't you just go out for coffee like you used to?'

Nardo squared off in front of me. His lips were drawing back, the street kid was coming out again. I stepped back and measured him for a kick in the groin. It would be nice to wreck McClough's library. Nardo probably thought so, too, but he restrained himself.

'I do the talking about the kid, Krales,' he said. 'Or else there's no talk.'

'Give up, will ya?' I said. 'You can't charm me, and you can't scare me, either. . . .'

'Can I buy you?' he asked.

'What?'

'Somebody we both know says you need money. That true?'

'Who's this somebody?' I asked.

'What difference does that make? The important thing is, do you need money, and will you do a very simple thing to get it?'

'Which is?'

'Tell us where Artis Pettibone is, and don't tell the rest of the world.'

'And why do you want him?'

'That's a long story,' Nardo said.

I sat down and folded my hands. 'I love long stories,' I said.

'Do you love $5,000 as much?' Nardo asked.

'I'd have to hear the story first,' I said. 'Tell me the story, Daddy.'

'He has something of mine, Mr Krales,' the Ambassador said.

'Which is?'

Nardo became very agitated. 'Arnold, I won't be responsible for. . . .'

Ambassador McClough raised a hand wearily to silence Nardo. 'He has a very valuable family heirloom.'

Nardo stared at McClough in disbelief, then backed into a chair in the corner. The Ambassador turned kilowatts of counterfeit sincerity on me, and continued: 'Under ordinary circumstances I'd call the police, but that would mean publicity. . . .'

'So you call a newspaperman to avoid publicity,' I said.

'I want this . . . heirloom back, Mr Krales. I don't want anybody to know he had it, or how he got it.'

'A private detective would be a better bet than a big-mouth reporter,' I said.

'We already tried that,' he said. 'Mr Nardo recommended a very good man, or so he said.' The Ambassador threw up his hands, one reasonable man appealing to another. 'So far we've had no results and don't anticipate any.'

'Also,' Nardo said from his doghouse in the corner, 'you know where the kid is. You're our fastest route to him.'

'What is this heirloom he has?' I asked.

'My great grandmother's pearl necklace,' McClough said. 'A string of seventeen flawless pearls in gold settings encrusted with diamonds, so you can see it has more than sentimental value. In its day it was condemned as vulgar. My grandmother saved clippings from the Charleston *Observer* about the stir her mother had caused when she wore it to a ball given in honor of John C. Calhoun. It was made for her by a Frenchman who had been court jeweler to the Duke of Orleans during his tenure on the French throne. My grandmother carried the necklace in her jewel box when she escaped Atlanta. . . .'

'Her name wasn't perchance Scarlett?' I asked.

The Ambassador regarded me with the hauteur of a Southern gentleman. 'Of course Northerners, and, if you'll excuse me, people with certain Middle European roots. . . .'

'Eastern European,' I corrected.

'Yes . . . well, you might find this funny, but you don't know what a tragedy that war was for millions of people. The necklace came to symbolize the resiliency of our family. I remember it was kept in a glass case at our home. It was history, not adornment. We all heard its story, and heard how my grandfather had come home from serving under Robert E. Lee to find himself pauperized by the carpet-baggers who cut up his land into parcels ostensibly given to the slaves, but really controlled by them. How he pawned the necklace to get working capital, and years later, when every foot of ground had been restored to him, plus hundreds of thousands of acres he had acquired along the way, he searched it out and paid triple the price he had pawned it for.'

'Mighty stirring story, suh,' I said. 'The vindication of the aristocracy. My favorite theme.'

'I'm sure it is,' McClough said. 'Anyway, the thought of that. . . .'

'Nigger?' I supplied helpfully.

'Criminal, Mr Krales. A boy who has carried a grudge against our family since his childhood, and announced to me over the telephone that he was going to ruin us. The thought that he has destroyed one family treasure and now is in possession of the other is intolerable.'

'And. . . .' I said.

'I want it back,' he said. 'I don't know what plans he has this time, but I want to get to him before he puts them into effect. It's already too late to save Pammie Sue.'

'How was he involved with your daughter?' I asked.

'He stole her, like he stole the necklace. He was a bad, resentful boy from the start, the image of his father. Nathan Tyler was a tenant farmer on our land in Pulham. After the war, when tobacco farming became automated, we didn't need him, or the two-hundred-odd other families we were carrying. But my father kept them on. Nathan paid him back by being drunk and unreliable. His yield was worthless, and he and his family were nothing but trouble-makers.' McClough's voice was heavy with the lachrymose self-righteousness of the misunderstood rich. 'Finally, the inevitable happened, and Nathan was sent off to the chain gang. Of course the whole family went to pieces. The mother – what was her name?' My skin crawled as lewd reminiscence glittered in McClough's eyes. 'She was a wild one in her own way, and she up and disappeared one night. Sarah took the children in, gave them her name because the name of Tyler had become anathema among the colored people in the county. Serena was sent off to school, the older boy Dean couldn't be handled and was dispatched to an orphanage, and Artis was put to work in our stables and around the house. Artis was a fighter and a vandal. I can't count the number of times the troopers brought him home instead of to the reform school, out of respect for Sarah. One morning he attacked Pammie Sue as she was about to go off for a ride. She couldn't have been more than thirteen. I've always thought that experience unbalanced her and led to the problems she had later on. . . .' The Ambassador gulped and looked down at his shoes for an appropriate interval. He would have to do that every time he mentioned his daughter.

'My father was an old-fashioned man,' he said. 'He wanted to shoot the boy right there, but we prevailed upon him to let us send Artis away, and we did, to a combination reform school-clinic for black children that they had in Charleston.'

'Father Divine's Boys' Town,' I said.

'It was better than the chain gang, Mr Krales, much better. And if you can forget your liberal concern for the criminal, think of the victim. Pammie Sue was hysterical for weeks afterward. And she never was the same. She became quite wild herself. Her mother, of course, was no help, and I was away most of the time, so Aunt Sarah filled in as best as she could. When we closed the house, Sarah and George came up here with me and looked after Pammie Sue. We thought the move would be good for her, but it wasn't.'

'New York has its own type of regional peccadillo,' I said.

'People like you always feel they have the right to be cruel about the rich and successful,' McClough said. He stabbed at one of his sagging jowls with his forefinger. 'We build a world for you to exist in. We take the risks. . . .'

'I'll be happy to discuss your contribution to civilization some other time, Mr McClough,' I said. 'But let's get back to the point – if there is one – to this story.'

The Ambassador pinched the jowl until it reddened. I wondered if there was any sensation in those pendulous pieces of flesh, testaments to his idle, indulgent life.

'Pammie Sue was a tribulation to me,' he said. Sure enough, he looked down at his shoes. 'I was constantly flying back from wherever I was to deal with her latest escapade. She went from one school to the next. There was a procession of boy friends, an abortion in Puerto Rico. She got no pleasure out of anything she did. . . . Always hysterical, crying. We tried one kind of therapy and medication after another, but nothing worked. I sometimes thought her only mission in life was to make me unhappy. In the last year she took to disappearing for weeks on end. We never knew where she was, or who she was with. But as long as the Saks and Bendel's bills kept coming in, as long as she signed for her monthly checks, her legacy from my wife, we knew she was in the city and at least healthy enough to go shopping.

'But then this last time the bills stopped coming in. I had, by this time, received my appointment and had been in Germany for almost six months. It seemed to me then that the challenges of such a crucial diplomatic post took precedence over the problems of a spoiled, unhappy child whose condition seemed quite hopeless by then.'

'Sure,' I said. 'If I had bought myself an ambassadorship, I'd want to enjoy it too.'

'I don't expect you to believe in patriotism any more than

you do in parental concern,' McClough said. 'The old-fashioned virtues are not in fashion in these days. Nevertheless, I was worried when the bills just stopped. And a few weeks afterward the man from Chemical Bank who handles my wife's estate sent me a batch of checks all endorsed over to Artis Pettibone. I flew home immediately. I left my post and my responsibilities out of concern for my daughter.' He stopped and looked at me as if he expected a round of applause.

'When I got back, I discovered that Pammie Sue had moved in with him,' he said. 'I don't know how he met her, but I'm sure it was a deliberate, calculated plan. He as much as admitted it to me over the phone. They were somewhere on the West Side, just across Central Park, but we couldn't find them. They would call late at night and taunt me. Pammie Sue seemed totally under his spell. The way she laughed and cursed. Even her voice had changed.'

'Why didn't you call the police?' I asked.

'Frankly, because I thought this kind of story would force my resignation. There had been a lot of controversy surrounding my appointment, if you remember. My closeness to the President was held against me, although I never understood why.'

'It may have had something to do with your qualifications,' I said.

'I think I have proven myself as capable a diplomat as any career man in the Foreign Service,' McClough said.

'No doubt you have,' I said.

He squinted through to the veiled irony in that remark. He was controlling himself remarkably well, and Nardo was keeping silent in his corner. They obviously thought they needed me very much.

'Didn't you fear for your daughter? After all, she was in the hands of the man who had raped her.'

'Of course I was afraid,' he said. 'But she didn't seem to be there against her will. She seemed in good physical health, at any rate.' The Ambassador checked his loafers out again. 'My God, I didn't want to embarrass the President. I had to balance a lot of considerations in my mind.'

'And your daughter came out with the short end,' I said.

'I thought she would come back,' McClough pleaded shrilly. 'She always had. I stationed a private detective at the bank to get her when she came for her monthly check. I had another man combing the West Side, checking on Artis. It all came to naught. They came to the house one afternoon when I was away, and took the necklace. That was two months ago. They called me once after that and said they were holding the necklace for ransom, and would phone with further instructions. I never heard from them again.'

'And now you want me to tell you where Pettibone is,' I said. 'What makes you think I know?'

'You were with his sister last night,' Nardo piped up. 'She must have told you.'

'Somebody else was with her too,' I said. 'Know anything about that?'

Nardo scowled and slammed at his pockets for a cigarette.

'The police would be very interested in that story you just told me, Ambassador,' I said. 'And so would the reading public.'

'You won't make five thousand bucks by going that route,' Nardo said, 'C'mon and stop the shit. We know your story.'

'Okay, so you know my story, but you don't know my price,' I said. 'Ten thousand American, okay?'

'Ten thousand,' Nardo said, without consulting McClough.

'I'll call you in two hours and tell you where to stash the money,' I said. 'As soon as I've got it, I'll tell you where the kid is. From then on, I never heard of him or you.'

'Fair enough,' Nardo said.

The Ambassador simpered triumphantly. 'Well, Mr Krales. Thank you.'

'Stay off the hot line for a while, Your Excellency,' I said. 'I don't want any busy signals when I call.'

CHAPTER FOURTEEN

Artis Pettibone had never been so popular in his life, and for so many different reasons. He was worth ten thousand to McClough, and ten thousand to Skivoso and Iboopa; that was, unless their hatchet man had extorted his whereabouts from Serena, and it didn't look like he had. Twenty thousand dollars just to set the wolves on a rapist, a thief, and maybe a murderer. That was a lot of overtime. I could quit, write a novel. My severance came to a little over five thousand; I could get another fifty dollars if I sold my furniture. Even with the alimony I'd be home free for at least a year. Time enough to write *War and Peace*, paint the Mona Lisa, die of cirrhosis. I set off for the Village to see if the deal was still hot with bread barons.

The bakery was closed, but light gleamed through the Venetian blinds over the door, and I heard movement inside. I knocked on the window, pounded on the door, and shouted:

'Hey, Skivoso, Iboopa, anybody home here?'

The blinds rustled, and a bloodshot brown eye glared at me.

'Store's closed,' the eye browled.

'I want to talk about Artis Pettibone,' I said.

The eye seemed to hang there, as if it had been stuck between the blinds while the rest of the body went back into the store. Then the door opened, and a chunky little guy in a leather jacket and a battered felt hat looked me over.

'Who are you?' he asked.

'Krales from the New York *Event*. Your associate knows me. May I come in.' I brushed by him before he could say anything. Iboopa was coming out of the back, wiping his hands.

'What the hell do you want?' he asked.

'I heard you were offering ten grand to anybody who could

locate Artis Pettibone. I wanted to know if the deal still stood.'

'You crazy?' he said.

'Who tole you this?' the little guy asked.

'Mr Skivoso, I presume,' I said. 'The point is not who told me, but if it's true. Because I might be able to help you. You see, I think I've got a lead on him.'

'Wait here,' Iboopa said.

He disappeared into the back, followed by Skivoso, who turned and shook a stubby forefinger at me.

'Just stay right dere,' he said, pointing to a spot on the floor, which I obediently occupied.

The place was quiet except for the tinkle of rock music coming from a transistor somewhere in the back. I cremated a Camel and was just beginning to regret my importunity when they returned.

'Okay, I made a call,' Iboopa said. 'C'mon with us.'

The bakery was empty. There were racks, but no oven. The place didn't look like it had seen a sesame seed in years.

'Where do you do your baking?' I asked.

'Next door, in the pizza joint,' Iboopa said.

The sound of music grew stronger as we headed into the back. Purple light came from a little room near the rear exit. I went to take a look, proceeding gingerly at first, but when nobody tried to stop me, I lengthened my stride.

The room was dark except for an Indian red glow coming from some fluorescent lamps over a long table. Seated at a bench in front of the table were three black women and one black man. They were wearing surgical masks and motorcycle goggles. The man was bare to the waist and was wearing dayglow bikini underwear; the women were wearing bras and panties. They each had a small sack of white powder and a jar of white powder. They were putting a little of the white powder from the sack, which they measured out with a spoon, and a lot of the white powder from the jar, which they took out with a scoop, into little glasseine envelopes. A fat white man in a Mets T-shirt was sitting on a high stool, smoking a cigar and watching them.

So that's how it's done, I thought. The workers wear the goggles and the masks to make sure none of the stuff gets in their noses. The stuff in the jars must be quinine or milk sugar or some kind of thing they cut it with; the other stuff is heroin. They have to strip down to their shorts so they won't be able to conceal any of the stuff on them; the overseer just sits there and watches them.

'So that's how you make your dough,' I said.

'Dat's funny,' Iboopa said, unamused.

He opened the rear door, and we stepped out into a little alley. Behind me Skivoso cleared his throat, as if he were about to burst into song. Iboopa clasped his hand and hunched over prayerfully. Then he rammed his clasped hands into my stomach.

I fell forward with an 'oof'. Skivoso bounced something off the back of my neck, and the world faded out. There were lead weights on my eyelashes, and the stone of Sisyphus kept my back bowed. I felt my insteps scraping along the ground. What extraordinary virtuosity, I thought. They must have done this thing a million times before to be so deft and assured about it. Gratified by their craftsmanship, I fell into a blissful slumber.

I dreamed I was lying on the beach at Cannes. The sun beat down quite pleasantly, but a bunch of starlets in string bikinis had played a silly trick on me. They had poured buckets of ice water over my ankles. How naughty. I got up to chastise the little darlings, and my head collided with the the sun. It was made out of hot metal and scorched my forehead. Now I was worried. What was I doing so close to old Sol? I opened my eyes and looked up into a grid of pleasantly glowing heat coils. I wasn't on the beach. I was in an oven.

'Help,' I yelled. My hands were tied to a board. I was too tall for an oven, so my feet stuck out. I kicked, and something tightened around my ankles.

'Help. Get me outta here?' I writhed and wriggled. It was useless. The coils were getting hotter. I could smell my own singed flesh. They were going to burn me alive. I heard voices.

'You bastards,' I cried, kicking desperately. I could see daylight through the crack in the oven door. Hands were holding my ankles, gripping tighter as I struggled. It was useless. I closed my eyes and prayed to pass out.

I was starting to go under when the oven door opened, and I felt myself sliding out. Room temperature was like a blast of frigid air. Whoever was carrying me laid me on the counter.

'You guys crazy?' he whispered, and then shook me. 'Krales, you okay?'

It was Carbonaro. He was sweating, his eyes were bulging, and his hands shook as they wandered over me. He looked down with the same distraught expression I remembered seeing on my mother when I fell off a seesaw, so many years ago. And I loved him for it.

'They tried to make a pizza out of me, Frankie,' I said.

'I know, I know,' he said, untying me and sliding the board out from under my back.

'But they didn't put any mozzarella on,' I said.

'You gonna be a smart aleck now?' he asked. 'Can you get up?' I rolled off the counter into his bear hug.

'Don't say nothin',' he whispered. 'Just let's get the hell out of here.'

Skivoso and Iboopa were standing in the corner, pouting like naughty schoolboys. Carbonaro propped me against the counter and turned to them, shaking his head and laughing nervously.

'Hey, you guys gotta owe me this time,' he said. 'I really saved your asses.'

'We made the call, Frankie,' Iboopa said. 'Dis guy comes in with a story. That's the thoid time he stuck his nose in, so we made the call.'

'How many times I gotta tell yiz, yiz gotta clear it with the old man?' Carbonaro said. 'He's lookin' to do yiz in now, anyway. You're lucky I'm lookin' out for yiz.'

'The guy knew about the nigger, Frankie,' Skivoso pleaded. 'That means he's trouble, and when he tried to make a deal, we figured if he's like that, then we can take him out.'

'So he knows about the kid,' Carbonaro said. 'That can't hurt you.'

'Yeah, but he knows about the operation too, Frankie,' Iboopa said.

'Ah, whaddya mean. . . .' Frankie said. 'He thinks. And he can't put what he thinks in the paper.'

'No, no, Frankie.' Iboopa's eyes glittered with malicious cunning. 'He seen the room as we were walkin' him out. He seen everything. So we gotta put him to sleep.'

'Smart,' Frankie said, rapping his knuckles against his forehead. 'Smart like a *gabone*, you know. So you show him the room just to have an excuse, huh? But it's no good, and you just made it worse for yourself. 'Cause this guy don't get touched, y'understand?'

'Does the old man know?' Skivoso asked.

'And if he did, he'd know yiz were tryin' to blackmail him, and he'd come over here and blow yiz away personally,' Carbonaro said. 'You don't get cute like that in the Village.'

'He seen the operation, Frankie,' Iboopa said.

'We made the call,' Skivoso said.

'We gotta put him to sleep,' Iboopa said.

'I'm takin' him outta here,' Frankie said. 'You got my personal guarantee that he won't make trouble.'

'We can't let you do this, Frankie,' Iboopa said.

'What? You don't accept my word?' Carbonaro flushed. He pushed me aside and advanced on the two men. 'You callin' me a liar now?'

'Nothin' personal, Frankie, but we made the call,' Iboopa said.

Skivoso took a revolver with a chipped wooden handle out of his jacket pocket and pointed it at the floor.

'What's this?' Carbonaro demanded. 'You gonna shoot me now, huh?'

'Put it away,' Iboopa said harshly.

Skivoso shoved the gun back in his pocket and retreated. 'I'm sorry, Frankie. I didn't mean. . . .'

'*Figlio di butana . . . desgraciada*,' Carbonaro said, raising his hand, letting it hang menacingly over the cowering man, and then bringing it down with stinging force on his head.

'Y'see this hand?' he said, grabbing the hand in which Skivoso had held the gun. 'I should cut it off.' He shoved Skivoso's hand into the oven, slammed the door on it, and held the door closed. Skivoso whined, turned purple, and fell, clutching with his free hand at Frankie's sleeve. Frankie kicked him in the stomach and stepped away. Breathing through his nose, Skivoso pulled the door open and inched away on his knees, cradling his injured hand.

'You show me disrespect in my neighborhood?' Carbonaro shouted at Iboopa, who hadn't moved a muscle during the destruction of his partner and who watched him with careful, squinting concentration, wary but unafraid. 'I got a little talkin' to do now too, and in the meantime I'm takin' this guy outta here, and you keep your brudder-in-law away because he's like a fish in a barrel on Bedford Street, starting yesterday. Y'understand?'

Iboopa nodded, moving his head and nothing else. 'We're gonna have to talk this all over, Frankie. I gotta make another call.'

Carbonaro dropped a dime on the floor. 'Here, call up all your friends.' He grabbed me by the back of my singed jacket. 'C'mon, you stupid bastard.'

Uncle Al was outside opening the back door of the Mercedes. 'Those bastards hurt you, Mr Krales?' he asked, full of tender solicitude.

Carbonaro pushed me into the back seat. 'Let's get outta here,' he said.

The car glided away, and the partition slid up again. Carbonaro smacked me on the forehead with the heel of his hand. 'Stupid. . . . You okay?'

We were pulling away from a joint with a big red sign. 'Pizza di Palermo,' I read. 'Is that where I was?' I asked.

'Yeah, and you weren't the first,' Carbonaro said.

'You mean they bake people in there, and then they make pizzas, in the same oven?' I asked.

'You wanna call the Health Department?' Carbonaro said. 'You in shock or something?'

'Why did you do it?' I asked.

He shrugged. 'I like you, and I don't like them. They

called their man, and he called my Uncle Victor to clear it, although it was just a courtesy call, because my uncle can't go up against him. But when I heard about it, I came over and pulled my godfather act. Pretty good, huh?'

I didn't answer because my lips were trembling. My body held the heat of the oven; I could almost hear my entrails crackling. I sat there, watching my hands shake, feeling the muscles pulsing in my legs. Carbonaro put his arm around me.

'Hey, my friend, don't be embarrassed. Whaddya usually do when you been through something like this?'

'I don't know. I've never been baked in a pizza oven before,' I said.

'Always with the jokes,' he said. 'I can't get over that. I meant, you wanna take a shit, you gotta throw up? Anything you want.'

'You know what I want to do?' I said.

'Anything you want, I told you.'

'I want to cry,' I said.

'Hey, you deserve it,' Carbonaro said. 'Go ahead. Forget I'm here.'

I put my head in my hands, and immediately tears poured in hot freshets from my eyes. I saw things. Images clicked on and off in my mind. A home movie of my nervous breakdown. My wife sat on a deserted beach, brushing her hair back from her eyes and rummaging in a picnic basket. My little boy ran toward me, his arms out, laughing. The eyes . . . the eyes were the same. My mother standing in the cold, crepuscular air of a cemetery, just standing there by a stone, her arms folded. Serena Pettibone looking at me, searching in my face for a sign. But of what? WHAT? WHAT DID THEY ALL WANT?

I cried for a long time. A hot, painful lump formed in my throat, the first sign of returning consciousness; then I became aware that I was saying things, crying out names and questions. I became embarrassed, but did not stop. Instead, my thoughts turned to vengeance. By the time I had mastered myself enough to speak coherently, I wanted to kill Skivoso and Iboopa. I wanted to skewer them the way they had skewered poor Pamela Sue McClough, to burn them the way they had burned Serena Pettibone, to pull out their fingernails, slice off their testicles. I wanted to keep them alive as long as possible, make them suffer and scream and beg for death.

We had driven over to the docks on the West Side. Uncle Al went into a diner for coffee. He pressed a steaming container into my hand.

'Wanna nice cheese danish?' he asked gently.

I shook my head.

'Maybe a bagel?'

'I want to kill them,' I said to Carbonaro.

'Sure,' he said, wiping doughnut sugar off the side of his mouth. 'I don't blame you.'

'You can get me a gun,' I said.

'Hey, I can get you a tank, but what good's it gonna do? Look, don't get mad at me, but the only thing you ever killed is a fifth, you know what I mean?'

'You're right,' I said, plunged into hysterical despair. 'I'm not good for anything.'

'I didn't say you couldn't do it,' he said. 'All's you gotta do is pull a trigger, or do a little carving, or maybe a little yank with a rope. It ain't hard. I mean, writin' a newspaper story is a lot harder. You wanna find a killer? Lemme say this: you take a guy drivin' a garbage truck for two-fifty a week. An ordinary guy with the wife, the kids, the color TV. You tell him, "Tony, you makin' two-fifty a week, I'll give you two-fifty a night. Just push this old lady down the stairs, poison this baby, cut this old man's throat." Anything you want, they'll do.... And then on Sunday they sit home and watch the football games. So go figure it out.'

'Those guys tried to make a pizza out of me, Frankie,' I said. 'I'm gonna have them arrested.'

'Uh uh, no cops.' He wagged a schoolmasterly finger at me.

'That's the only way I can get them....'

He shook his head vehemently. 'No cops. Everything can be worked out, you know what I mean. But no cops.'

'I'm not one of your little toy soldiers,' I said.

'No cops,' he said.

'Will you have me killed if I call them?'

He looked stricken.

'Beaten up?'

'You think I'm an animal?'

'So?' I challenged.

'So, there's this little thing about savin' your life,' he said softly. 'I mean it could be said that you owe me.'

I had forgotten that. 'Okay, no cops,' I said.

I got the sniffles again on the way home. Uncle Al whistled, and Carbonaro looked out of the window until I pulled myself together.

'Better put some Vaseline on your head,' he said as I got out. 'Get a good night's sleep.' He pulled a roll of hundreds out of his pocket. 'Need some money?'

I turned away from those Gorgon-like bills. 'I've got enough Vaseline in the house,' I said.

Carbonaro laughed. 'You don't like money, do you?'

I swayed like a drunk. 'Thanks,' I said. 'I'll do the same for you sometime.'

Carbonaro laughed. 'He's a pisser,' I heard him say as he closed the door.

CHAPTER FIFTEEN

I collapsed on the horsehair sofa in my living room. As the adrenalin dissipated, the shakes increased, and I discovered blisters on my neck and back, each discovery bringing me back to the time I spent in the oven, each return trip intensifying the horror. Now, an hour after the fact, I was weak with panic. I staggered up to double-lock the door, then went back to put a chair under the knob. Every creak became a careful footstep, every voice in the hall the whispers of

Mafia hit men casing my apartment. Iboopa would be sure to get me. Carbonaro's protection didn't extend beyond the Village. It would be a simple matter to find my address: just call the paper. Or even easier, look me up in the phone book. But then they'd only find my old address. And my son!

I called my old number. My wife answered sleepily. I could hear 'I Love Lucy' in the background; the same shows I grew up on, and now my son was watching them and getting another insane perspective on domestic life to go with the one he'd developed with his own parents.

'Are you awake, Sandy?' I said. 'Wake up, because I don't want you to forget what I'm going to tell you.'

'Please, Josn, no histrionics,' she said. 'You brought it on yourself.'

'You know about the oven?' I asked, amazed.

'Oh c'mon, don't make Auschwitz analogies. It's not as bad as all that.'

'You callous cunt, what do you know? I called up to save your life, and you give me this? I'm not asking for sympathy. God knows that would be too much. But a little intellectual recognition of what it's like to be almost burned to death. . . .'

She was silent – properly rebuked, I thought. 'What are you talking about?' she finally asked.

'The pizza oven,' I said. 'What were you talking about?'

'Alimony jail,' she said.

'Let's back up a minute,' I said. 'I was almost baked in a pizza oven a little while ago. The guys who did it might still be after me, and they might come up to the house. So I called to warn you, and to tell you to get Quentin over to your mother, or my mother, if you can stand it. Now, what were you talking about?'

'Well, I called the police last week, and the warrant officer at the precinct was trying to get in touch with you. But you kept discovering bodies all over the place, and I guess you weren't home too much, so he called me today and said he was sending two patrolmen over to arrest you.'

'How can you do that to me?' I said.

'And how can you pull this ruse on me? Do you have some complicated legal reason for trying to get me out of the house?'

'I was almost murdered.'

'Well, I'm sorry to hear that, Josh, but you have certain responsibilities which you are not fulfilling. . . .'

'The guys who did it might come over there and murder you.'

'Well, Herb is here to protect me, if that's the information you're trying to pry out. I'm sorry, Josh, but I've just gotten tired of chasing you around with my hand out. I have a legal and a moral claim. And your son certainly should count for something. . . .'

'I can't believe the woman I lived with for six years is having me arrested,' I said.

'Oh, don't be so melodramatic,' she said, a note of contrition creeping into her voice. 'You'll have plenty of other deadbeats to commiserate with, and. . . .'

'Did your lousy dyke lawyer put you up to this?' I shouted, forgetting my pain, my anxiety, everything, in the joy of marital conflict. 'And all your ball-breaking friends from your women's group?'

'No, it was strictly my idea, although I'm sure nobody will care one way or the other. Most people don't like you, Josh. I'm sure you won't have any visitors. Except, of course, your mother. She'll probably bring you a pot of chicken soup with a file in it. . . .'

The intercom buzzed.

'Two cops on their way up to see you,' the doorman said.

I left the phone off the hook. My wife was still talking. After a while she'd hang up, but as long as my phone stayed off the hook, she wouldn't get any calls for the rest of the day. I rushed down nineteen flights of stairs in thirty seconds.

'You prick,' I panted at my doorman. 'If Raquel Welch came to see me, you'd tell her I'd moved out. But the cops, you let 'em right up. See if you get your two bucks this Christmas.'

I ran into the gay bar across the street. 'Got a public phone in here?' I asked the bartender.

'Oh my God, a booth queen,' he said, pointing limply to the back.

The Sullivan Street Social Athletic Club wasn't listed. I called Solo's Restaurant and asked for Carbonaro, but he wasn't there. So I called Victor Lupo's house in New Jersey.

'I have to speak to Frankie Carbonaro,' I told the goon who answered. 'My name is Krales. He knows me, and he'll want to talk to me.' I gave him the number of the bar and hung up. Five minutes later the phone rang.

'Hey, tough guy,' Carbonaro said. 'I was just tellin' my uncle how you got big balls, you know, for the way you acted.'

'Look, you gotta do something for me,' I said. 'I'm afraid Iboopa's going to send that Albino up to my old address where my wife and kid are. Can you put a couple of guys up there, discreet guys, to watch out for them?'

'I would be honored to,' he said. 'And I would like to apologize for not having thought of it myself.'

Next I called the office and had the switchboard read me my messages. Captain Boyd, chief of Manhattan South Homicide, had called a few times. He was my man for nailing Duffy. I was about to hang up when the traitorous clerk put Kettle on the phone.

'Where have you been?' he boomed.

'I'm working on the Village murder story,' I said. 'New angle.'

'You're fired,' Kettle said. 'We've notified the union, and we're ready for arbitration. We've got you on insubordination, drunkenness, and the union's so sick of this they won't even put up a fight.'

'McClough's involved,' I said.

'Don't try to wave a story in front of me,' Kettle said. 'Because nothing you can bring in is as important as your effect on the morale. . . .'

'His daughter was living with Pettibone,' I said.

'That's just a cheap scandal,' Kettle said.

'And it will sure look cheap in a big headline in the *News*,'

I said. 'Or maybe on TV: "CBS News has learned that Pamela Sue McClough. . . ." Think I'd look good with a mike in my hand?'

'They wouldn't. . . .'

'Oh, that's only part of it. I just told you enough to make your spotted tongue hang out. I've smeared him pretty good, but now it's going to be a mud slide. A Republican, a friend of the President whose nomination was opposed by this newspaper. A millionaire who's backing a loser. Clobber him, and the liberals will choke you in Pulitzer Prizes.'

'When do we get this story?' Kettle asked, resigned to a few more days with me.

'You get the first installment in fifteen minutes,' I said. 'And if I can't get more, then I'll quit. Happy now?'

I hung up and called Boyd at Manhattan South. He gave me a big Rotarian hello. Old play-it-by-the-book Duffy was probably breathing down his red neck, and he wanted him out.

'I was very concerned about what happened between you and Lieutenant Duffy,' he said. 'I don't like my people punching civilians around.'

'You probably prefer a rubber hose.'

Boyd laughed. He wasn't about to antagonize me. 'Duffy admits doing it,' he said. 'His attitude about the press has always been poor. I think if you made a complaint to the deputy commissioner, I'd have to recommend a hearing.'

One hearing, no matter what the disposition, would darken Duffy's fair hair, and that was all Boyd needed to keep his job.

'Well, he refused to give me just rudimentary information about the McClough killing. . . .'

'Which it's his duty to give,' Boyd said righteously.

'I know,' I said. 'And life can be so simple with a guy like me. Anybody who wants to be my friend only has to give me a little edge on the competition, that's all. And then I'll cooperate in return.'

'Maybe I can help you,' Boyd said.

'And maybe I'll cooperate,' I said. 'Why are you after Pettibone?'

'His brother Dean was one of the McClough victims,' Boyd said. 'Dean Tyler, that's his real name, was a member of the biggest heroin-dealing syndicate in Harlem. Narcotics Squad people had films of him and his brother Artis making drops all over Harlem. They had a, uh . . .' he cleared his throat, 'unofficial, off-the-record sort of tap on his phone, and heard him make an appointment with his brother for the night of the murder at what both referred to as the "pad".'

'Was there a tail on Tyler?' I asked.

'Uh . . . I imagine so, but something snafued, I guess.'

'Must be an invisible shield around Greenwich Village which narcos can't penetrate,' I said.

'That's not my concern,' Boyd said. 'I'm a homicide detective. Since it came out in your stories that Pettibone worked down the street from the murder apartment. . . .'

'You mean the Narcotics Squad didn't know that?' I asked.

'If they did, they didn't tell us. All they told us was that Tyler had set up a meet with Pettibone. This other information places him at the scene, so we want to talk to him. Of course, right now we don't know if he's hiding out or living under a pile of newspapers in a vacant lot somewhere.'

'You don't think he had anything to do with this, do you?' I asked. 'The killings have Mafia written all over them.'

'There's a black Mafia too,' Boyd said. 'And it's very active in drugs.'

'Well, how do you figure the debutante's involvement?'

'She liked 'em black,' Boyd said. 'They're supposed to have rhythm, you know.'

'You don't need rhythm to put a hole in somebody's chest.'

'I've been in this business twenty-five years,' Boyd said, 'and I have one operating principle: use what you've got. And that's all I've got on her. The only real way to solve a murder is to retrace the last five minutes of the victim's life. We can't do it with any of these people. And with the girl, the closest we come is three months ago when she was in Germany visiting her father. The poor guy was so overwrought he forgot about it, and we had to show him her passport.'

'Poor guy,' I said. 'How long was she there?'

'Coupla weeks. She went to Sweden after that and took a freighter home. That one that was just in the collision on Thanksgiving, the "Charles XII".'

'Was she alone?'

'She was on the boat, that we know. Whoever she was hanging out with in Europe didn't have dinner with Daddy at the embassy.'

'Hey, Captain Boyd, we're getting along great, you know that,' I said. 'Just talking to you makes me madder and madder at Duffy.'

'Well, we want to do the right thing,' he said.

'Sure. Unofficially and off the record, what's your take on Ambassador McClough?'

'I think he's a very patriotic and very misunderstood man,' Boyd said piously. 'You can't blame a guy for being rich, especially if he was born that way.'

'Especially,' I said.

'I had a long talk with the guy, and I think if the press would leave him alone, he'd do fine. But they got this goddamn witch hunt goin' for people in the Administration. You know, when the liberals in the media. . . .'

'Save that for another interview, Captain Boyd,' I said. 'I appreciate your help. Gosh, I only wish every cop I had to deal with was as open and straightforward as you.'

I hung up over his unctuous rejoinder and called Homicide for Duffy. They gave me a number I knew quite well – the Beat Bar and Grill across the street from headquarters. Duffy came to the phone half in the bag.

'I just wanted to tell you that I'm not going to make any trouble for you,' I said.

'Hah.'

'And I don't want you to think it's because of the power you sicked on me, or anything else you might have done that I don't know about.'

'Yeah, it's just because you think I'm a great guy,' he said.

'I hate your guts,' I said. 'But I also don't like the people who don't like you, so the whole thing would become too complicated if I started.'

'Yeah,' he sneered. He didn't believe me, but it didn't matter.

'Now, one good turn deserves another, so answer me just one question. Where's Artis Pettibone?'

'In my other suit. I'm lookin' for him, ain't I?'

'What do you think he'll tell you when you find him?'

'You mean if he still can talk?'

'Yeah.'

'That's two questions,' he said, and giggled spitefully.

'You're on McClough's team too, huh, Duffy,' I said. 'Never met a cop yet who didn't kiss rich people's asses.'

'Fuck McClough,' Duffy shouted, and I could imagine the assembled flat feet pivoting to frown on his heresy. 'He looks like a dickie waver I once arrested in the balcony of the Radio City Music Hall. He don't mean nothin' to me, y'understand? I'd lock him up just as quick as that dickie waver.'

'We'll see,' I said.

The telephone was Zeus's thunderbolt in my hand. It crackled with retributive lightning as I called the office. 'Chapter One,' I told Kettle.

They put me on with Potosky again. 'I'm dictating, you're typing,' I told her.

'That's what's known as breaking into the business,' she said sourly.

'Artis Pettibone was a most-sought-after man today,' I dictated. 'New paragraph. The police want to question him about his knowledge of the Greenwich Village massacre in which his brother and his erstwhile mistress were killed.'

'Mrs Schwartz in Brooklyn is never going to understand "erstwhile",' Potosky said.

'That's Mrs Schwartz's problem,' I said. 'If *you* don't want to be erstwhile, keep your mouth shut. Now, picking up the story from "killed". Pettibone's brother, Dean Tyler, alleged by police to have been one of the biggest heroin dealers in Harlem, was found shot through the chest in a

Greenwich Village apartment. The girl Pettibone had been living with, Pamela Sue McClough, was found pinned against the door downstairs by an undertaker's implement known as a trocar.'

'I know that phrase causes *frissons* of horror in our readership, but don't you get tired of writing it?' Potosky asked.

'Mrs Schwartz will never understand "*frissons*",' I said. 'Now, if I may. . . . Picking up from "trocar". Pettibone's sister, Serena, was tortured and slain in her Harlem apartment by someone who, police now believe, was seeking information about her brother.

'New paragraph. Among those in the search are . . .' (Dammit, I didn't know Iboopa's first name.) '. . . Fat Augie Iboopa, a Greenwich Village bakery owner who claims that Pettibone impregnated his teen-age niece while working for him as an apprentice baker. New paragraph. Another most anxious to know Pettibone's whereabouts is Ambassador Arnold McClough, father of the slain girl, who says that Pettibone stole a diamond-encrusted pearl necklace, an heirloom that has been in the McClough family for 150 years. McClough is so concerned about retrieving the necklace that he has not informed the police of its theft, but has preferred to work through private detectives, and even offered this reporter $10,000 to find Pettibone for him.'

'That's slander,' Potosky said.

'That's show biz,' I said. 'And I'm a star.' I dictated the rest of the story, plus a memo to Grissom on the estimated size of my overtime.

There was a police car in front of my building. It could have been for a burglary, a leaky pipe, a dead pensioner in a bathtub, or for my alimony bust. Three blocks away a black Cadillac was easing in front of my former residence with two vigilant Sicilians inside. My story was in, my son had better protection than Caroline Kennedy – all was well with the world. Now all I needed was a place to sleep.

CHAPTER SIXTEEN

People don't look at each other on the streets of New York; one errant blink can get you maimed or married. So when you draw horrified stares, you know you've really blotted your copy book.

I checked my zipper and then looked in a store window to see what was amiss. A huge blister had bubbled off my forehead, my cheeks were peeling, and my coat sleeves were scorched. I looked exactly as if I had just come out of a pizza oven. People jumped out of my way as I weaved down West Seventy-second Street.

I took the subway to Times Square and walked over to the periodical annex of the public library, an old gray building where the library stores bound copies of newspapers, magazines, and old books that were never requested. Five densely-packed floors of forgotten print. I thumbed idly through a couple of years of my own paper, catching my by-line here and there. Through history with Josh Krales, the original man of dead letters. The riots, the murders, and demonstrations, the interviews with people now dead or obscure, the issues that once had burned and now hardly smoldered.

The *Times* had the text of the McClough confirmation hearings, wherein he was needled by the Democratic senator from his own state.

SENATOR STITT: Well, we've established that you do not speak German. Do you at least have a knowledge of German history? Do you know who Bismarck was?

MCCLOUGH: Well, Senator, if you just give me a minute. . . .

It hadn't been that long ago. McClough had been the buffoon of the month for a while. Comics made jokes about him; newspapers ran ominous editorials about his nomination. The appropriate scandals had been dredged up: the land sold to the army for three times its assessed value, the stock deals, the involvement with a high-rolling financier who had gone broke. An earnest McClough telling senators: 'I don't have as much money as you think, believe me.' A vigorous presidential defense, a refusal to withdraw the name from nomination, and then. . . .

A week after confirmation, McClough was on his way to Bonn. A year later he was the Hon. Ambassador, and everything else was forgotten. Did it matter that he wasn't a career diplomat or a great intellect? Was he going to drive Germany into the arms of the Bolsheviks with some horrible faux pas! No way! A photograph of McClough on the steps of the Capitol with his attorney, Preston Parker. Sure, there's the kind of guy he would hire. I wrote myself a note: 'Who is Peter Nardo?'

Who's Who had a thumbnail sketch of McClough. B.A. from Tulane – wasn't that the Harvard of the South? Family business, Republican politics, membership on a couple of presidential commissions under Eisenhower. No military pedigree, though; little Arnold must have had flat feet. Preston Parker was in there too. But there was nothing on Peter Nardo.

While I was at it, I wrote down all the questions still to be answered. 'Who told Nardo I could be bought?' And 'What does Artis Pettibone have that types as diverse as McClough, Iboopa and Breitel could possibly want?'

Loose ends, too many of them. The Village murders were the easiest to tie up. It had been Albino and friends, obscure executioners who watched football games on Sunday. It seemed rather brazen and unprofessional of Albino to leave his calling card, but maybe he hadn't had time to pull the trocar out; another pressing matter had been brought to his attention. Maybe my arrival had spooked them, although as far as I could remember, the street had been silent and empty.

Concentration had blurred my vision. As it cleared, I saw a group of grizzled, shirt-sleeved horse-players searching old copies of the racing forms for some obscure bit of history that would give them an edge over the odds-makers. At the table in front of me sat a girl in a black dress and dark glasses, her blonde hair tucked under a little fur cap; spiked heels dangled from her nyloned toes. Her pose was vacant and voluptuous; women are at their sexiest when they don't know they're being observed. She sucked on a pencil, slowly and lasciviously scratched her calf with long vermilion nails, Serena's color. There was a pile of magazines in front of her, but she was lost in lubricous reverie. She shifted her thighs slightly to let the fantasy phallus enter. A little twist of the profile, and I realized it was Potosky.

I eased out of my chair and sneaked around behind her. Her shoulders tensed at my approach. I slid my hands around her neck.

'LIBRARY RAPIST STRIKES AGAIN,' I said.

'You wish,' she said. 'It's a good thing I recognized you, or I would have doubled you over with a karate punch to the solar plexus.'

'Not the scrotum?' I asked.

'Oh no. We liberated women do all our emasculating verbally.'

'So I've heard.'

'What happened to you?'

'A bunch of goons tried to bake me in a pizza oven,' I said.

'Serves me right for asking,' she said.

'But what's with you looking like a fifties hooker?' I asked.

'I have a date with a man who needs a lot of incentive,' she said. 'Stephen Skutz, the stage designer.'

'But he's gay.'

'Let's say he's a reluctant bi,' she said. 'But also the sweetest, most nonhostile, and beautiful man. Do you know him?'

'He's a skinny, bleached-blond fairy,' I said. 'You're gonna have to snap your garter belts for the whole weekend to get any action out of him.'

'He's a wonderful man,' she said, 'and I don't want to talk about him any more.'

'That's fine with me,' I said. 'Because I need a big favor from you.'

'Which is. . . .'

'I need a place to stay tonight. I can't go to my place because my wife has a warrant for my arrest for nonpayment of alimony.'

'You must have a black book full of willing young things who would just swoon to put you up,' Potosky said.

'I'd rather impose on someone who's not so anxious, if you know what I mean.'

'Yes, yes, fear of possessive females, of making commitments, a common syndrome these days.'

'Well, if you're bringing your friend back to the apartment. . . .'

'No, he's more comfortable in his own place.' She fished a key ring out of her pocketbook and handed it to me. 'It'll be all right for tonight, but if you don't solve your domestic problems by tomorrow, you'll have to look elsewhere.'

'Fine,' I said, examining the key ring. 'Which is the door key?'

'They all are,' she said. 'This opens the bottom lock, this the top, this the police lock, and this little one shuts off the alarm over the door. You'll have to do that as soon as you get in, or you'll have the entire precinct on your hands. They love coming to my apartment.'

'So,' I said, twirling the key ring around my finger, 'it's set.'

'And take that triumphant look out of your eye,' she said.

'There'll be no seductions tonight.'

'Are you including your own efforts?' I asked.

She turned back to her research. 'I'll be home about two, if I'm home at all, so be awake,' she said.

'I'll have the cocoa bubbling on the stove,' I said.

Potosky lived in one of those new buildings where a snoozing doorman mans a fuzzy closed-circuit television set that is focused on an empty garage, where Muzak tinkles in the elevator, and the wind whistles through the cheaply-constructed walls. It took me fifteen minutes to open

Potosky's door, during which time her neighbor, a chubby girl with a McDonald's bag and a copy of *New York* magazine, arrived and gave me a significant look as she diddled with her keys. Poor kid. She probably languished at the peephole, peeking out at the constant procession of jet-set men who escorted her neighbor. One day, out of desperation she'd take up with a slightly *louche* character, and the next morning they'd find her in pieces all over the bedroom.

The smell of incense was in the air. I groped for a light. Something small and furry ran between my legs and snapped at my ankles. A rat? I finally found the switch. The rat was a Yorkshire terrier you see on the leashes of berouged middle-aged ladies with skinny legs and aluminium hair.

The apartment was the type every Radcliffe girl dreams of having. It was full of chic, book-store art in metal frames: sketches by Grosz, posters by Dali and Picasso, a huge, ungainly oil of a nude girl sitting by a window, which had to be collegian Potosky painted by a Harvard lover. Globular Swedish lamps hung over potted plants; an old captain's chest sat in front of a leather couch. Record albums lay in piles all over the room; a bookcase bulged with paperbacks, all neatly arranged by subject, with a whole shelf devoted to porno.

There was a corner left in a bottle of J & B. I threw it down and got undressed, throwing my clothes all over the living room. She had a huge brass bed so big you could hardly walk around the bedroom; a little television had its face turned to the wall in shame at the goings-on. The bathroom was moist and warm; here was a girl who bathed a lot. The medicine chest was full of oils and lotions, an electric toothbrush, a Water Pik, a vibrator with a little grease at the tip. I ran the bath and threw everything in until the room was thick with redolent steam, and greenish bubbles floated on the surface of the water. There were bruises on my thighs that I could not trace, but otherwise my body was a map of where I'd been the last few days. My back and arms were crisscrossed with Serena's nail marks, my eye was slightly swollen from Duffy's fist, and skin hung from scalded patches on my arms and legs. The hot, scented water flowed maliciously through my scorched and wounded crevices. I stiffened against the pain; my nerves whined and sparkled like loose connections; my teeth ached, the soles of my feet tingled and throbbed. But after a while the agony subsided to a tedious twinge. Swirling my feet in the fragrant suds, I fell asleep.

The phone woke me up. Potosky had an extension on the wall by the tub. All I got was heavy breathing when I answered.

'Do you call here often?' I asked.

Heavy breathing.

'Because this isn't the party who's usually here.'

More heavy breathing.

'I'm a dwarf with a hump,' I said. 'I have hairy toes, a big nose, and bad breath. My ears and nose run, and pus comes out of my eyes every Saturday.'

'Will you shut up!' the breather shrieked. 'You're ruining everything.' And he hung up abruptly.

I slipped into Potosky's terrycloth robe and killed the half-bottle of cooking sherry I found in the kitchen. Then I got into Potosky's bed between her Saint Laurent sheets. There was a phone on the night table. The bath had made me pleasantly drowsy; the cooking sherry gave me an edge. With a sigh of lascivious contentment, I dialed Sarah Pettibone's number.

The old woman's voice was faint and quavery, as if she'd been crying or starving . . . or both. 'Artis ain't been back,' she said. 'We been waitin' for him to come and do the shoppin'.'

I asked her about Serena.

'I know it would come to this,' she said. 'My sister was cut up by some man in St Louis. And now Serena. . . . The sins of the fathers. The police told me about Dean, and I wasn't surprised. He was another bad 'un. Mad and ready to fight. Never did know how to behave. He and Artis were goin' to burn down the big house one night. I told the boys: if God had meant for us to be livin' there and the white folks breakin' their backs in the fields, well, that's the way it would be. I told my sister, and so did Reverend Cleveland: some peoples is so full of the devil that they have to pray extra hard to get him out. You have to be strong to resist.'

She was wandering, her voice rising with the onset of a new memory, falling with its melancholy conclusion. She spoke in her natural accent, too weak to maintain the proper diction of her commerce with white folks.

'I'm going to call some people in the Welfare Department to come over and help you out tomorrow,' I said.

'Ain't never been on Home Relief, ain't never will be,' she said. 'In the Depression you could see people eatin' the bark off'n trees, scrapin' it with their fingernails. There was some colored people who was eatin' this white clay you could find in Indian Gully in back of the property. My husband and I – thanks to God and Mr Sam McClough – always had a roof and food on the table. Ain't never been on Home Relief.'

'Where do you think Artis might be?' I asked.

She laughed. 'Oh, that boy's a terror. He's only hidin' with his brother. Most prob'ly they down in Mr Tatum's shack by the fields. Plannin' and dreamin', you know, like little boys who don't know the world. Artis say he gonna make a lot of money in Charleston and come back with a big Cadillac and buy me the whole property, big house 'n' all. I told Mr Sam about it, and he like to bust he laughed so hard.'

'What about Pammie Sue, Sarah?' I asked.

'Lord, don't let it come out,' she said, and sniffled a bit. 'If God had meant for us to mingle, he wouldn't have made us different colors. Ain't that as plain as the nose on your face? But Artis is a good boy, yes he is. Poor little Pammie Sue never really had a mother. She was so sick they thought she was goin' to die. Turned blue. Lord have mercy, I never seen anything like that. We all thought the poor little child was gonna die.'

'I'm going to send some people to take care of you,' I said.

'Artis'll be back,' she said. 'He's just

down to Mr Tatum's, tellin' stories with his brother. He be back.'

I hung up and called Breitel's little hideaway. His girl friend answered.

'Abe isn't here,' she said plaintively. 'He told me to wait, but it's been two hours. I hope he's all right.'

'Don't worry,' I said, 'you can't break your neck falling off a bar stool.' I gave her Potosky's number. 'Tell him I've located Artis Pettibone,' I said.

Now I had nothing to do. I smoked my last cigarette and went on a search-and-destroy mission to find more. In the living room the terrier came at me with fangs bared. I kicked him in the face with my bare foot. He flipped over, whined reproachfully, and slunk off into a corner to go to sleep. I went through every drawer and closet in the house, through all Potosky's pockets, even looked under the bed. Potosky had albums full of pictures, mostly of herself at the various watershed stages of her life – high school, graduation, proms, pimply escorts in dinner jackets. There were special-occasion shots of the handsome Potosky family, all sleek and beaming. Old iron-gray, distinguished Dad; the trim, competent little Mom; two super-clean younger brothers in blazers. I found her address book and looked myself up. There were two *x*'s next to my name; at least I merited a coded entry, no matter what it meant. The dog snarled, and I hit him square in the noggin with my shoe. A trickle of blood seeped from his nose and he crept off with a cowardly whine.

I finally found a package of Virginia Slims under a cushion in the couch. There were three joints in it, but no cigarettes. I smoked one of the reefers and took the pack with me into the bedroom. The dog tried to follow me in, and I slammed the door on his neck.

The hours went by pleasantly. I depleted Potosky's marijuana, listened to her records, and tortured her dog. I was just starting to doze when the bell rang.

I ran to the door, unlocked it, then jumped back into bed. The dog yelped and ran weeping to his mistress, who crooned endearments to him.

'Ajax, what did you do?' she said. 'Oh no, no . . . bad dog.' She came into the bedroom holding a soggy piece of newspaper. Her hair was in disarray, and her eyes roved wildly, lighting only briefly on me.

'My dog pissed in the living room,' she said. 'You must have upset him.'

'Stick his nose in it,' I said, and ducked as the canine speciment whizzed wetly by.

'I'll stick your nose in it. What did you do to him?'

'Showed him who was boss.'

'Yeah, he's about the only person you could do it to.'

'He's not a person, he's a dog.'

'Yeah?' She approached the bed, squinting angrily into my face. 'You've had a real nice time, haven't you?'

I smiled and snuggled under the covers. 'I took a bath, Mommy.'

She pried up my eyelids with a cold thumb. 'Smoked a little dope too.'

'Yes, Mommy. It stops me from wetting my beddie.'

'Mommy's going to spank you,' she said, slapping me lightly on the face.

'Oh do, Mommy,' I said. 'Do.'

'You're sick,' she said, with a look of disgust. 'I'm going to take a bath.' She kicked off her shoes and without a blink pulled her dress over her head.

'Do you usually undress in front of strangers?' I asked.

'I'm not ashamed of my body. Are you?'

'No, I'm not ashamed of your body.'

She was wearing an incredibly ornate network of underthings, complete with black garter belt with shiny snaps, mesh stockings, black panties. . . . Her ivory legs gleamed like a virginal smile amidst all this depravity. It was very enticing. I rose to help her.

'Please,' she said, 'I've seen enough flaccid male flesh for one night.'

'Nothing flaccid about me,' I said. Her pointed look changed that, and I slunk back to the bed, drawing the covers up over my head. 'It's not fair for you to torture me like this,' I said.

'This is my house,' she said. 'You smoked my dope, beat up my dog, and I can do anything I please.'

Her breasts were larger than they seemed when she was clothed. Her hair fell almost to her buttocks, which jiggled assertively as she walked into the bathroom and clicked the lock. Lust crept over me on little cat feet. The bath roared. Steam seeped through the cracks in the bathroom door.

'Are you okay?' I yelled. 'Not slitting your wrists, are you?'

'Stay out of here,' she shrieked.

In a minute she was out, wrapped in a white towel, a blue towel wound around her head.

'You look all red-cheeked and Nordic,' I said.

She unwound the blue towel and shook the damp tendrils of hair off her shoulders. She fished an electric hair dryer out from under the bed. It roared like a chain saw and blew the dark, wet strands into floating, golden gossamer. I touched her hand.

'You're still warm from the bath,' I said. She didn't reply, so I moved two more fingers onto her wrist and slid them up her arm to the nape of her neck. How pathetic and asinine is the aroused male, the anxious organism in search of release. I lowered my voice seductively, all the while wanting to apologize to her for this idiot who was lowering his voice seductively. 'Want a massage?' I asked, stroking the soft flesh under her ear.

'At least be original,' she said. 'I get that line from off-duty cops.'

I slid my hand over the fold of the white towel, drawing it open. My hands were mere centimeters from those two fleshly globes, cynosures of my dreams. I leaned forward, deferring the moment of contact, and whispered in her ear, 'Let's be friends.'

'Oh shit, all right,' she said. Throwing her arms back, she flopped down on the bed. 'All right,' she gasped, spreading her arms and legs in a position of total surrender.

'Jill,' I murmured, moving over her, forgetting even my own absurdity in the drama of the moment.

'I have to go to work tomorrow,' she said. 'You have five minutes to turn me on.'

Somewhere, I thought, a man and a woman are sweating and straining in the carnal death dance. *Le petit mort,* the French called it. Shakespeare and Donne begged to 'die' in their ladies' arms. I, too, had died. There would have to be an entry in the *Guinness Book of World Records* for this: the man who became tumescent, detumescent, retumescent and then detumescent in the shortest time. I looked at her lying there, her eyes squinted closed, her lips pursed – like a little girl waiting for a penicillin shot – and I knew in a blinding flash that I was finished for life. Never again would I be tickled by the rub of love.

I got out of bed and began dressing.

'Is that how you respond to a challenge?' she asked.

'I don't provoke,' I said.

'I guess if I had endured your tedious little advances, it would have been okay, but I didn't feel like being seduced tonight.'

'You're not normal,' I yelled at her. 'You hang out with stud coke dealers who rape you, gay guys who reject you. You don't know what it's like to be with an ordinary guy with love in his heart and something between his legs.'

'And I'm not interested in ordinary guys,' she said.

'You've never lived with a man, washed his socks, smelled his farts, done his laundry, cooked his dinner. You've never sweated up the street with thirty pounds of groceries, stayed up all night with a colicky baby, projectile vomits and flying shits all over the place.'

'Ecch, sounds awful,' she said.

'My wife,' I said, 'money-grubbing, hardassed bitch that she is, never did a number on me like this.'

'You must really be upset if you're using your wife against me,' she said.

'My wife is fifty times the woman you'll ever be,' I said.

'Maybe she is,' Potosky said, and somewhere I discerned a glimmer of sadness in her. 'Why don't you go back to her, so she can smell your dinner, cook your socks, and wash your farts, or whatever that litany was. . . .'

I ran out into the living room to retrieve my jacket. The dog growled, and held his ground. I place-kicked him over the living room table.

'Don't take it out on the dog,' Potosky said.

I slammed the door.

'Ajax!' I heard her calling. Take your goddamn dog and shove him up your lap, I thought. The lonely neighbor's door seemed to bulge out, begging to be knocked. It would serve Potosky right to see me and the neighbor arm-in-arm in the elevator the next morning. Nah, she wouldn't care. Besides, I had to find Artis Pettibone.

CHAPTER SEVENTEEN

I lurched out into the street, grimacing against the icy November wind. Girls with short skirts and open shoes, the backs of their legs whipped crimson by the weather, yearned for the warmth of their little flats, yet were alert enough to search the faces of every man for a possible Prince Charming or Jack the Ripper. And this was the good part of town, where the oldsters were swathed in fur coats, where cabs rolled in front of buildings, and people sprinted into their lobbies, bracing against their split second in the cold. A mere three blocks to the east, families huddled in their overcoats next to the kitchen stove, or ran the hot water to keep warm. A stone's throw to the west, homosexuals in skimpy leather jackets braved the weather in doorways and on corners, waiting for their Prince Charmings or Torquemadas. Junkies lay petrified in the gutter; bums washed gelid windshields with trembling hands. Street lights gave off little illumination and no warmth. I met an angry gust around every corner.

It was cold, but colder in Sarah Pettibone's apartment tonight. Icicles surely hung in Jill Potosky's labial cavern.

McClough had to be shivering in his dark, drafty corner of deceit. It was cold in the *Event* press room now that the last edition of the paper had rolled, and the floor was littered with gently flapping sheets. Duffy, drunk as he was, had been numbed by snowdrifts of brooding and self-doubt. My wife, her extremities eternally icy, languished palely in the embrace of her lover, turning tepid at best from his ministrations. In a bedroom as dark as the cold side of the moon my son slept by the flickering warmth of the TV. How sad it was. All of us were Rorschach splotches of blood and reflex negotiating with snail-like pace the cheerless tundras, the impossible expanses of our lives. Serena Pettibone lay alone and forgotten in her cubicle at the Bellevue morgue. The world had honored its last obligation to her with an autopsy, a careful survey and preservation of the damaged organs, a routine inventory of her possessions. She would be no colder in potter's field, graveyard of the poor and unclaimed, than Pammie Sue McClough was in the family plot. If potter's field was where Serena was going. . . .

I wedged through the twisted door of a phone booth. Standing up to my shoelaces in slush, garbage, and what I hoped against hope wasn't urine, I called the Bellevue morgue. The attendant was singularly unexcited when I told him who I was.

'What's the story on Serena Pettibone?' I asked.

'She's dead,' he said.

'Oh yeah, look behind you,' I said.

'That's not funny,' he said. 'I got enough trouble sittin' in this place forty hours a week.'

'Is she going to potter's field?' I asked.

He shuffled some papers. 'Let me see. . . . Nope, she's goin' home, looks like. She's a shipper down to Pulham, South Carolina.'

'Who's paying the freight?' I asked.

'Next of kin, the brother. He claimed the body and laid out the cash.'

'What's his name?'

'Nathan Tyler, Jr.'

'Did he show any identification?'

'Hey, look, this ain't the New York Athletic Club. Guy wants to take a body off the city's hands we don't go lookin' up his family tree.'

'Burke and Hare could make a fortune at Bellevue,' I said.

'Who are they?'

'Two hunchbacks with sacks who are sneaking up on you,' I said.

'Don't make jokes like that,' he said.

'What did this Tyler look like?'

'Decedent is a black female. I assume the brother is a black male. I wasn't here when he showed. . . . Hey, this is funny. . . .'

'I thought you didn't like jokes?'

'Well, I'm just pushin' the sheets around here, and I see that this guy who was killed in the Village, this Dean Tyler, he was also sent down to Pulham. Body left this morning. Should almost be there, huh?'

'But who's gonna meet it?' I asked.

'The same guy, Nathan Tyler, Jr. Jeez, I don't think we've ever sent anything down to Pulham, South Carolina, before.'

'Well, you might have a few more candidates before the week is over,' I said.

Two bodies rolling down to a small town in South Carolina. Who would be there to meet them? There was no one left in the Tyler family but a younger brother. He was the sentimental type too, taking care of his aged aunt, buying his sister a color TV. He was given to making gestures, like seducing the aristocrat's daughter, stealing the family heirloom, making idealistic threats, romantic promises. Would he let his brother and sister rot in paupers' graves? Not Artis Pettibone.

I knew Pettibone was in Pulham. It wasn't the best place for him to go. It's hard to hide in a small town where everybody knows you. Better off sticking to one block in Harlem than the whole state of South Carolina. But he was there, I could feel it.

As I dashed down the street, I saw a redhead flash and

then disappear in a car a few yards in front of me. Breitel was lying on the floor under the driver's seat, his hand over his face. I banged on the window.

'Peekaboo, I see you.'

He sat up in the driver's seat and rolled down the electric window. 'Hullo, Krales,' he said.

'What were you doing on the floor?' I asked.

'Tryin' to find my goddamn cigarette lighter,' he said.

'Oh, I thought maybe you didn't want me to see you. . . .'

'Nah, why would I hide from you?'

'I dunno, maybe it's my breath.'

'Whaddya talkin' about?' he said, lighting a cigarette from the car lighter.

I reached around the half-open window and unlocked the door. 'Going my way?' I asked, sliding into the seat.

'Sure, I'll give you a lift,' he said, blowing casual smoke rings. 'I'm on a job, but. . . .'

'Stop the shit, Abie. How long have you been on my tail?'

'Whaddya mean? You're paranoid.'

'I'm not going to jerk around with you here,' I said. 'I'll just tell Duffy that you're the one who tipped me about the murders. I'll tell him you also called me from Serena Pettibone's apartment. He knows you were with me in Bed Stuy; the old lady'll make you for him.'

Breitel examined a blister on his finger with great care. 'And what if I just take out my gun right now and blow you away,' he said. 'Think I wouldn't do that?'

'I think you'd do anything you thought you had to,' I said. 'And I know some cops who agree, and would believe anything I said about you. So you've got your scenario, I've got mine. Let's see whose makes the drive-ins first.' I pushed open the door to leave.

'All right,' he said dully, like a crook caught with the goods, 'I was tailin' you. I tailed you that night you balled the hooker too. I knew she wouldn't open up with me around, but you go good with the broads. . . .'

'What's this?'

'It's true, you got a knack with these bimbos. They all

like you, and I thought that you'd be able to cop the kid's address or make a meet with him or something.'

'Okay, but why did you want him in the first place?'

Breitel started the motor. The car stalled. He cursed and started it again, racing the engine until the whole car vibrated around us.

'I was hired to find him,' he shouted over the roar. 'McClough.'

'McClough?' I shouted as the noise abated.

'Yeah, Petey Nardo turned him on to me. We was partners on the force for years. Petey went to law school and put in his papers before the Knapp Commission started to break balls.'

'I should have known that creep was a cop,' I said.

'A smart cop who could buy and sell you even when he was poundin' a beat,' Breitel said. 'Nobody ever closed Petey Nardo down, and nobody ever will.'

'How does he come to McClough?' I asked.

'Yeah, that made me curious too,' Breitel said. 'Petey's got heavy connections in Brooklyn. His godfather, I mean his real one, you know, the one who shoved the wafer up his ass or whatever they do, is Joe 'Blue Ribbon' Ribone. Old-fashioned stuff, a piece of Vegas, the docks, trucking companies. A little dope too, to pay the phone bill. Petey always played both ends real good, and took care of me too. Even set me up busts for my promotions. So I didn't get too deep into what what goin' on between him and McClough. This was three months ago. The daughter was gone with this fancy necklace. Sendin' them dirty telegrams and callin' at three in the morning. They wanted to find the kid, and. . . .' He suddenly became very busy pulling into traffic.

'And what?' I asked.

'And they wanted to burn the nigger,' Breitel said, and turned on me. 'Tell anybody this and I'll kill ya.'

'Were you the burner?' I asked.

He shook his head. 'Strictly the finger. They wanted the girl and the necklace. It was Petey's move, and he's smart.

Let the kid slide a coupla days, and then put him to sleep. But I wouldn't do it. When I burn, I burn alone.'

'How much were you getting?'

'Standard fee, five bills a day plus expenses, and a ten-thousand-dollar bonus OTB when I found her.'

'What's OTB?' I asked.

'Off the books. The Ambassador was pissed. So was Petey, which I couldn't figure out, 'cause it wasn't his necklace or his daughter. There was a lotta things that didn't make no sense. . . .'

'Like what else?'

'When it came out that Pettibone had been workin' in Iboopa's factory there,' he said. 'I mean, that's part of Joe Blue Ribbon's operation, and you figure Petey would know about it, and at least would tell me. I found it out from readin' your story.'

'And I got it from a hood in the Village,' I said.

'Who's this?' Breitel asked.

'Frankie Carbonaro.'

'Never heard of him,' he said.

'You will,' I said. 'But tell me why you couldn't find the girl.'

'I squeezed every grifter, junkie, hooker, and pimp in the fuckin' city,' he said. 'McClough was payin' and I was playin'. I put guys on it and spent bread. That's usually enough. But this kid was layin' low. He had her money, plus they were sendin' him money, which they didn't tell me until she was iced. They said he threatened to kill her if anybody jammed him when he picked up the bread. They said they had wanted me to pick him up on the sly, and that's how they were gonna get him.'

'Did you believe that?' I asked.

'Not for a jerk-off second,' Breitel said. 'But by then they had raised the ante. No more per diem, just fifty grand in cash money if I spotted Pettibone. And lemme tell ya, they were sweatin' piss, the two of them. You know, Petey's got a temper, and I had the feeling he wanted to hit this nigger himself, that's how mad he was.'

'What do you think they're up to?' I asked.

'I think this kid walked out with more than just the family jewels,' he said. 'But what he took, I don't know.'

'Skivoso and Iboopa had their hitter looking for Pettibone too,' I said.

'Albino,' Breitel said, nodding. ' 'Cause he knocked up somebody's daughter, according to the New York *Event*.'

'Do you believe that?' I asked.

'Not for a. . . .'

'Jerk-off second,' I finished for him. 'So what do we have? A bunch of liars. Except for you and me, and I have doubts about you.'

'Well, what are you bustin' your ass for?' Breitel asked. 'There's nothin' in it for you.'

'First of all, I'm curious,' I said. 'Second of all, I've got a grudge against Skivoso and Iboopa because they tried to bake me in a pizza oven.'

Breitel looked me over. 'They will do that to folks from time to time,' he said.

'And third of all,' I said, 'McClough and Nardo offered me seventy-five thousand for Pettibone's address.'

'It was ten grand,' Breitel said. 'Stop tryin' to get a rise outta me. And I was tailin' you because we all thought you had the kid salted away somewhere.'

'I do,' I said.

'Uh huh,' Breitel said. His hands trembled momentarily; wincing angrily, he steadied them.

'Wanna see him?' I asked.

'Why not?'

'Got your overnight bag?'

'Where we goin'?'

'I'll tell you when we get there.'

'Okay,' he said, 'but first I gotta make a stop.'

We drove up Third Avenue to a gigantic white building on Sixty-fourth Street, where Breitel had his hideaway. All the way uptown he made small talk, trying to seem unconcerned. But I could sense his excitement; whistling to the Muzak in the elevator is always a dead giveaway.

Breitel lived on a floor as long and narrow as a bowling alley.

'Stay out here,' he said, as he fiddled with the keys. He opened the door just wide enough to permit his entry. 'Decent, baby?' he called.

'Yeah, babes.' It was the same voice I had heard on the phone.

'Don't get cute,' Breitel warned, sticking a stubby forefinger in my face. 'She's a little dizzy, but a nice, simple broad.'

The apartment was done in wall-to-wall Astroturf. A pair of bare legs culminating in turquoise toenails were propped on the arm of a couch that looked like it was covered in white poodle fur. Vincent Price, wearing a black cloak and a purple face, was menacing a green girl on the 'Late Late Show.'

'I couldn't get the color right,' the legs pouted. A frizzy blonde head appeared at the other end of the sofa and blinked me over. 'Ooh, we have company!'

'Why d'ya think I asked if you were decent?' Breitel grumbled. He went to the television and began turning dials.

'Ooh, lemme button up.' A pneumatic blonde wearing dungaree shorts cut to the crotch and a T-shirt with a huge salami and the legend 'Take a bite of this' arrayed across the bosom got up, yanked a zipper over what at a cursory glance seemed to be pubic hair. Her penciled eyebrows were raised in perpetual surprise; her pontoon lips pursed interrogatively. 'Are you the guy from *Playboy*?'

'No, he ain't,' Breitel said.

'Didn't you say you were gonna bring him around?'

'Yeah, but this ain't the guy,' he said.

'I'm from *Penthouse*,' I said.

'Wait here,' Breitel said to me, 'and don't start in.' He pointed an admonitory finger at Little Annie Fannie, but let it droop and shook his head, mumbling something to himself as he walked into the bedroom.

'He said three weeks ago he knew the art director at *Playboy*,' Marie Curie complained. 'You know, and he was going to get me a centerfold.'

'Well, I'm a photographer over at *Penthouse*,' I said.

'You really are?' she asked dubiously.

'Oh yes,' I said. 'We'd be glad to consider you. Of course, we'd have to see the way you photograph.'

'Gee, I've got a great portfolio. I've done straight modeling, head shots, nudes. . . .' She was easy to convince.

'Nudes is what we'd be most interested in,' I said, ever the sincere professional.

'I've worked with a lot of photographers,' she said. 'We get along, usually. I like the photographic karma, if you know what I mean.'

'Exactly,' I said.

She sucked her thumbnail, still unconvinced. 'But you know I can't work with some signs. What sign are you?'

'Sagittarius,' I said, with a silent prayer.

'I'm Libra,' she gushed. 'That's perfect. We complement each other emotionally, you know.'

'Oh, I know,' I said. 'My best subjects have always been Librans. My wife was a Libran.'

'Was? . . .' She sucked her fingernail in puzzlement.

'Oh, she died,' I said. 'Plane crash. On her way to help the Nicaraguan flood victims.' I looked at my shoes. 'We were very happy.'

'Oh, what a sad story,' she said. 'Do you have any children?'

'Twins,' I said. 'Scott and Heather.'

'Oh gosh,' she said, near tears. 'Isn't that awful? Scott and Heather.'

Breitel came out of the bedroom with a gym bag and an attaché case. He looked suspiciously from her to me. 'You been running your number, Krales?'

'You're the only person in the world who thinks I've got one,' I said. 'What's in the case?'

'My survival kit,' he said, snapping open the case to reveal several guns and gun barrels arranged neatly on purple velvet. 'This,' he said, pointing to a luger-shaped gun, 'is my 357 Magnum, the stakeout gun, we used to call it. It'll go right through an engine block and into the driver. It'll knock a goddamn door down.' With a flourish he snapped a barrel onto another piece, threw two shells into it, and snapped the thing and pointed it right at my testicles. 'This is a precision sawed-off shotgun. One buckshot shell, so I can knock anybody down without hardly aiming, one dumdum shell, so I can put them away without worrying about where I hit 'em.' He snapped and dismantled it, replacing the shells in their plush little niches, and held up a tiny two-barreled gun. 'This is a derringer.' He slipped it into a tiny holster on his belt buckle. 'I can put it right dead on my spine too, and nobody who frisks me will pick it up. One bullet for the other guy, and one for me, if it comes to that.'

'Which it won't,' I assured him.

'You never know,' he said ominously. 'Sometimes it's better to kill a guy and sit a coupla ten years for it. Sometimes it's better to turn the picture off right then and there, know what I mean?'

'No,' I said.

'Anyway, I don't want this Pettibone slippin' out. If he's there, he's mine, or he's nobody's. Understand?'

'We'll share him,' I said. 'And we'll share the fifty grand – I should say sixty, counting my end – for finding him. Understand?'

He nodded. It was easy for him to make a deal he had no intention of honoring. 'Now, where we goin'?'

'Away down South in Dixie,' I said. 'He'll be waitin' on the levees. You know, the Jewish neighborhood.'

CHAPTER EIGHTEEN

We weren't too far out of New York when it hit me – that good old rural paranoia. Not that the New Jersey Turnpike is Tobacco Road, but as soon as the houses detached, the vacant lots become fields, and the police begin wearing boots and Stetsons, I know I'm in trouble.

I'm a city boy. Drop me drunk and in my jockey shorts in the middle of Harlem, and I'll keep my head. Stick a knife to my throat on the subway, and I'll negotiate; mug me on an elevator, and I'll make it to my floor. I'll always survive in New York: that's the principle I have always operated on, and I won't be gainsaid, even by violent death.

But those wide open spaces, buttons and bows, and overall country, fat, laconic rednecks with straw hats and shotguns, farmers' daughters wearing calico dresses with nothing underneath – as far as I'm concerned, that mythic landscape begins slightly south of Newark and continues on to the Florida Keys. And everyone there is out to get me. As I whiz through their sordid little enclaves, they see my city duds, my wallet a riot of colorful credit cards – all canceled – my New York license plates, in themselves sufficient provocation for summary arrest and execution. They know I'm Jewish, all of them; don't ask me how, but they do. They know I work for the liberal press. They know I'm no match for them. There isn't a rural bully between Maine and Acapulco who would hesitate to spray buckshot at my feet to make me dance, rob me, rape me, string me up, or throw me to his pet water moccasin. Sheriffs have been alerted to stop me for some contrived violation, throw me in some hick hoosegow, and then frame me for a crime of passion committed by the son of the local Snopes. Alone and bruised in my cell, crying out for justice, pounding rock on a chain gang, dangling from the end of a rope, or shot between the eyes while trying to escape: that's how I'll end my trip south of the border.

The first Holiday Inn sent me into a panic. It was somewhere between New Jersey and Washington, D.C. Breitel insisted on stopping. 'It has the best coffee.' Sure, and it also had a parking lot full of foreign license plates. The jaundiced Jersey tags, the seamy off-white District of Columbia plates, Maryland's ersatz royal blue outnumbered our grand Empire States entries, by at least five to one. We were wandering cold and hungry into the bosom of our enemies.

O men of the hinterlands, full of hate! I almost expected them to be distributing copies of the 'Protocols of the Elders of Zion' with the menus.

Breitel ordered coffee, and I decided to risk the bathroom. I got as far as the vending machines in the lobby. A slender young man in a chartreuse shirt looked provocatively at me. Two boys with long eyelashes and short shorts lounged against the candy machine, deep in conversation. A middle-aged chap with an angry face and a tight dungaree suit ran a comb through his hair. I fled back to the dining room.

'The lobby's full of gay guys,' I told Breitel.

'These joints are all faggot hangouts,' he said, forking up a piece of cherry pie that looked like it had been made with Elmer's Glue and nail polish.

'Yeah, but in Pisspot, New Jersey,' I said. 'How can there be so many in such a hick town?'

'They come from all over the area,' he said. 'They can't get too much action at home, so they come here to pick up on the truck drivers, the travelers. Every Hojo and Holiday Inn and whatever else is the same up and down the road. And if you can't handle it, you're gonna hafta shit on the highway.'

Now I had a new detail for my mental fresco of Middle America. A streak of crimson lechery slashed across the cheerful, Rockwell hues; secret passions contorted the wholesom› faces. Watchful, lissome creatures all mascara and fulvous yellow, with blue veins on their limbs, posed at the edges of my canvas. Vampires lurked within these bland precincts. Solid burghers wore their wives' panties underneath drab business suits. Every evening while the TV flickered in the parlor window – merely to lull passers-by – they writhed in some secret place, mate-swapping, devil-worshiping, torturing urban strangers who had stumbled innocently into their midst. Those motels with the incomplete neon signs – the CAPITAL MOTE. – an obscure biblical threat if I ever saw one. Those antique shops, friendly hand-painted signs: ANTIQUES, PEWTER, COLONIAL CHAIRS. . . . Only the letters were diabolically askew; the paint had dripped like a murderer's warning. I needed a drink.

Breitel had a flask in his glove compartment: your essential whiskey, warm, metallic, uncompromising. It made me gag and brought tears to my eyes.

'Ambrosia,' I told Breitel.

He was driving with the arrogance of a cop, doing seventy-five, eighty, zooming past timid nocturnal motorists who were observing the fifty-five-mile stricture.

'C'mon, baby,' he urged his Buick, 'kick ass.'. He hollered at the other drivers. 'Get outta the passin' lane, you creep.' He chain-smoked, chewed gum and took frequent hits from the flask. The back of his shirt was soggy with perspiration. He was having a ball. Several times I volunteered to drive, but he wouldn't relinquish the wheel. 'We'll make better time with me,' he said.

We drove around the Capital Beltway, an elaborate circular piece of road designed to keep the horrors of the Washington ghetto from the carefree traveler. Industrial dawn splotched the horizon as we continued on into Maryland and Virginia. The flatulence of refining oil, the morbid sweetness of percolating chemicals came into the car. Patient working men, sleep still clinging to their eyes, drove by. Smokestacks decorated the morning with a Looney Tunes pollution – they almost seemed to be pursing like giant lips and gently blowing their soot into the sky. Communities huddled under this smoky coverlet; people lived with the stench and the darkness. Boy, if they ever got mad. What would Kissinger do then?

We followed Interstate 95, the bucolic route where even Howard Johnson was loath to tread. Breitel had a pocket full of quarter slugs for the tolls. We stopped for breakfast at a little diner dwarfed by huge trucks parked at crazy angles. Breitel straight-facedly repeated the old saw about truck drivers and diners. The place was almost empty, and I realized that the trucks had merely pulled over for a little snooze. Two middle-aged ladies in greasy aprons squinted across the counter at us. An old, bent black man threw a gob of lard on the grill for our eggs. The coffee tasted like

Mississippi mud. I put my cigarette out in the yolk of one of my sunny-side ups. Breitel ate his breakfast and the rest of mine, and ordered a cheeseburger for the road. I picked up the check.

'Wasn't that the worst shit you ever ate?' he asked, as if that had been reason enough to eat it. He unwrapped his cheeseburger. 'Let's see about this.' He took a bite and shook his head. 'This ain't meat, it's dog.' He threw the cheeseburger into the first toll machine we came to. There was a metallic grunt, then a bell rang and a sign that read 'Thank You' flashed on.

'Machines ain't got no taste,' Breitel said.

Virginia seemed to go on forever. And when it ended. North Carolina began, which wasn't much of a sensory shock, although the color of the road signs did change from green to blue. I knew we were heading south when octagonal orange buildings materialized advertising 'Sorghum, Country Hams and Fireworks', an unlikely inventory but one that had to be profitable, judging by the number of such operations we passed, some directly across the road from one another. Every five miles we came across a billboard featuring a little man in a sombrero, advertising a motel about seven hundred miles away: 'Speedy Gonzales always has time to stop at the Jumping Bean Motel . . . Bring the family.' The road was clogged with signs, some elaborate, some painted on the backs of barns, advertising 'Cigarettes, $2.80 a carton.'

'Everybody's in the cigarette business around here,' I said.

'I used to know a guy in Fayetteville who'd go twenty-five cents under the road price,' Breitel said. 'He was the sheriff there. He'd stop the smugglers at the state line, fine 'em, take the cigarettes, and then resell 'em back to the dealers, or anybody else who came along. We'll see if he's around.'

'I don't want cigarettes,' I said.

'The way you smoke, you could save a fortune,' he said.

'I'm going to make a fortune in a couple of hours,' I said. 'I'll be able to buy all the cigarettes I want.'

'You hope,' he said.

'Money's all I care about, anyway, right? That's what you told Nardo, isn't it?'

'Huh?'

'Didn't you tell him I'd do anything for money?'

'Nah. Listen, if I wanted to get to you, I'd use pussy. That's your weakness.'

It exasperated me that a man who hardly knew me could pretend to understand me so well. 'What makes you think I'm such a Don Juan?'

'Who's Don Juan, a Puerto Rican pimp?' Breitel laughed. 'Never mind explaining. Look, Krales, the book on you is you're cut-crazy, okay? And from what I've seen, I agree. You're a Jewish fag. You like girls more than money.' Breitel wheezed and turned red. When it looked like he was going to explode, a percussive 'hah' issued forth. I dove into the back seat and fell asleep.

I awoke at midday. We were crawling along behind a school bus. The road had narrowed and gotten very rural. Gray clapboard shacks teetered on the shoulder. Roosters strutted importantly in the dirt; scrawny pigs glared from behind tattered wire fences. Old black women called to each other from rickety porches; old black men squatted by the roadside, smoking and looking into the cars. Automotive cadavers were scattered about – ancient, rusted pickup trucks, wrecks that had been stripped of everything but their damaged hulks, wheel-less tractors, seatless motorcycles. I could feel the heat, even though the air conditioner was blowing on my neck. I sensed it in the slow movement of the kids walking up the road with their books, that horrible schoolday languor I remembered so well. It hovered in the stillness around the country stores on the side of the road, cars and trucks parked out in front. 'Cold Soda, Cold Beer' read the signs. Everybody was inside, huddled around the fan, cradling bottles of Dr Pepper. Beyond the roadside civilization, fields stretched right to the horizon, barren and unattended now in the fall. A TV antenna rose out of every shack. I got the feeling that if a tornado hit this patch of road, the televisions and the antennas would be the only things left standing.

'Where the hell are we?' I asked.

'Ever heard a nigger talk about home?' Breitel said. 'This is it.'

'We have to turn off on 317,' I said. 'That'll take us to Pulham.'

'We're still in North Carolina,' Breitel said. 'Can't you tell?'

I fell asleep again. When I awoke an hour later, the back seat was a paradise of malignancy; cartons of every brand of cigarette were strewn all over me. Breitel had more piled neatly next to him in the front seat.

'Why didn't you put this shit in the trunk?' I asked.

'I did, but I ran out of room,' he said. 'Two hundred cartons at two and a quarter apiece. Not bad, huh?'

I dug a carton of Camels out of the debris. 'Who's going to buy all these?'

'I'll sell the Salems to my mother.'

'Your mother?'

'Yeah, I'll give them to her a little above cost, and then she'll deal them to the other old farts in the nursing home. Picks herself up a little spending money that way. The rest. . . .'

'I don't want to hear about the rest. You're probably smuggling them into emphysema wards.'

'You owe me four and a quarter for those Camels, wise guy,' he said.

No trumpets heralded the passage into South Carolina, only the smell of pulp factories spreading over the landscape like ink through a blotter. The same signs, the same shacks and screened porches, and then suddenly the view changed. Neat red brick houses replaced the squalid clapboard.

'South Carolina is the nation's number-one producer of brick dust,' Breitel explained. 'Bricks are cheaper than cigarettes down here. These niggers can build themselves houses for three grand that would cost fifty up in New York.'

The houses were short and squat, like the one built by the wise little pig. Aside from tiny glass slits for windows, they were all of brick, and there were brick patios, brick driveways, brick walls fencing in each plot.

'They must be hot as hell in there,' I said.

'Fuck 'em,' Breitel said.

The weird orange buildings now added peach wine and pecans to their list of commodities. Pecans, bricks, tobacco, cheap labor for the fabric mills, the paper factories; and brick houses for the peasants. Was that what South Carolina was all about? I wondered if the McClough mansion was made out of brick.

We stopped at a pecan store on a particularly noisome stretch of road. The proprietor, an old white man with a long jowl that flapped against his collar, jumped at us as if he hadn't seen anybody for years.

'You fellas bring the stink with you from up North.'

Breitel picked up a bottle of peach wine. 'Got any real booze for sale here?'

'Hold your horses a second, and I'll give you a treat,' the old man said. He went into the back and came out with a bottle. 'Stonewall Jackson, finest bourbon in the South. Makes Jack Daniel's taste like sow piss.' He opened the bottle and poured drinks into three jelly jars. The liquor was smooth and languid, like a South Carolina afternoon. Breitel threw a ten on the table. 'How much'll that buy?' he asked.

'Two bottles, and another drink out of this 'un here,' the man said.

'Know how far Route 317 is?' I asked.

'Just a mile or two down the road,' he said, stuffing the bottles into a box marked Pecan Candies.

'We're trying to find Pulham,' I said.

The old man made a face. 'What y'all wanna go there for? Nothin' but coons there now.'

'The McClough plantation?'

'Ain't nobody there now. He sold it all to the government to put some kinda buildin's up. All the ole folks is just waitin' around to get booted off. Don't grow as much tobacco as they used to around here. Used to be all there was. Now you got those goddamn pulp mills. People come by and ask me how I live with that smell. Well, I tell 'em, it's bad in the mornin', when they start the machines up, and it's bad around quittin' time, when they flush 'em out. And at least I don't have to work in one of 'em.' He nuzzled his jelly jar. 'I do well enough. Got my son livin' in Charleston. He worked in the McClough curin' sheds. Shoot, just about everybody worked for the old man at one time. . . .'

The old man talked us to the door, and was still talking as we drove off.

There was a gas station at the junction. We got a road map of South Carolina, but couldn't find Pulham. The attendant, a young man with pimples on his face and tattoos on his arms, who called us 'sir', sent us down 317. We drove for miles down a rutty country road. On either side of us were gray mills, shimmering slightly in their gaseous discharges; a brick house or two; a little clot of stores with the now-familiar signs. The road narrowed, and gave up all pretense to asphalt.

'Think that kid gave us the right directions?' Breitel asked.

'The South Carolina AAA says Pulham is in the western part of the state, at the end of Route 317,' I said. 'Now, they may all be trying to fool us.'

'What if Artis isn't there?'

'Then you break even on the cigarettes,' I said.

We hit a belt of rural towns. Clebs, Farnham, Wilson's Creek. Tobacco fields had taken over from the factories. People stopped what they were doing and squinted at us. We'd gotten to that part of the world where everybody knows everybody. The towns were getting smaller. Soon the tobacco fields gave way to truck gardens, orderly furrows amid backyard debris. It was dark; we had to slow down and turn the headlights on the town markers to make them out. Semple's Crossing, Prescottville, Kilcayne: every debtor and desperado and carpetbagger, every disappointed empire-builder had immortalized himself on these patches of moribund territory. There was no town called McClough. Or Rockefeller, come to think of it.

Finally the sign came out at us: Pulham. The main street

was full of potholes. A few black men were lounging on camp chairs in front of a barbecue restaurant.

'Open your mouths so we can see your faces,' Breitel muttered.

'Know where the McClough place is?' I hollered out at them.

An old man wearing an army fatigues jacket approached the car. 'Ain't nobody out there,' he said.

Breitel leaned forward. 'We're from the FBI,' he said to the old man. 'Mind telling us how to get there?'

The old man gulped and shuffled back a few steps. His arm shot stiffly out from his body, and he pointed down the road. 'You don't have fur to go, gemmen,' he said. 'Just straight outta town and turn right when you see this here gummint sign. It's just a little bit out the way after that.'

'Right,' Breitel said. He floored the car. The tires squealed, and we slid around the dust until we straightened out. 'Kid's there,' he said. 'Anytime somebody doesn't answer your question, you just turn around what they said, and you got the truth. That's a little trick of the trade, my boy.'

Outside of town the road became smooth again. Our headlights picked up an imposing sign done in South Carolina red: 'Fort Omar Bradley, US Army Engineers Training Center, First Field Medical Division, Military Data Processing Center. . . .' And then the name of every ward heeler in state government from the governor on down to the commissioner of highways. They had planned a big installation on McClough's land. Or had they? Serpentine blacktops had been cut into fields. A ditch or two pocked the landscape, and that was it. No work, not even the beginning of an excavation. McClough had made his six-million dollar deal; everybody had been paid off. The South was probably full of such backroad boondoggles.

We glided silently up to a cluster of buildings. The Carolina moon shone its light on an old mansion with pillars and porticoes and little spires cutting like pencil points into the night sky. A light burned in one of the downstairs windows. Breitel took the derringer from its jewelled scabbard.

'Don't slam the door,' he whispered.

A shiny red sports car with New York plates was parked in front of the mansion. We almost fell through the porch. Breitel cursed. The light went out, and we heard footsteps. I banged on the door, getting a handful of splinters.

'Artis, you in there?' I called.

'Get away from the door,' Breitel whispered, pulling me back.

'This is Josh Krales from the *Event*,' I said. 'Did your sister tell you about me?'

The door flew open off its hinges. A dark figure with something glittering in its hand came rushing through and slashed out in the darkness. I felt the breeze and fell back against the house. The figure turned to me. I could dimly make out Serena's high cheekbones, her near-Oriental eyes. 'You better get off my case, man,' it said.

By this time my knees had dissolved, and my larynx was frozen. 'I'm not on your case,' I croaked. 'I want to help.'

'Help by stayin' the fuck away,' he hissed. He lunged at me, and I ducked under him, rolling over a rail into the remains of what in ante-bellum days had been some kind of thorny porch creeper.

'Breitel,' I shouted, as I heard my attacker's footsteps on the leaves.

The headlights of the sports car clicked on. Pettibone looked up and froze in the beams like a frightened animal. Then he moved forward, brandishing what I now saw was a kichen knife.

'That knife spit bullets?' Breitel said from the void beyond the glare. ' 'Cause if it don't, you're in a lot of trouble.'

Considering the circumstances, his tone was not at all unkind.

CHAPTER NINETEEN

'Okay, you caught your nigger, now what you gonna do?' Pettibone said.

Breitel had him spread-eagle over the hood of the sports car, and was searching him, gently and methodically. He hadn't pulled his gun, hadn't even said he was carrying one. The kitchen knife was leaning against the windshield, only a few inches from Pettibone's outstretched hand, but light years away as far as he was concerned. The kid was cowed. The fear was obvious, showing through his trembly defiance. Breitel went on patting and probing; his silence was more terrifying than the most grisly threat. Finally he turned to me.

'It ain't on him, unless he shoved it up his ass,' he said.

'What do you want?' Pettibone asked.

'Let's go into the house,' Breitel said to me. He tapped the kid on the back of the neck. 'C'mon.'

The kid walked ahead of us. Breitel nudged me. He was playing his cop game and enjoying it. Pettibone and I were both too frightened to be a match for him.

Pettibone guided us unerringly through the moldering mansion; only a man who had walked the place many times in his dreams could step so sure-footedly through the darkness. Boards creaked beneath our feet; somewhere a shutter flapped forlornly in the breeze; squeals and the patter of little feet told us that McClough Manor had some new residents.

A large stairway bisected the house. Pettibone took us through a little door in the stairs, down to the kitchen and the servants' quarters. He was light-skinned enough to have sprung from house servants; the field hands were always the darker Negroes. His face showed enough of a confusion of strains to make him the great-grandson, perhaps, of a proprietary coupling of master and slave. I shivered, overwhelmed by the guilt and horror of it all.

Pettibone was living in the remains of the kitchen. It was a big room, with shelves along the wall and a long table in the center. I could imagine a corps of happy Aunt Jemimas humming in rich contraltos while they kept time on their mixing bowls. A flourishing, happy plantation, singing darkies, courtly whites, and the necklace that had scandalized New Orleans. And now, a hundred-odd years later, a few cans of pork and beans, a six-pack of Coke, and three people struggling in history's Hollywood grasp.

'Okay,' Pettibone said. 'What do I do now?'

Breitel looked at me and shook his head. He balled his right fist behind his back and hit the kid in the face. There was a pock, like the sound of a home run. Pettibone seemed to leap backward off his feet; he landed against the wall. Breitel was on him before he had a chance to wipe his bloody nose.

'The family jewels, you nigger cocksucker,' he snarled, lifting Pettibone by the collar and the belt buckle, and shoving him against the wall. 'Unless you want the next dance with me.'

'What the hell are you talkin' about?' Pettibone mumbled.

Breitel hit him in the forehead with the heel of his hand. The kid's head hit the wall and immediately went limp. He seemed healthy enough, but I felt sick. I was tired and sweaty, my underwear was sticking to me, my mouth was dry from too many cigarettes, and all that bad road coffee was chanting in my bowels. I'd even forgotten what had possessed me to come down to South Carolina. All I knew was I didn't want Breitel to hit the kid any more, even if he was a murderer.

'Abe,' I said.

'Stay out of it,' he said. 'The kid knows what I want. I want him to know I'll kill him if I don't get it.' He stuck his thumbs in Pettibone's bloody nostrils and began tearing them apart. 'Do you know that, pretty boy?'

Pettibone gasped and nodded. 'Uh huh, uh, uh.'

'You gonna get us the shit?' Breitel asked, tearing harder.

Pettibone's arms flailed helplessly. His grunts became more hysterical. I turned away and thought I heard the sound of ripping flesh.

'He said he would, Abe, so let him go.'

'Awright, awright.' Breitel stepped back and let the kid wobble along the wall. 'Guy never lets me have any fun. . . . Now you get your brains together and turn the loot over.'

'Yeah, yeah.' Pettibone slid to the floor, where he sat for a while with his head in his hands. 'You a cop?'

'Whatever turns you on,' Breitel said.

'How the hell did you find me?' Pettibone asked.

'My associate here,' Breitel said. 'He knew.'

Pettibone labored to his feet and looked at me for the first time. 'My sister tell you?' he asked.

'No,' I said, and flashed back to Serena's mangled body. 'She kept your secret. I just knew this was the only place you could go.'

'Boolsheyut,' Pettibone drawled, and turned to Breitel, apparently more willing to deal with a sadist than a hypocrite, which is always a mistake. 'I guess I can't get outta the house with the shit. I was just stashin' it when you came. You never woulda found it.'

'If we found you, we would have,' Breitel said.

Pettibone smiled bitterly. 'You sure do lay it out, my man.' He took us into a pantry off the kitchen. The light didn't penetrate, and we had to strike matches to see where we were going. In the wall there was a hole leading to a blackness that was blacker than what we were coming from.

'White people lived in this house for 150 years and never even knew about this place,' he said. 'Every kinda nigger, from Uncle Tom on down, knew about it and never tole 'em.'

The walls were made of hard-packed earth, and the dirt floor was smooth. It was a makeshift secret tunnel constructed with such care that it had stood up better than the house about it.

'Where does it lead?' I asked.

'Out about a hundred yards to a spot in the fields,' Pettibone said. 'Ain't nothin' there now. When we were kids, the story came down that some field nigger whose wife had been taken away from him had dug the tunnel to get to see her at night, when she wasn't with the Massa, you dig?' There was no anger in his voice; only amusement at the quaint ways of his forebears. 'That sucker must've been in love, huh? Next thing is, they were hidin' runaway slaves, and then later, anybody else who needed a secret flop. My old man lived here for a coupla weeks while the state police were after him. My Aunt Sarah brought him his food and stole money, a little bit a day, until she had enough for his bus ticket to New York. Never did tell her own husband about it, either. . . . Maybe they had something goin'.'

'Your aunt's very loyal to you,' I said.

'Really got next to my family, didn't you?' Pettibone said. He seemed to resent me more than all the Massas who exploited him and the Breitels who beat him. 'My sister tried to get me to come around and see you. Said you were all right. But, shit, Serena was meetin' Jesus Christ every other day. Especially if he was white.'

'Must be a family trait,' I said.

He stopped, and I brushed against him. For a moment I thought he was going to swing at me. Then I could feel him sag and sigh. I knew that gesture – total despair and resignation. I'd made it myself several times.

'I guess I got better taste in honkies than her,' he said. 'I ain't dead. . . .'

'Yet,' Breitel said, and shoved him against the wall. 'I think this Martin Luther King lecture here is a fuckin' stall.'

'Hey, man, you got it,' Pettibone said. He reached down into a hole so freshly dug we could smell the wet, rich earth, and came up with a suitcase. 'You got the power now.' He slid it across to Breitel, who shook out his match and picked it up, grunting under its weight.

'Jesus, did you put rocks in here?'

'You showin' your class, baby, if you can't figure how much a score like that would weigh,' Pettibone said.

'Shit, it's only a. . . .' Breitel clicked the latch and lit another match. He froze, then mumbled, 'What the hell. . . .'

I looked over the top of the suitcase. Little packets of hundred-dollar bills, each with a rubber band doubled around it, lay snugly within. There were a lot of those little packets. There was a lot of money there. I looked at Breitel. His head was down, and it looked like he was going to fall into the valise. The match he was holding burned down to his finger. He yelped and dropped it on the money, then cursed and picked the burning match up between his fingers.

For a moment the three of us stood in the darkness. Pettibone was chuckling softly. 'Whatsa matter, ain't you dudes never seen two million bucks before?'

Breitel cleared his throat. 'I think we all could use a drink,' he said.

CHAPTER TWENTY

I went out to the car for the Stonewall Jackson. By the time I got back, Breitel was sitting in the kitchen with the money spread out on the table.

'One million, nine ninety-nine, nine,' he said.

'What?'

'New money,' he said. 'Hundred bills to a stack. Two hundred stacks.' Breitel looked confused. 'The kid used a hundred to get down here. Gas and food and cigarettes.' He shook his head, and I thought he was going to burst into tears over the missing hundred.

'Got any glasses?' I asked Pettibone.

'Got the Coke cans,' he said.

'Forget it.' I slammed the bottles down between the stacks. 'Let's have a drink and figure this out.'

'I don't drink,' Pettibone said.

'Never heard of a nigger who didn't drink,' Breitel said. 'Don't think that we're gonna get drunk, and you're gonna slide outta here. Don't think that, or I'll put two thirty-eights in your knees, and you'll be happy to crawl to the toilet. Awright?'

Pettibone reached for the bottle and took a healthy swig. Breitel passed the bottle to me.

'Everybody drinks,' he warned.

'Since when do I have to be forced?' I asked, and took a careful hit, holding the liquor in my mouth before swallowing, on the off chance that some of it might evaporate. 'I want to know how you got this bread,' I said to Pettibone. 'Then, when we know that,' I said to Breitel, 'maybe we can figure out what to do with it.'

'Fair enough,' Breitel said, taking another gulp. 'I wanna know too.'

'Sure,' Pettibone said. His Adam's apple bobbed as he drank, and he was pie-eyed when he came up for air. The kid hadn't been lying: only a nondrinker could have such little respect for alcohol.

'I took it,' Pettibone said. 'That's how I got it.'

'Wait a minute,' I said. 'We know you took it. But how? Why?'

'Okay.' He took another drink. 'It was her idea. I just went along like I always did. That bitch never had no trouble with me.'

'Which bitch?' I asked.

'Pamela Sue McClough, that's which,' Pettibone said.

'Listen, you black. . . .' Breitel said, leaping up and raising his hand.

'Are you defending American womanhood, you phony bastard?' I said. 'After all the goddamn chippies you've boffed.'

Breitel sat down. 'I apologize,' he said to Pettibone. 'Please continue.'

'It was her idea,' he said. 'She got this sailor on the Swedish boat to bring the shit in. . . .'

'Wait a minute,' I said. 'Just start from the beginning.'

'From the beginning?' Pettibone asked.

'That's right.'

'From the time when I was ten years old?' he shouted.

'What happened then?' I asked.

'That's when I first balled her,' he said.

'Whaddya talkin' about?' Breitel mumbled. 'People can't fuck when they're ten years old.'

'Okay, motherfucker,' Pettibone screamed, 'that's when I first stuck it in. . . .'

Breitel got up again, a bit slower this time, and pointed a crooked finger at Pettibone. 'You watch the way you talk about this girl. . . .'

'You at it again?' I said. 'Who do you think you are, Bert Parks?'

Breitel sat down. 'You're right,' he said. 'I apologize,' he said to Pettibone. 'Please continue.'

'I was raised no more'n five hundred feet from here,' Pettibone said. 'My mother was up to the house a lot, and she would take me along to sit in the kitchen with Aunt Sarah, or hang around out in the garage with Uncle George. He was chauffeurin' for them then. My old man was layin' up juiced most of the time, and he'd beat the piss out of us if we was there when he showed up. So they shipped Dean and Serena off to school. . . .' Pettibone began to sob.

Breitel leaned over and whispered to me, 'What's he doin' that for?'

'His brother and sister are both dead,' I explained.

'Oh, I'm sorry.' He bowed to Pettibone. 'Please continue.'

Pettibone took another drink. 'Maybe I was six, I don't know, but anyway, she'd bring me up to the house, and I'd sit in the kitchen and have milk and cookies. It was always dead quiet. There weren't but four of them livin' there – Grampa Sam, Mr Arnold, Miss Florence and little Pammie Sue. You never heard nothin' goin' on upstairs, and all the niggers tiptoed around like somebody was dyin'.

'The first time I seen that bitch she was kickin' and cryin'. Her face was all red. . . . They were takin' her into the car. I remember Aunt Sarah tellin' Uncle George' – his voice became shrill and feminine – ' "Don't you touch her now." She was wearin' a white dress, and shiny black shoes, and those legs . . . I mean, shit, if I was six, that means she was five. How many five-year-old bitches you know got sexy legs?'

Breitel rose again, raised his hand like an orator, opened his mouth, and then sat down. 'Please continue,' he said.

Pettibone took another drink. 'Sexy ain't even the word for that bitch. I mean, you'll see a chick with a beautiful body that you wanna ball. That don't mean shit compared with this bitch.' He used the word with anger, admiration, and despair. I tried to picture that skewered corpse alive and animated. I didn't have to: Pammie Sue McClough had been seductive even after she'd been dead for fifteen minutes.

'Six years old,' Pettibone said, 'and I couldn't get the bitch outta my head. You know, I don't think I'd ever seen a white girl my age before. Or if I had, 'cause I must've, she just chased 'em all away. I went home, and I couldn't get those laigs outta my mind. And that pretty blonde hair with a little permanent wave, or whatever, down at the bottom. Shit, I never felt any more about a woman in my life than I did then.'

'What's this got to do with the bread?' Breitel asked.

Both Pettibone and I took another drink and ignored him.

'I found out later that they were takin' her away to some boarding school,' Pettibone said. 'Rich white folks got a problem down here. You got so much trash, where you goin' send your sweet little girl to school? So they had this boarding school for all the rich folks in the state. Somewhere round Charleston, I never did know where. Even later on, when she was always runnin' away. . . .'

'Would somebody tell me what this has to do with the money?' Breitel asked.

'It was her idea,' Pettibone said, slamming his fist on the table. 'She got my brother into it, and I didn't even know. She was the hardassest bitch you ever saw.'

Breitel rose slowly and shook his finger at Pettibone. 'Now, I told you. . . .'

'Stop jumpin' around,' I shouted. 'We'll get to the money. Just work up to it. That's the best way.'

'I'll tell ya,' Pettibone said, reaching for the bottle. 'I'll tell ya everything.'

'Don't niggerlip that bottle,' Breitel said.

'Let's get back to Pammie Sue,' I said.

'Right on, baby, let's get back to the pussy,' Pettibone said. 'Shit, yeah, why not? I got it, didn't I? A lotta cats wanted it. . . . Comin' around with their cars and all. And me layin' out down in the stable, waitin' for her to show. 'Cause that's where it all went down. They put me over to the stable when I was about eight. The old man, Grampa Sam, wanted to raise racehorses, but everything he got into just went and died on him, even the goddamn tobacco after a while. Hell, he was rich enough to fool around and have himself a little pickaninny cleanin' out the shit and liftin' his fat old carcass onto some old swayback plug. I was workin' around there after school. Only thing I knew was, do what you're told. Don't be like your pa or your brother neither, 'cause Dean had gone to reform school, and everybody said it wouldn't be long before he'd be doin' it again. And my sister sat out back, lookin' at picture magazines and not gettin' into nothin'. Ma was drinkin' so bad she'd beat on us once in a while if we was just underfoot. So Aunt Sarah told me to be a good boy and work hard, and Mr Sam – how she loved his ass – would get me a scholarship or put me in his will. Hell, I never did know what he was gonna do for me.

'Anyway, I'm nine years old one day, and I'm in the stables, and Pammie Sue comes down for a ride. Home from school and shit, and wearing shorts and sneakers. The old man dug where she was comin' from too, lemme tell ya. He had his hands all over her. Those white legs just layin' against the brown horse. The horse heavin' and snortin' 'cause he knew too. Everything with a dick knew about her shit. Fuckin' grasshoppers must've been whackin' off in the fields. She had the whole goddamn place turned on. And she loved it, even then. Just touch the bitch, that's all you had to do. Anybody – pops, grampops . . . but especially that pretty little nigger stableboy. You got it. Especially me. One mornin' after a coupla weeks – it was durin' the summer vacation, hot as hell and nothin' to do – she comes down by herself. I can't even open up my fool mouth, you dig. I get out this big old stud that the old man's got her riding. Motherfucker's got a rod as big as a baseball bat. 'Cause he dug where it was at.

' "What's that?" she says. First words she ever spoke to me.

'I said, "I don't know." What the hell else could I say? And she laughed and laughed like I was the stupidest thing. "Is yours as big as that?" she says. "My papa's is." Dig the bitch. Bringin' it right down on me. Shit, I believed her. Far as I'd heard, white folks were some kinda animals, anyway, right. "Lemme see yours," she says. Well, I know I ain't got the horse or her old man beat. But I follow her up to the hayloft and take off my pants while she just stands lookin'. And meanwhile I ain't said one word, you believe that.

' "You wanna marry me?" she says. Dig what I tell the bitch. I tell her. "We can't, we're too young." Oh man, I was a very lightweight little cat.

' "We're kinda brother and sister, anyway," she says. "Your mom is married to my papa. They do all that married stuff every afternoon."

'Now is that a way to find out your mamma is fuckin' some old dude, with you not really knowin' what fuckin' is, but knowin' that only your pop was supposed to be into it? And a white man too. First thing was I got scared, but she kissed me. Right there in the haystack, with my pants down, she kissed me. "That's what your mama does," she says. "And you wanna see what else?" And she goes down on me. Poor old good boy Artis is cryin'. He so scared, he don't feel nothin'.

'Anyway, she's been peekin' in on 'em and knows everything. So next thing, I'm on top of her, and tryin' to get it on, you know. And forget about it. Man, I ain't ready. And I really hear about it from her. 'Cause she always wanted to show her daddy that she could have a nigger too.'

'So what's this story that you raped her?' I asked.

'Pops tell you that?' Pettibone snorted and leaned forward with that same angry, grieving look his sister had. 'Hell, she raped me, and she tole him about it too, 'cause there wasn't nothin' she wouldn't say or do to get at that man. Every time she came home from school, every summer, it was me and her. By the time I was thirteen, we were really gettin' it on. She was twelve, but she looked like twenty. Goddamn tits had popped out over the winter, and what a surprise that was. She was big too, just about as tall as me, with a big body all over. And she had more goin' on in her pussy than any hundred-dollar hustler I ever knew. Man, for five years I thought screwin' was the greatest thing goin'. You know what? I thought all you had to do was lay back, close your eyes, and imagine somethin', and it would happen, without you even havin' to say one word about it. Man, I thought it went down like that with every woman. But I ain't seen nothin' like that bitch for pure squeeze in my life. And I never will.'

'So how'd you get caught?' I asked.

'Usually, Pammie Sue would take old Samson out for a trot right down into the gully where the Indian burial ground was supposed to be. I'd wait, and then I'd run – dig it, man, I'd run my ass off to catch up – goin' through the clay pits so's I wouldn't be seen on the road. We'd just lay there all mornin', ballin' and kissin' and gigglin' . . . laughin' at the grownups, her at her pops – her mom was dead, or on the way by then – and me at my people, 'specially Aunt Sarah and Uncle George. We figured they never got it on. And my mom. Pammie Sue really hated her.

'So this one day it starts to rain, and she wants to go up in the hayloft. Well, I was scared, but I went. She dug takin' chances like that. Sure enough, we ain't up there fifteen minutes when old jiveass Grampa Sam comes in. Man, that bitch up and starts to yell, and jumps down, almost breakin' her neck, and goes cryin' to the old prick. And me up there, tryin' to pull my pants up. Now, what the hell was I gonna say? I knew well enough not to deny anything, 'cause then they'd have me callin' her a liar. Best to admit you acted like a nigger than to accuse her of actin' like a pussy.

'The old man wanted to kill me, but Mom and Aunt

Sarah like to went down on their knees to Mr Arnold. . . .'

'Where was your father?' I asked.

'Long gone, baby. Mr Arnold took care a that. My dad got tore up one night and cut some dude over in Farnham. The cat was just a jiveass nigger like him, and it didn't have to mean nothin', if Mr Arnold had said the word. But instead he got the patrol down on my ole man's case. So Pops went and hid out in the tunnel for a coupla weeks. They got him at the bus station and beat one of his eyes right out his head. Then they had him diggin' ditches on the goddamn work gang till he just fell over and died. He wouldn't have done much anyway. He was a mean little black cat. Call his own kids "high yaller." That man hated everybody. Anyway, fuck him, right?' He directed this at Breitel, who was staring morosely at the money, his chin in his hand.

'Right,' Breitel said.

'They sent me away,' Pettibone said, turning back to me. 'Booker T. Washington School. My brother was there when he wasn't breakin' out. Hell, I ain't sorry about that place. I learned how to fight. Them goddamn preachers they had there shove a Bible in your face and a ruler up your ass, and you better sing purty for Jesus. Shit, me and Dean got pretty tight in there, and we used to talk about how we were gonna go back to Pulham with a million bucks and two purple motherfuckin' Cadillacs, and blow all them white motherfuckers away. I told him about Pammie Sue, the real truth, and we had a lotta good laughs about that. We hung together like brothers, man. Kicked a buncha ass, and everybody respected us. Shit, when I came to New York, I met cats who'd heard about us in other joints down home.'

'You never did go back to Pulham after that,' I said.

'No, man, they woulda shot me on the spot. I hung around Charleston for a while with my brother. He was into pimpin', and doin' all right. My sister couldn't get it together for nursin' school. She came and stayed with us, but her and Deanie never got it on, so she went up to New York, and I didn't hear from her until I went up there myself.

'Which was last year. I was hustlin' down in Baltimore, and I got hung up. Coupla dudes were really out for me. So I went lookin' for Dean 'cause he was up there. And so was Serena. Dean was livin' over in Lenox Terrace with white rugs and a big ole Cadillac. Him and some other home boys was dealin', and they had Harlem wrapped up tight. Motherfucker had a gun in every room, one in the glove compartment, and another one in his belt. Had chicks fallin' in and fallin' out. I mean, you'd just step over fine bitches everywhere you went in his place. And across town my sister's hustlin' in some bust-out dealer's bar. Takin' care of the visitin' personnel, you know, from Newark and Detroit. Shit, I hadn't been runnin' chicks for the last coupla years not to know that Serena didn't have no hustler in her, man. I told that to Dean, and he said, "Hey, man, I got her the gig." So I knew that my brother was heavy into the power scene. And money, man, like you seein' here. In fuckin' shoeboxes in the closet, in pillowcases. Motherfucker didn't know what to do with it, didn't know where to put it. Can you dig that?'

'So he got you a job,' I said.

'Yeah, he got me somethin'. First I was pushin a gypsy cab for some West Indian dude who had about thirty of them. You pay the cat twenty dollars plus fillin' up at his station, and you keep what you make. You gotta push for ten hours to make thirty bucks. Man, I told Dean, "Dig it, I can't cut this work scene, just ain't used to it." So he gets me a gig collectin' rent.' Pettibone shook his head in disbelief. 'Some other black dude who was investin' all his skag profits in slum buildings. And I gotta go and get the bread from these people, right. Welfare days you can see me comin'. And just in case it gets heavy, they give me a gun, right, so I can blow the brothers away.

'Well, that wasn't up my street, either. So Dean tells me, "Man, go out and score yourself a coupla holes, and I'll put you right in midtown Manhattan where the fifty-dollar tricks are layin' out in the gutter." Shit, I ain't puttin' it down. I had two chicks in Charleston when I was seventeen, had three holes in Baltimore. Sittin' up in my little pad, listenin' to music while they were out bustin' their tails. But New York, man, you gotta be a psychologist and a dresser. You know, you got these honky pussies from Pennsylvania and even down South, and they got this thing about black cats. You know, that we're all supermen. Not in ballin', 'cause the worse thing a pimp can do is ball one of his holes after he's pulled her. You see, 'cause if he has an off night, the mystique is gone, and that hole gonna find some other dude. It was just style that they dug. And also it was a nigger. 'Cause they run you up here. Man, you takin' their bread, beatin' 'em up, and gettin' 'em high, but they're runnin' you.

'So I score me a coupla holes, and then I cut 'em loose. And Dean, he ain't mad. Now he gets me into the factory down on Bedford Street. Five bills a week. I got there at three in the morning and cut skag until seven. Three days a week, sometimes four. There's enough dope goin' in and outta there for the whole city. These Italian cats have got it controlled. My brother's in an out with them. But he's a buyer, so he ain't really shit.

'Okay, so I get myself straight behind this job. Why not? I'm makin' good bread, got a lotta time to myself. I moved into a little brownstone pad in Brooklyn. And, you know, I started goin' to night school, finishin' up; I even wanted to go to college. Plus I was takin' care a my aunt and uncle, 'cause nobody else in the family would go near them. I was doin' okay. Had me a coupla chicks on the scene, a little Mazda. I was just bein' cool. No big-money dreams. And then I'm talkin' to my Aunt Sarah one night, and she tells me Pammie Sue's in town. Now, why did she do that? Even people who love you like to see you messed up every once in a while. She must have known, 'cause soon as I got home, I called that house. And a hour later the bitch was standin' at my front door.'

'And it started all over again,' I said.

'Hey, man, your friend's asleep,' Pettibone said. Breitel, head in hands, spittle on his sleeve, was snoring peacefully away.

'What are we gonna do about the money?' I said loudly.

'Huh?' Breitel looked up, blinking.

'It's impolite to fall asleep during somebody's story,' I said.

'I apologize,' Breitel said. 'Please continue.' And his head drooped into his arms again.

'Why do you wanna hear all this, man?' Pettibone asked me. 'You gonna put it in the paper?'

'Some of it,' I said. 'The rest I want to know. Because I'm the kind of guy who has to know everything. And I'm a good listener.'

'Shit, I ain't never had nobody listen to me like you do,' Pettibone said. 'It makes me nervous. I feel like I'm sayin' things I shouldn't.'

Reporters and psychoanalysts know how to make people talk. Just keep silent, look expectant or even a little bored if you want to be mean. I kept silent and looked bored. Sure enough, Pettibone started talking again.

'The chick had growed up. She wasn't little-girl mean, she was big-woman evil. And crazy too. She'd been through a lot and was into coke. An ounce a week, which she got by ballin' some cat up in the Bronx. Man, the way she could boogie, I'm surprised the cat didn't turn his whole stash over to her.

'You know what it's like to ball a chick who's all kissin' and carryin' on and moanin' and grabbin', just every fuckin' thing anybody ever thought of . . . doin' that one minute, and then spittin' like a goddamn cat in your ear about this 'n' that? But mostly her father, what a badass he was. She really had a hate on for him. Said he'd murdered her mother. Talked about all the boozin' and the bitches and how he was rippin' everybody off with this and that deal. I guess one of the boots she'd been ballin' had been political, 'cause she had this whole thing about black people, like she just discovered that we weren't exactly runnin' things, you know? Well, it didn't take much to get me started. I mean, I would've voted for George Wallace just to keep gettin' that pussy, but I could really get into cuttin' Mr Arnold up. I remember me and Dean had even talked about icin' him. Dean with all his guns and all, and thinkin' he could beat the world, anyway. When I told her that, she freaked and said, yeah, why didn't we. But do it real slow, she said. Shoot him in the kneecaps, then the balls. Can you imagine a chick talkin' that way about her own father? Somethin' bad had gone down between them. I thought, at first, maybe he tried to ball her, but with a chick like that, she'd get madder if he didn't.

'Anyway, she started hangin' out with me. The block was cool, young-married and faggot, one of those scenes. We got along good, as long as I let her carry on about her old man, and makin' revenge plans. One was we write letters to the FBI with all kinds of shit about his business dealings. But all that was coming out in the papers anyhow, and it didn't seem to matter. The other was we kidnap him. She was really hot on that. But, fucked up in love as I was, I backed off. I knew they'd put my black ass away for good behind that. So here comes the good part.'

Breitel mumbled and snored. I took another drink. There was a corner left in one bottle; the other was down to a drop. I pushed both bottles across to Pettibone and shook Breitel.

'The good part's coming,' I said.

He farted in response. Pettibone carefully poured the booze from one bottle into the other and took a drink. He threw both bottles in the corner.

'You ain't shit,' he said to me. 'Now that your man's passed out, I could get outta here right now with the bread, and you couldn't do nothin' to. . . .' He stopped in mid-sentence.

I followed the path of his glazed eyes, and saw that Breitel, his head still on the table, was waving his derringer around in the air. 'Please continue,' he mumbled.

'Look, man, I wanna know what your plans are,' Pettibone said.

Breitel just waved the derringer again. Pettibone looked at me.

'I just want to hear the good part,' I said.

Pettibone started to cry again. 'My brother and my sister went down behind this hustle. You motherfuckers gonna kill me too?'

'The only thing I ever killed is a fifth,' I said. 'We'll decide what to do with you after we hear the good part.'

Pettibone shook his head like a wet dog. 'Okay, man,' he said groggily, 'the good part is I found our Mr Arnold was smuggling smack into the country for the Mafia. That good enough?'

Breitel stirred, the succubus of blackmail whispering in his ear. I blinked away visions of Pulitzers and big book contracts.

'It's good enough if it's true,' I said.

'Ain't the bread proof enough?' Pettibone asked.

Breitel looked up, suddenly very alert. 'You know what I think,' he said. 'I think we need another drink.'

CHAPTER TWENTY-ONE

The four of us (including the suitcase) got into Breitel's car. Pettibone drove. I sat next to him, instructed by Breitel to 'watch the bastard', while he sat in back with the valise on his lap, stroking it absently like a pet Siamese.

We drove down a bumpy back road into a little shanty town on the edge of a huge, deserted field.

'Ain't no lights burnin',' Pettibone said doubtfully. 'Besides, it wouldn't be right to take these people's wine.'

'Take?' Breitel started to laugh. 'You know what you're gonna do? You're gonna make yourself so popular. . . . Here.' He passed a hundred-dollar bill into the front seat. 'Go out and get a bottle. And don't take change.'

Pettibone came back a few minutes later with an armload of bottles, lurching and laughing hysterically.

'Motherfucker almost had a heart attack,' he said. 'He had all this shit out in the shed 'cause he didn't want his old lady to know about it. I think he's gonna get in the wind himself right now.'

A motor cackled like an old man clearing his throat, and a few seconds later a rickety pickup truck jangled past us, sparks shooting out from its dragging muffler.

'He is.' Pettibone said. 'Old bastard's gonna drive all the way to Charleston and have himself a time. Sonofabitch. . . .' He was laughing so hard he could hardly speak. 'You know what he said to me? You know what that joker said? He said, "Jesus sent you to me, boy. Jesus sent you." A little bread can make anybody crazy.'

We put on the light and took inventory. There were two bottles of Old Magnolia Blossom Peach Wine, a half-dead bottle of Alamo Spanish Red, and a nondescript jar of clear white liquid.

'Sneaky Pete,' Pettibone said, tapping the jar. 'Home brew, man. Killed more niggers than the dry shits.'

Pettibone drove back to the mansion, but turned away and headed for a row of dilapidated buildings.

'Wanna see where we used to live?' he asked.

'I wanna know how come McClough was a courier,' Breitel said.

We got out in front of another old shack. Pettibone sampled each of the bottles and decided on the Old Magnolia Blossom. The Carolina sun was inching over the rim of the world now. Pettibone walked the ground in front of his ancestral home.

'Out there was my father's land,' he said. 'I'll bet you every buck in that suitcase that there's a rusty old tractor sittin' out there right now. You could hear him just about every day, cursin' and yellin' at the goddamn thing. He never could get it fixed proper. . . . Over here was the garden. We had sweet peas and greens and tomatoes and onions. Sweet corn too, man. We called it Country Gentleman. Ever have that?' He was testing us now, dancing around in the dust with the bottle in his hand.

'What about McClough, Artis?' I asked.

'Mr Arnold is a bad cat,' he said. 'Think of all those sufferin' brothers in the ghetto who died because of Mr Arnold. Makes you wanna get a rope, don't it?'

'How did you find out?' I asked.

Pettibone sat down on the porch steps and leaned against a rail. 'It was my brother. Y'see, the Italians had the network; they brought the shit in. And you had to buy from them and pay their price. The Harlem dudes were on their own. They weren't workin' for no godfather. They kept lookin' for a way to get the shit in themselves so they could save seven thousand a key.

'Dean wanted to find out how they got the shit in. 'Specially those two Italian dudes, 'cause they had always had the goods. Quite naturally, they wouldn't tell. I mean, you got stuffed in a trunk even if you asked 'em. But Dean figured if he could get onto their source, he could make a better offer to the cat and still save money.

'Now, the black dudes had a little somethin' goin' for them. A lotta cats in the army were bringin' tastes over from Vietnam on military planes. Nothin' big. One a these cats got himself a black major over in Germany. Graves Registration, you dig. He'd be sendin' tons of the shit over in coffins to his man on the other side. Perfect. Then the major started sendin' coffins without any bodies, just a phony name and a lot of skag. So he got popped, and he turned in everybody. Man, they couldn't shut that cat up. So Dean and the fellas picked up on this and said, listen, we gotta work with the pros, code of silence and all that shit. These GI turkeys can bury us all, and they ain't bringin' more than a coupla pounds at a time.

'I remember, Dean told me, "Look around, man, and see what you pick up. You get the name of their connection, and I'll give you a hundred thousand cash money."

'Well, I looked and listened, but those cats don't talk. Man, they don't have to. One cat'll start a sentence, and the other one finishes it. I ain't never seen anything like that. The Italians are together, man, you gotta admit it.

'But my brother was on the case too. I think he'd been seein' too many Superfly-type flicks. He was into power. He'd talk about buyin' up politicians, runnin' this and runnin' that. He thought he was livin' in the Roarin' Twenties.

'He checked the Italians out and found a pigeon. That

little Vern, who was blown away. Vern was the spotter. He'd sit there every night, and. . . .'

'We know what he did,' I said, anxious to get to the end of the story before the sun rose, as if I were on deadline.

Pettibone looked hurt. The one person who'd shown interest in his life had now deserted him. But he continued: 'Vern liked pussy, and he was just too mixed up to get it. Dean, bein' a pimp and all, picked up on the john in Vern, and brought Zarita around. Now this chick is a slave, y'understand? A stone junkie who'll do a hundred tricks a night and make 'em all think she loves 'em as long as she's got her strong pimp and a half a load waitin' for her in the pad. She's been doin' the sidewalks for months, and all of a sudden she's gotta turn all that power onto one cat. And these chicks are strong, the strongest. When they got their looks, and dope ain't totally ate their brains away, they're strong motherfuckers.'

'So Vern told Zarita who the courier was, she told your brother, and he told you,' I said.

'He called me up one night, laughin' like a crazy man. "Your father-in-law," he says. "Old Mr Arnold's the man. He's even slicker than we thought."

'When Pammie Sue heard this, she freaked. She was gonna get the bastard now. Turn his ass in. I said, okay, but lemme get the hell out, 'cause the whole scene's gonna get popped. And then she said, wait, she had a better idea. But wouldn't tell me what it was. Only thing I knew was, she made me get a passport. And then she took her inheritance check and signed it over to me. I said, "What you doin' that for? The check'll go back to the bank, and your old man'll see."

' "That's just what I want," she says. Man, I took one long look into that bitch's face and knew it was over. She had flipped. I guess what had always been in her had come out.'

'So you went to Germany with her,' I said.

'Yeah, we went. She packed all her clothes. I was just along for the ride, 'cause for two weeks I never saw her. Didn't even stay in the same city. I was in Munich, and she went to Bonn to stay with her father. Before she left, she cut her hair and took off the make-up, tied her tits down, and walked around drawlin' and curtsyin' for a couple days just to get into practice. We laughed and laughed. And then she'd start to cry and curse him out, gettin' so loud that I'd have to put a pillow over her mouth. Then she'd get on me, screamin' and throwin' things. I'd just try to quiet her down, you know, and she'd get madder and start scratchin' at me. I'd hold her down for a while until she relaxed. Then things would be okay until the next day.

'She was gone for a coupla weeks, and then she called me one night and said she knew how he was doin' it. He was sendin' big loads back in his baggage. Takin' the plane and sendin' the shit in by boat under diplomatic immunity. Nice, huh? The shit went right to the house on Sutton Place, where the people had some old broad who looked like a housekeeper – you see, that was why he had ditched my aunt with a coupla hundred walkin'-around money – and took charge of the shit.'

'I met her,' I said.

'It was a good hustle,' Pettibone said. 'From Sutton Place right down in a cab to Bedford Street. Two hundred pounds at about seven grand a pound.'

'A million-four OTB,' Breitel said. 'Nobody could turn that down.'

'Did you find out how McClough got the dope?' I asked.

'Some low-level dude in the German Foreign Office. He was there the nights the dope was dropped. Kept comin' around with his little attaché case, stay for drinks, then split without the case. A little while later Mr Arnold would go up to his room with the case. Pammie Sue saw it all. She even knew what valise he was stashin' it all in. Only it was heavy, 150 pounds, she figured. She needed a nigger to tote it for her. That's why I was there.

'I rented a car and drove to Bonn. "Wait down the block," she said. A coupla cops passed me, then came around the corner and passed me again. Mr Arnold's limo passed with him sittin' in the back, all styled up for a party. He looked me right in the face, and I like to shit in my pants right there. But he didn't recognize me. He probably didn't even know what I looked like when I was livin' down the road from him.

'It made me nervous, anyway, thinkin' he might put the cops on me, or somethin', so I decided to split. And just as I start the motor, I see Pammie Sue comin' down the street, draggin' this suitcase after her. She's all messed up, dungarees, blouse unbuttoned, boots droopin' down to her ankles, hair flyin' all over the place. And suckin' wind like a dyin' cow. But she waves me away and drags the valise right up to the car. "Let's get the fuck outta here," she says. And you know, with all she had done, that was the first time I ever heard her use a swear word. I shoulda known then.

'We drove right up to Sweden. On the ferry, just before we cleared customs, Pammie Sue opened the valise. It was just what she had said, 150 pounds wrapped up in packages like hamburger meat. I said, "Man, they're gonna bust us." But she smiled and showed me her passport. She had that diplomatic shit too, from her old man.

'Dig, how smart the chick is. The Swedes are used to mixed couples and don't even give us a second look, anyway. But then they almost break their heads salutin' when they pick up on the diplomatic passport.

'We checked into a little hotel in Stockholm. Pammie Sue was laughin' and carryin' on, then she got down and lay in bed, cryin' the whole night. Wouldn't let me near her; I had to sleep in the goddamn chair. You can see all the shit I took from this bitch.'

Pettibone threw the empty bottle of Old Magnolia Blossom out into the empty field. It bounced and shattered against a half-buried shovel. Pettibone stared after it, looking again at that bitter black man coaxing his wheezing tractor. When Pettibone turned back to us, the anger was out of his eyes. His voice was calmer; the words came more slowly.

'Next day she left. I had been tellin' her it would be dangerous to try to get the shit into the country if her old man was onto us. I could see the goddamn Mafia waitin' at the dock with the FBI and everybody else. He could just turn us in and not worry about anybody believin' our story about him. So she says, "I'll find a way to get the shit in. You just wait here."

'Well, I waited. Sittin' on a million-dollar stash, I waited like a damn fool. I was afraid to go out, and when I did, I couldn't look at nobody. Kept the valise under the bed and stood around every morning when the maid came in to clean. She got so paranoid about it that I figured I better come on, so I talked some shit and ended up ballin' her on the bed, all the time thinkin' of all that money and death underneath. Then every morning I had to score. Last thing I felt like doin' was ballin' some fat, old red-faced chick who bit my shoulder and scratched my back. But I did it just to keep everything cool.

'Two weeks or maybe even more went by, I can't remember. And one night, must have been after two in the morning, someone knocks on the door like they're gonna break it down. Man, by then I was goin' nuts. I open up the motherfuckin' window, gettin' ready to jump out. Then I said to myself, "Nigger, you done anyway. Might as well keep breathin'."

'So I open up on this big, dumb-lookin' blond-haired cat with a pea jacket, or somethin'. He don't look like no fuckin' cop. He's a sailor off this freighter that Pammie Sue had taken back to the States. She worked some shit on him, and he's ready to take the stash back on his next trip, which is in a few weeks. How do I know he's for real? He's got a letter from Pammie Sue and $1,000 cash for an airplane ticket. The man can't hardly speak English. He asks me if Pammie Sue and I are – what did he say – fiancé or somethin' like that. The cat's in love. She probably put out for him on the poop deck and really turned his head around. "Hell, no," I tell him. "We're just friends." I think I coulda told him we was brother and sister, and the cat woulda believed it.

'I flew back the next day, happy to get off that load. Pammie Sue's at the airport, and my brother's with her. She brought him on it, she says – a cat she could never stand when we was all kids. But I can tell they're tight, real tight.

I didn't know whether to cry or kick ass, so I cried. That night I just cried like a baby right in front of her. Any pimp can tell you that if you show weakness to a hole, you're finished, and that goes for straight chicks too. 'Cause when you come down to it, they're all holes. I knew that. I knew she wanted me to kick her ass. She wanted me to do a street-nigger number on her. Man, she wanted to get hit. Maybe even die. Made believe she was happy, runnin' this game down on Pops, but she wanted to get hit. But I wasn't the cat for it. And she just cut me loose.

'From then on, it was her and Dean. They got crazy, breakin' into the old man's house and takin' the necklace, callin' him up in the middle of the night and makin' believe it was me. Dean started takin' Pammie Sue around uptown, over to the Nirvana. . . . That's how I knew about it, 'cause Serena told me. They were havin' a blast, and meanwhile the old man's out lookin' for me. There was nothin' I could do about it. Couldn't go to the cops, sure as shit didn't wanna hip Mr Arnold. I mean, he ain't nothin' to me.

'I didn't know what Dean wanted with the shit, but I knew he didn't have it yet. That Swedish cat was bringin' it in. So I figured to get myself a little taste. I call up Mr Arnold and tell him I'm holdin' his stash for ransom. The motherfucker jumps down my throat, 'cause that's just what Dean was doin'. "You don't have to repeat yourself, Artis," he says. "We're prepared to pay. All your instructions will be followed. Now, if you're drunk or doped up yourself, or if my daughter has a few more choice words to say, I'd rather not hear them." And he hangs up. Hand me some of that white lightning, man.'

Breitel passed him the jug, and he took three long swallows, doubling over in a coughing fit as soon as he put it down.

'My father used to drink this shit by the bucket,' he said. His eyes were tearing, but not from the booze. He sat down on the wet earth with the jug between his legs, 'I wanted to get her,' he said. 'You think I was wrong?' He looked up at us pleadingly.

'She had it coming,' Breitel said.

'They both had it coming,' I snarled, surprised at my own vehemence.

'And they got it,' Artis said, nodding slowly. 'I remembered it was the "Charles XII" that this cat had shipped out on. It was due back on Thanksgiving Day. So they couldn't touch the stash until then.

'Man, I just sat in my apartment for a week, not goin' out or nothin'. My sister called. She was the only one. Every day that other bitch didn't call I just kept thinkin' about cuttin' her and shootin' her, buryin' her alive. Like a kid, I thought of killin' myself even, and how she'd cry. But I knew she wouldn't. So I had to get her.

'Day before Thanksgiving I call Mr Arnold. "You want your dope?" I say. "The drop's been changed." I didn't know where the drop was supposed to be, but I got that turkey to tell me. "Go to the phone booth on the corner," I tell him.

' "Hold it," he says. I hear him speakin' to somebody. "You mean the one on Bedford, off Seventh Avenue South?" he says.

' "That's it," I say. "You drop the bread there a half-hour before the appointed time, you dig. Now repeat the time for me." ' Pettibone chuckled. 'Motherfucker repeats the time. Three-thirty in the mornin'. "Okay," I tell him. "My man's gonna pick it up, and if he's interfered with in any way, you don't get your stash. I don't want nobody around there, at all."

'Quite naturally he agreed with everything I said. I didn't even know how much bread they had settled on. But it was a combination drop and blackmail, so it had to be a nice chunk. And it was.

'Thanksgiving morning I turn on the radio, and the motherfuckin' "Charles XII" is sinkin', and this one cat who went down with the ship, he's gotta be my man. Well, I laughed so hard the neighbors was bangin' on the walls. Then my brother calls real early for him and asks me do I want to make some bread. Five thousand dollars just to show up at this address in the Village. Only a little ways down the block from the bakery. Everything's cool, he says. There's just a little deal cookin', and he needs cats he can trust.

' "Yeah, baby," I tell him. "No hard feelings. What time is this now? Four o'clock in the morning? I'll be there. Bring my piece? That's the way it is? Shit, we brothers, ain't we?" '

Pettibone spat into the dust. 'Shit, we're brothers. Like Cain and Abel. I'm on your case like white on rice, my man. I know every move you're makin'. Sure he needed help. With that boat sunk, he didn't have nothin' to trade. He was gonna try to rip that money away. Only there wasn't even gonna be any money. Little brother Artis had taken care of that.

'I hopped down to my Aunt Sarah's and laid a little shoppin' money on her. Just straightenin' out all my shit in case somethin' went down. I called Serena and told her to stay by the phone that night 'cause I might need her. Then I went to the movies. I saw *Superfly*. . . .'

'You're gonna make your fortune by and by,' I said.

'That's it, baby,' Pettibone held out his palm, and I slapped it. And then, as the first rays of morning sun prickled on the backs of our necks, we began to laugh. Breitel looked at us in amazement and then joined in. We laughed and slapped each other's palms.

'That night I get in my car and drive to the Village,' Pettibone said. 'I sat on the corner of Carmine Street, a coupla blocks away, lookin' through my rear-view like James Bond, you know?'

'Like James fuckin' Bond,' Breitel roared, slapping me on the back hard enough to disgorge a little magnolia-colored saliva.

'Soon enough I seen these cats roll up in an old Caddy, drop the bread, and split. Before they left, they hung a little sign over the booth; Out of Order. I mean, can you imagine some cat poppin' in to call his old lady and findin' two million bucks? Like this nigger with the hundred dollars, he'd be long gone. Only he'd have two million. Nobody would ever find him.'

'They'd never find him,' Breitel shrieked, pounding the dirt. That fresh gust of hilarity blew me over onto my back. Now all three of us were on the ground, crawling and giggling and clutching each other, and kicking up dust. It occurred to me that we were drunk, but I quickly banished that blasphemous notion in favor of the more obvious conclusion that here were three good friends enjoying a marvelous after-dinner anecdote, albeit in somewhat rural circumstances.

'You're gonna make your fortune by and by,' I sang.

'SUPERFLY,' Breitel shrieked à la Aunt Jemina. 'That's you, baby,' he said, shaking Pettibone.

'Bet your ass it's me, baby,' Pettibone said. 'You wanna hear what Superfly did?'

'Yeah,' Breitel and I shouted in unison.

'Okay. Superfly cools over to that phone booth and picks up the suitcase.'

'Beautiful,' I said, full of admiration for this resourceful youth, this self-made man.

'Then Superfly calls up his sister and says he's comin' for the night.'

'Right on,' Breitel said.

'Then Superfly hops back in his little short. . . . But wait.' Pettibone pointed across the street. 'He sees his brother Dean pullin' up. He sees Pammie Sue. And a whole army of other cats that he knows from uptown come rollin' out. They all go up into this little pad. So Superfly decided he wants to see what's gonna go down. He hangs out. Superfly is very cool.'

'Very,' I agreed.

'So Superfly kinda ducks down a little bit and waits. After a while old Vern, you remember him, comes up the block with Zarita. They go upstairs. Everybody's waitin' around for the payoff. Then this Oldsmobile with Jersey plates comes up, this big old black El Dorado. Two cats get outta the Olds and go upstairs. A big, mean-looking motherfucker gets out of the El Dorado and stands by the door.

'Well, Superfly knows what's goin' down, even if he ain't there. Mafia's askin' for its dope, and it don't get it. Niggers is askin' for their money, 'cause they ain't got it. Each side thinks the other side is runnin' a game. And it don't take long for the shit to hit the fan.

'I heard the shootin',' Pettibone said, sobering up a bit. 'The big guy by the door had a gun under his coat. He opened it up and took a coupla pops at somebody. Whoever it was didn't come out. Then these two white cats came staggerin' down. One of them looked like he'd been belly-shot, looked like he was holdin' his balls in place. The big guy pushed them both into the Olds, and it took off. Then he goes through the door – the big guy does – and comes down in a little bit with Pammie Sue.'

Pettibone drained the jar of Sneaky Pete and took a deep breath. 'He's holdin' her by the hair, yankin' her back and forth. Ole Superfly that we were talkin' about almost went out the car after her. But everything went down so fast. Shit, that's a lie. I was too scared. I knew they'd burned everybody up there. I was scared.'

Breitel cleared his throat. 'Nothin' wrong with bein' scared,' he said.

'Ain't nothin' wrong with nothin',' Pettibone said. 'It's just the way you feel about it, and I didn't feel so damn good. She was scared and cryin'. Didn't look that different from a lotta the times I'd seen her cry, right from the first time I ever seen her when they was takin' her away. Just scared. . . .' His voice broke. 'Then some other cat got outta the Caddy and went over and slapped her right in the face like she was a goddamn whore or somethin'. I couldn't see her, he was standin' in the way. He stepped back and said somethin'. The other cat was holdin' Pammie Sue by the hair. He just stuck her with this blade or whatever. Jammed her right into the door. Her arms reached out, then went down. Her head kinda slid over. Wasn't no way she could be alive. Then they just drove away. Just for a goof I followed them down Seventh Avenue for a while. But the farther away from that door I got, the more I thought about the bread, as if I was gonna run 'em off the road and ice 'em both like Superfly would do, and finally I went up to Serena's house. Real cool dude I was. . . . I never even told her about the bread. Just that people was after me. I split so she could bring you around, hung out in Riker's downtown, and saw the cops when I come back. My sister was the best woman I ever knew – Dean and Pammie Sue, too, but they was messin'. Serena didn't do no nothin' but be born my sister. So I had this money, and I thought, why not bring her and Dean back home to the Baptist cemetery where they put my old man and my moms too.'

'And that's how we found you,' I said.

Pettibone nodded. 'My sister told me I had too much soul to be a hustler. I was insulted when she said it.'

'You're gonna do a lot better than all the hustlers in this little scam,' I said. 'Right on up to the Ambassador himself. You didn't know the dark-haired guy who slapped Pammie Sue, huh?'

Pettibone shook his head. He had told his story and was tired of talking.

'Know what he looked like?'

Pettibone shrugged and looked up. 'He looked a little bit like that cat comin' toward us right now.'

CHAPTER TWENTY-TWO

Peter Nardo, darkly immaculate in a short leather jacket with down trim, a Tyrolean hat with a rakish feather, and a large-bore shotgun which he cradled loosely over his forearm, was walking toward us. He looked like a saturnine squire out for a morning's shooting. I quailed in my shoes at the sight of him, but Breitel came out grousing.

'Hey, Petey, what's this? What's with the piece?'

Nardo stopped, and lifted the gun slightly. 'You holdin', Abie?' he shouted.

'Nah,' Breitel said, tugging at his belt. 'I'm clean.'

The gun was raised up a bit more. 'I want the money,

Abie.' Nardo nodded back toward the El Dorado, which was bouncing through the field toward him. 'I got some other people here. You don't have any muscle that I can see.'

'Get behind the car,' Breitel whispered. 'Do it slow while I'm talkin'. Hey, Petey,' he shouted, 'this ain't a war, is it? I mean, we're all on the same side....'

'Stay where you are, Krales,' Nardo shouted. I dived behind the car, and he shot. It sounded like the A-bomb. The shell crashed through the window on the driver's side.

'Shoot the motherfucker,' Pettibone said, huddling against the right rear hubcap.

'Can't.' Breitel hissed. 'Can't get any distance with the derringer.' He moved out toward Nardo, his arms spread, the perfect supplicant. 'Hey, Petey, what are you shootin' my car up for? C'mon, let's talk this over.'

Nardo snapped another shell into the gun and waved to the men in the car. Trocar Albino came out from the driver's side. A little guy with a ski jacket, holding a rifle, got out of the back.

'I want the money, Abie, and I want the nigger,' Nardo said. 'You and Krales can go. I know you got the money and your traveling kit in the car. So stay away from it and clear those two assholes out too.'

Breitel looked back at us. He could see us, but Nardo couldn't. 'They're scared, Petey,' he said. 'I think Krales just passed out.'

Nardo stopped and waited for his two hatchetmen to join him. Then all three of them marched on the car. 'Stay clear, Abie,' Nardo warned.

'You know how to shoot?' I whispered to Pettibone.

'No time,' he whispered. 'I'm gonna run. . . .'

'Hold it.' I grabbed him just as he was taking off. 'Wait a second, and maybe we'll be able to walk away.'

The back door of the car was already off the latch. I inched it open and got my fingers on the suitcase. Then I opened the door....

'Stop,' Nardo shouted. He threw another shot at the car, this time into a tire. Air sizzled out, and the car began to sink. I pulled the valise out and stood up, lifting it to shoulder height and propping it against the rear fender. 'Want the money, Nardo?' I yelled, slipping the lock and taking a neat stack of hundreds out. I slipped the rubber band off it and threw the money at him. 'Here, take it.'

The bills flew out in all directions. Nardo and his gorillas stopped in their tracks and watched as the money scattered over the dusty fields, soaring away on the wings of a slight morning zephyr.

'Krales! ' Nardo shouted in agony.

'Krales! ' Breitel screamed, his hand over his eyes, as if the sight was too painful for him.

I dipped in and threw another stack to the winds. 'You want the bread, go and get it! '

The little guy dropped to one knee, and I ducked behind the fender. A bullet whined off the trunk. I scattered another stack over the top.

'Every one of you freeze,' I shouted, 'or I'm gonna dump the suitcase, and you pricks'll be playing fifty-two pickup for the next three weeks.'

'Hey, man, what are you doin'?' Pettibone asked.

'I'm trying to save your life, shmuck,' I said. 'You're the first one to go.'

'Yeah, man, but the money,' he said.

'Not the money, Krales,' Breitel shouted. 'Not the money.'

'You're ditchin' your own money, Krales,' Nardo said.

'Bullshit,' I hollered back. 'You'd never split with me. You were going to kill us first chance you got. So now you got your guns, and I got your money. It'll take you at least thirty seconds to get to me, and by that time I will have dumped a million bucks. If I start running, a quarter of a million more will go before you bring me down.'

'All right, let's talk,' Nardo said.

'Throw your gun away,' I shouted.

'You're nuts,' he said.

I loosed another stack of hundreds. Breitel moaned as if he'd been stabbed.

'Your boys can keep their guns,' I said. 'I know they can't make wee-wee without them. But you dump yours.' I threw a green grenade out into the Tyler fields. The bills were rolling like tumbleweeds over the deserted landscape. Albino bent down to retrieve a few that had blown his way.

'Will you lose the piece, Petey?' Breitel pleaded. 'The guy's gone berserk.'

Nardo threw his gun out in front of him and walked toward the car. 'Okay, now we talk.'

I threw a stack at the little guy. He got down on his hands and knees, and clutched at the fluttering bills. I launched another mammon missile to keep Trocar busy.

'Throw one more dollar away, and I'll kill you with my bare hands,' Nardo said. He sounded close to tears.

'Slip that gun case out of the car,' I whispered to Pettibone. 'The money for the El Dorado, Nardo,' I said. 'You move away from the car. Far away, out of range. We get in and drive off, and drop the suitcase at the entrance to the estate.'

Pettibone had the gun case out. Breitel was trying not to watch him.

'How do I know you won't keep the bread?' Nardo asked.

I threw another stack into the fields. 'Yes or no is all I need from you,' I said. 'No questions.'

Nardo was close enough for me to see the red streaks in his pupils, to hear rage pumping the breath out of him like bellows.

'Stop where you are, Nardo,' I said, brandishing another stack. 'The next step you take, I'm gonna empty this suitcase.'

'You bastard,' Nardo said, his voice breaking hoarsely. He didn't look behind him, but Breitel and I did. Nardo's backup contingent was scratching a payday out of the South Carolina dirt. They didn't even know he was alive. He was alone and unarmed, and he didn't quite realize it. But we did. Breitel's hand went to his belt.

'C'mon, Abie, let's get him,' Nardo said. 'Fifty-fifty.'

'You're a prick, Petey,' Breitel said. 'You were gonna kill me.'

Nardo backed off a few paces. 'You're crazy,' he said. 'We were partners, weren't we? Who got you into this in the first place?'

Breitel whipped out the derringer and ran for him. Nardo turned, trying to locate his gun. Breitel lunged forward, leaving his feet like a matador making the kill, and shot Nardo in the back of the head. Nardo slapped at his neck as if he'd been stung by a mosquito. He turned, and raised his hand. His mouth flopped open, and he said, 'Ah', as if he had a sore throat. He looked like a man who had started to say something, but had forgotten what it was. He took a few steps backward and fell on his back, his legs flying up in the air, then hitting the ground and twitching. Breitel stood over him.

'We ain't partners any more, Petey,' he said. He bent slightly and shot Nardo pointblank in the face.

Albino and the little guy had turned at the sound of the shots and were shading their eyes against the fast-rising sun. Breitel hit the dirt and bellied behind the car. He grabbed the shotgun, assembled it, and popped in the two shells. Then he threw the Magnum at me.

'Shoot this thing at the car when they drive away. Aim at the tires, and you might hit the engine block.'

'Why don't we let them go?' I asked.

'I want 'em,' Breitel said. 'They were gonna kill me, and I want 'em.'

Albino was lumbering for the car, bills flying out of his pocket. The little guy scampered after him. Breitel rose, braced himself against the fender, and shot. The little guy dropped the gun and clutched at his behind, then fell forward on his face.

'I got him in the shitter,' Breitel said.

'He won't enjoy the Sunday football games for a while,' I said.

'Maybe one of those pellets went right up his ass into his gut,' Breitel said.

But the little guy got up and limped over to the car, which was just starting to pull away.

'I guess it didn't,' Breitel said.

Albino opened the door and pulled his comrade in. He drove all the way around us, circumnavigating out of range and negotiating some pretty rough terrain on his way back to the road. Breitel grabbed the Magnum and emptied the clip. After the last shot had failed to even kick up a little scary dirt, Albino gave us a couple of scornful toots of the horn. Breitel dived for the shotgun and threw the last shot in a high, futile arc at the disappearing car.

'You prick,' he shouted, shaking his fist.

'Let him go, will ya,' I said. 'We've got a couple of little problems right here to settle.'

'We're alive, ain't we?' Breitel said, breathing hard. 'Nardo's the one with the problems.'

CHAPTER TWENTY-THREE

Nardo wasn't a pleasant sight, so I turned him over. The back of his head wasn't very inspirational either, so I slipped off his jacket and threw it over him.

'We've got a lot to discuss and no whiskey to do it with,' Breitel said. He and I retired to opposite sides of the Tyler field and took long, reflective pisses. Pettibone staggered around a bit and threw up. When we had finished, we wandered around, picking up some of the money. The bills seemed to wait for our approach, only to flutter away at the last second. After a while it became a chore like any other, and we tired of it. We sat down in old plow ruts. Breitel sifted a handful of dirt between his fingers. Most of it blew away.

'How can they grow anything in this junk?' he said.

'They can't,' Pettibone said. 'Tobacco uses the ground up. You gotta take care of it. But these people never did. They had enough land, enough trash and niggers to work it. . . .'

'Maybe all this money will fertilize it,' I said.

'Shit,' Pettibone said. 'Money ain't good for nothin' but spending. And not even that for some folks. Hell, I had two million a little while ago. Never got to spend more than a hundred of it.'

'How much you think you dumped?' Breitel asked.

'About a half-million,' I said.

'Man, that money's gonna float all over the county,' Pettibone said. 'People are gonna be findin' it in their backyards, on the ground, the highways. Gonna make a lotta folks happy.'

'Or unhappy,' I said. 'I can see guys killing each other over a couple of those bills, families torn apart, the works.'

'What are we gonna do about the rest of it?' Pettibone asked.

We looked uneasily at one another.

'We've got a problem,' I said.

'No, we don't,' Breitel said. 'I'll take a half of what's left, considering that I saved both your asses, and you guys split the rest.'

'That's our problem,' I said. 'We can't do that. We've got to give it back.'

'What for?' Breitel demanded. 'This is private money. . . .'

'There's no such thing. The wise guys know about it 'cause it's theirs. The cops know about it 'cause they're plugged into the wise guys. And the IRS will find out about it. Not to mention our wives.'

'Oh yeah, our wives,' Breitel said.

'I don't have a wife,' Pettibone said, 'but I sure could get me a fox with some of this bread.'

'He's got a point,' Breitel said.

'The cops wouldn't leave us alone if we came back empty-handed,' I said. 'We wouldn't be able to spend the money, but we'd spend a lot of time worrying about it. . . .'

'So that's what we're doin' now, ain't it?' Breitel said. 'Workin', stealin', knockin' our brains out to get money. Now we got it. Shit, I'm willin' to go three ways, if that's what's botherin' you.'

'You don't realize how much explaining we're going to have to do,' I said. 'There's this body here.'

'Petey,' Breitel said. 'We bury him in that tunnel and forget about it.'

'You can't just forget about a dead man,' I said.

'I've forgotten a couple in my time,' Breitel said.

'Look, the only way to cover yourself in this world is to be honest,' I said.

'Well, that just don't make no sense at all,' Pettibone said.

'You've got to assume that everybody knows what you're up to or will find out. There are cops like Duffy, reporters like me, greedy bastards like you, Abe, who get a sniff of something and never give up on it. Never. Shmucks like us working overtime are the kind of shmucks who bury shmucks like us. The only way to beat them is go the hero's route. Come back with the money and say we did it for Mom and America. Then they can't touch us.'

Breitel shook his head sadly. 'I'm sittin' here, listening to a guy talk me out of a half a million bucks. I can't believe it.'

'Well, you better,' I said. 'I wouldn't touch that money with your greasy fingers. It stinks all the way down the line. Not one penny of it came from honest work. A bunch of crooks and a cracker put it together.' I held up a hundred. 'If you could follow the history of this bill, see where it had been. . . .' I ripped the bill up and threw it away. 'I know you think I'm nuts, so I'll just lay it out. I'm writing this story the way it happened. That means if you two split the money, you'll be in trouble. Understand? You can kill me right here and try to forget about two bodies if you want.'

'You know goddamn well nobody's gonna kill you,' Breitel said. 'Even if you do deserve it. You pull every dirty trick goin', and then you turn around and get honest on me, which is the dirtiest trick of all, because now me and Artis gotta pay for your honesty. Is that fair?'

'No,' I said. 'So sue me.'

'The trip turns out to be a loss for me,' Breitel said. 'I got my car pretty much totaled. . . .'

I threw him a stack of hundreds. 'That plus what you glommed off the ground will buy you a new car.'

'I oughta get some kind of reward for protectin' the bread,' Pettibone said.

I threw him a stack. 'That's for being a nice little Superfly.'

'Now take one for yourself, so you can't turn us in,' Breitel said.

I put a stack in my breast pocket.

Breitel looked at the valise. 'Oh, Jesus,' he said. He walked out into the fields and threw up.

We locked Nardo in the trunk of Breitel's car to keep him safe from stray dogs, and the car safe from strippers. Pettibone brought his Mazda around. I got in back with the valise.

'You guys'll thank me for this,' I said.

'I'll thank you to shut your mouth,' Breitel said.

We drove all the way up Route 95 in silence. What can you say after you've turned your back on a million bucks? Especially if you've struggled and connived for money all your life. What do you tell an ex-cop who risked his job every day for ten bucks' worth of graft, a Southern black kid who went hungry, a reporter with a big alimony and a tab in every saloon below Fourteenth Street? United by their hatred for me, Breitel and Pettibone had become fast friends, and excluded me from their silences. I was all talked out, anyway, so I fell asleep. I dreamed my wife took two fangs connected to a golden chain out of her mouth and sank them in my arm. I woke up in self-defense. Pizza ovens and shotguns had no fury like an estranged spouse.

We hit the city after midnight. 'You guys want to see instant hero? Because that's what I'm going to make out of you.' I got out of the car, dragging the valise with me, and went into a phone booth. I called a federal attorney named Altman who lived on the West Side. While the phone was ringing, I opened the door of the booth and threw up.

'You want to make headlines, Altman?' I asked.

'What time is it?' he asked groggily. 'Who is this?'

'This is Josh Krales of the *Event*. Wanna make headlines?'

'Are you drunk, you bastard?'

'Altman,' I hollered, keeping my bile down.

'You woke up my kid and my fucking dog with this little joke, Krales.'

'Altman, do you want to put Arnold McClough in the slams for heroin smuggling?'

'What the hell are you talking about?' he asked.

'I'm dead serious, Altman. Say yes or no.'

'Got proof?' he asked.

'Got better. Got witnesses. Got 'em with me right now.'

'Well, why don't you come over for coffee, then, Josh?' he asked. 'I'll put the kid in the refrigerator. He won't bother us.'

CHAPTER TWENTY-FOUR

Altman made us wait outside his apartment while his wife got dressed. We heard a baby crying and a little dog snapping inside. Altman rubbed his eyes vehemently with his fist. His testicles peeked through the fly in his pajamas. The three of us stood around, trying not to look at them. Finally his wife gave the all-clear.

'This better be good,' Altman said, 'because between the kid and the mutt it'll be a two-Valium night for me.'

It was good, of course. So good that Altman decided we deserved coffee. His wife, looking very receptive in her peignoir, even brought out the Danish butter cookies.

Like all prosecutors, Altman loves a sure thing and, after hearing Pettibone out, he was sure he had one. He almost kissed me for laying the case in his lap.

'Why me, Krales?' he asked. 'You could have called any of the guys in the office. You could have called the chief. Why me?'

How could I tell him that his was the only name I had in my address book? 'Wanna know?' I bent forward to whisper in his ear. ' 'Cause I wanna ball your wife.'

Altman laughed. 'Whatever turns you on.'

His wife came in with a tray of toasted English muffins

and bagels. I blushed like a schoolboy caught with a dirty book, but Altman continued laughing.

'If that's all there is, then be my guest,' he said, secure in the knowledge that he was sharing a private joke with me. But his wife knew, as women always do, that some demeaning ribaldry about her had passed between the men. She glared resentfully. Altman, who'd been husband and father long enough to be amused by anyone with designs on his wife, laughed on, unaware that every snicker was another hundred added to the eventual divorce settlement.

'The case against McClough is strong,' I said, 'but there are some problems. For example, there's this body, this Mr Nardo.'

'No problem at all,' Altman said. 'Mr Breitel acted in self-defense. He wrested the gun from the decedent and shot him to protect you two gentlemen. It was the only thing you could have done, wasn't it, Mr Breitel?'

'The only thing,' Breitel said.

'And I'm going to call the FBI right now to make a superseding claim of federal jurisdiction on the body, so the field boys can retrieve it, and the local police need not be involved.'

'That's encouraging,' I said. 'But then we have Mr Pettibone's dilemma. He was in possession of the drugs for a short time, and was aware of the network. . . .'

'Mr Pettibone was working with us,' Altman said. 'Naturally, we had to keep it a secret for his own protection, but when he became aware that Ambassador McClough was a smuggler, he contacted us immediately, and we asked him to infiltrate the operation, didn't we, Mr Pettibone?'

'Yes, sir, that's what you did,' Pettibone said.

'So, you see, both Mr Pettibone – and yourself as well – are heroes, and I mean to emphasize that to the grand jury.'

'This photograph I found,' I said. 'There's a certain policeman named Duffy who'd love to put me in the slams for withholding evidence. . . .'

'I'm sure Duffy can be made to see that your actions, though unorthodox, were in the interest of an ideal higher than mere legality,' Altman said.

'Mere legality,' I said. 'I like that, but leave it out of your summation.'

He looked at the suitcase greedily. 'And now let's take charge of Exhibit A.'

Altman was a Democrat who saw the fulfillment of all his squalid ambitions in the person of a disgraced and convicted McClough. The Attorney General, a Presidential appointee, was not overjoyed at the prospect, but had to stand by as his middle-management of civil servants, old New Dealers to the man, funded Altman's investigation on two continents.

They sent Pettibone to Germany, where he identified the German courier, who turned out to be an official in the customs agency. After two minutes of lukewarm interrogation, the man broke down like a state Nazi, blubbering, begging for clemency, and implicating the whole network, from the Vietnamese pedicab driver right on up to McClough.

In New York the FBI waylaid McClough's housekeeper, put the fear of God and Hoover's ghost into her, and then sent her back into McClough's apartment to spy on him, with the promise of immunity if she would blow him away before the grand jury, which she did. Altman was offering immunity, bribes, even Nobel Prizes to anyone who could finger McClough. He was working eighteen hours a day, running from the grand jury to meetings with the U.S. attorney, to midnight consultations with his staff; doing it all with a song in his heart.

'This is going to be big for me, Krales,' he told me. 'I owe you a lot. How would you like to be PR man for a senator, eh? How would you like it?'

'You'll never get elected anything,' I said. 'You sweat too much.'

The insult rolled off his back. 'The sweat of honest toil, my boy,' he said. 'And the voters will see that.'

While Altman worked on becoming the first Jewish President, I went on sick leave. The story couldn't break until the indictment was returned, and I couldn't tell the paper about it for fear the bosses would sabotage my exclusive with leaks.

I paid off my wife with some of my Carolina money. And I sat home, avoiding the hangouts and fleshpots so nobody could spot me. After two weeks of this clean living, I came down with the flu, and my grand jury testimony had to be postponed. Altman sent me Xerox copies of memos from the Attorney General threatening mass dismissals. Even the President had weighed in with an Eyes Only, cloudily invoking national security to explain McClough's dope smuggling. It made good bedtime reading.

When I finally made the grand jury, Altman did a ten-minute prelude in which he portrayed me as a crusading journalist who had risked martyrdom to get at the truth. He harked back to the days of the Greek *polis*, compared me to one of Pericles's demos with the *logos* of justice, but stopped just short of phlogiston. The grand jurors were reluctant inquisitors. They were members of McClough's class, or aspirants to it – that's what grand juries are all about – and they could only view the mountain of evidence against him as an attack upon all they held dear. I was followed to the stand by McClough's bankers and brokers, all of whom had challenged the subpoenas and lost. They supplied records of McClough's paradoxical financial transactions, the brokers showing heavy losses in the market, the bankers heavy purchases of tax-exempts and commercial paper. The conclusions were inescapable. McClough was so devastated that I began to feel sorry for him. The memos from Washington had stopped. Everyone had jumped off his bandwagon. I could imagine him sitting alone in that apartment, now that his spying housekeeper had testified and gone. I wanted to call him, maybe even buy him a drink. His story was the one no one would ever know; his lawyers would see to that. He had claimed all along that he didn't have as much money as people thought. Had his heavy political contributions broken him? Was he smuggling dope to keep the champagne bubbling at the embassy? The McClough empire had abandoned the land and moved into dusty vaults where sharpsters shuffled paper and made millions disappear. Had he been caught in a squeeze, whittled down to his last three million?

But how long can you feel sorry for a rich man? Eventually, McClough, appropriately ashen and contrite, appeared to plead his case to the U.S. attorney. His attorneys – he had returned to the *Who's Who* variety – had advised him to co-operate, and the transcript of his interview became a collector's item around the federal building. McClough cried a lot, and said, 'I must have been out of my mind,' thirty-four times. One of his lawyers spoke darkly about a secret KGB operation which hypnotized American diplomats and forced them into compromising acts. Another asked in stentorian tones if McClough hadn't been punished enough by the death of his daughter. When reminded that Pammie Sue would never have been murdered if her father hadn't been a dope smuggler, the lawyer replied: 'That, sir, is the cruelest remark I've heard in thirty years of the practice of law.' McClough drew on his long career of public service, and promised that if exonerated he would never do it again. The next day the indictment came down.

I gave the *Event* front-page stories for two weeks running: 'AMBASSADOR LINKED TO MAFIA DRUG RING'. ... 'ATTORNEY GENERAL DENIES POLITICAL MEDDLING'.... 'PRESIDENT INVOKES NATIONAL SECURITY IN McCLOUGH CASE'.

McClough implicated Skivoso and Iboopa. The night before they were arrested, Frankie Carbonaro called me. There were no jokes, no flattery.

'How good is the case against the bakers?' he asked.

'McClough knew who was getting the stuff through Nardo and Joe Blue Ribbon,' I said. 'But he never met or spoke with them, so it's just hearsay.'

'So they won't be convicted,' he said. 'Another miscarriage of justice. You could charge them with attempted murder, but then I'll say I wasn't there to drag you out of the oven....'

'If you're going to talk to yourself, you don't need me on the other end,' I said, and hung up.

Skivoso and Iboopa were brought in. Scowling and handcuffed, they passed me on the steps of the federal courthouse. Carbonaro's Mercedes was parked across the street. They made three hundred thousand dollars' bail in fifteen minutes. Carbonaro's Mercedes pulled away. That night they disappeared. Smart money said Uncle Victor Lupo had made bail for them. The accepted version was that they had jumped. But a few weeks later, as if certain that their jump had been temporal as well as spatial, Carbonaro tore down their bakery and the pizza shop next door, and put up an Italian-style coffee house.

'My dream come true,' he said to me as workers brought in the marble tables, installed the espresso machine, and hung a Caffè di Napoli sign over the Pizza di Palermo sign. 'A nice place for nice people. Good coffee, sandwiches, Italian pastry, *gelati*. . . .'

'You won't make a nickel,' I said.

'Money isn't everything,' he said.

A shoe fell out of the pizza oven as it was being loaded in the truck. Carbonaro laughed. 'Hey, somebody's been usin' the oven for a closet.'

'You were the one who told Nardo that I was money-hungry,' I said.

'You figured that out,' he said. 'Y'see, you're a smart guy. That's why I like you.'

'I'm a pisser,' I said.

'Yeah,' he laughed. 'C'mon, have the first espresso served in the Caffè di Napoli.'

'You told him that I could be bought,' I said. 'You knew he'd try, and that would tip me about McClough. But it almost got me killed.'

'Hey, don't talk about it, I feel bad enough,' he said.

'You were behind everything,' I said.

'Hey, Giusep,' Carbonaro hollered to an illegal alien in a red and white striped shirt, '*due caffè espresso*.'

'You turned me on to Pettibone because you wanted me to run the whole scheme down.'

'You make me sound like a mastermind,' Carbonaro said. 'I'm just a street kid tryin' to make a living like a human bein'.'

'You knew about the dope, the blackmail, McClough, everything,' I said. 'You wanted Joe Blue Ribbon's family out of the Village, but didn't want to start a war.'

'What did they say in *The Godfather*, "hit the mattresses"?' Carbonaro shook his head. 'You know what life is like? I found out with the Jesuits. You take Albert Einstein – okay, you wanna make him Italian, we'll say Enrico Fermi. You tell him, "Enrico, no more nuclear physics. From now on, you're runnin' gamblin' and shylockin' on Bedford Street. And anything else that comes along." You know that Fermi would do a hundred-times better job than Victor Lupo or Frankie Carbonaro? You know that? Just on account of he's got a head. . . .'

'You've got a head too,' I said. 'It was pretty smart to use the press and the police to get your business done.'

'Hey, don't embarrass me.'

'So now your guys sell all the dope south of Fourteenth Street,' I said. 'Fermi wouldn't deal dope to strung-out kids.'

'He didn't have to. He was a nuclear physicist. C'mon, drink your coffee. It's good for you.'

'Enrico Fermi wouldn't manipulate an innocent reporter until he was almost murdered.'

'Enrico Fermi wouldn't go nowhere he could get killed, either,' Carbonaro said.

I drank my coffee.

CHAPTER TWENTY-FIVE

Who needs success? When the money is coming in; when you've earned the admiration of your colleagues, the respect of your enemies; when women want you before they've even met you, and other people's aphorisms are put in your mouth; when the world opens like a sunflower, the future is as smooth and predictable as a massage, then it's time to start looking behind you, brother, because disaster is dogging your path.

For two weeks it was all downhill for me. I had an absolute exclusive on the McClough stories. Beg and bribe as they might, the other reporters couldn't get near it. McClough's lawyers threatened suit and demanded a mistrial on the grounds that the publication of my grand jury testimony was unconstitutional. The case sped to the Supreme Court, with *Event* lawyers claiming that I was reporting as a participant, not a *journalist.* We won and the case became a precedent – *Krales* v. *McClough.* My place in history was secured; my son would read about me his first year in law school – Harvard Law School.

My overtime came to 213 hours, most of that at triple time. It was the largest claim ever brought before a Newspaper Guild arbitration proceeding. But I never got a shot at the precedent.

The *Event* management, fearful that payment of such a large sum would open the floodgates to similar claims, decided to negotiate. Grissom invited me for a drink; I insisted on dinner. He took me to a Broadway steakhouse where ex-pugs and bookies with fedoras gave him a big hello. I had three martinis before I would even look at him.

'You did a hell of a job on that McClough story, Josh,' he said. 'You've got to admit we gave you your head on it.'

'No,' I said. I had decided on monosyllables as the only way to avoid being trapped.

'But you're laying an awful big ticket on me. . . .'

'Uh huh.' I ordered a *chateaubriand* for two and proceeded to eat the whole thing myself.

'I mean, you shouldn't be greedy,' Grissom said. 'A little loose change must have dropped out of that suitcase between South Carolina and the grand jury. You could say that bonus came courtesy of the *Event.*'

I stared blankly at him, trying to remember the last place I had hidden that infernal stack of hundreds.

'Look, Krales, let's smoke the peace pipe,' Grissom said. 'You're a fractious bastard, but you're a good reporter. You're good for the paper, and that means you're good for me, because I am the paper. You understand that, don't you?'

'No,' I said, eating *sauce béarnaise* with a spoon.

'Cash is out of the question. If I pay you, every punk with an overnight story is gonna destroy me. I'm gonna have to show them that this act don't work. And the only way I can do that is to bury you. You know that, don't you?'

'No.'

'Word gets around you'd like a quickie divorce. Why not let the *Event* buy it for you? Plane fare to Haiti, a week at a hotel, the lawyer, the works. What do you say?'

'No,' I said.

'And throw in an American Express card for you.' Grissom had the look of a man who had played an unbeatable trump. 'Think it over, there's no hurry.'

I had a piece of chocolate cream pie and thought it over. A week in Haiti, a binge on the blue Caribbean, and freedom as well. Plus an American Express Card, a reward more valuable than a Nieman Fellowship to the true journalist. Either that or two thousand-odd dollars and a career of writing obituaries. Of course Grissom could bury me. He could put me in Coventry: a desk in the corner, no work at all, a man without a country. And if I quit, what paper would hire the man who had earned the highest overtime ever paid a reporter?

'Do I fly first-class?' I asked.

My wife's lawyer drew up the consent decree, and she signed it with unsettling alacrity. Two days later I was squinting into a Haitian sunset, trying to locate the charming gamines who had made off with my luggage. Haiti was scenic enough, but *National Geographic* hadn't mentioned its major industry – divorce. Every hotel provided hot and cold running lawyers. You could call room service for a consultation. I grimly resolved to go on the bender of the century. But after a few Planter's Punches, the Haitian girls began looking like Serena Pettibone, and in the half-light of a morning hangover all the incipient divorcées in the hotel reminded me of my wife. Meanwhile, my lawyer thought it only proper to inform me that the agreement my wife had so casually signed guaranteed her forty per cent of my income in perpetuity. So, instead of love or liberty, I got amoebic dysentery from an aged mango and was home after four days with sun poisoning on my nose.

Alas, a reporter is only lionized for the duration of his exclusive. As soon as the proverbial fish are wrapped in it, and it is clipped and filed in the morgue, he sinks like a stone to his former lowly station, permitted a cackle or two at a yellowing memory, as long as he doesn't reminisce aloud.

My co-conspirators made out a good deal better than I did. Breitel was appointed permanent consultant to the State Investigation Commission. The publicity had made him so rich that he could afford to leave his wife. Pettibone entered the Police Academy and was appointed detective upon graduation. He went to work in Homicide under Duffy and managed to gain forty pounds – all in his gut – in two months. Carbonaro's caffè was always empty, except when he dragged me in for a *cappuccino*, but he didn't seem to mind. The only other person I ever saw in there was a greying, extremely correct member of the Paraguayan diplomatic mission. Carbonaro had co-opted himself a diplomat, and, I assumed, had picked up where Skivoso and Iboopa had left off.

One night, after my return to obscurity, I wandered into the Hyena. It was Thursday, payday in most of Gotham's publicity mills, and the place was jammed. The same people who had apprised me of my genius a scant fortnight before, favored me with tired greetings. The women who had pursued had to be wooed again; the bartender asked me to pay my tab. I was dreaming of fame, fortune, and meaningful relationships with Las Vegas chorines when a blonde woman waved to me. She was wearing a print dress featuring tilting Eiffel Towers, saluting gendarmes, strolling lovers, and a place called Café de Paris. There was a doorman standing next to her with his nose in a beer.

'Too snooty for your colleagues?' she called.

It was Potosky in another metamorphosis. She had cut her hair and was wearing wing-tipped glasses with rhinestones on the frames. Under her dress I caught the outline of what looked like a cast-iron bra ending somewhere around her rib cage. She looked like a transvestite trying to imitate a Mid-western schoolteacher.

'I didn't recognize you,' I said.

'Yes, I suppose there has been quite a change.'

She had put on a little weight – which is supposed to be a sign of a happy (or unhappy) sex life – and her cheeks were radiant without the aid of make-up.

'Have you met my fiancé?'

The doorman took the mug out of his face. It was Goldburg, the Coast Guard Information officer. He definitely remembered me.

'We've met, Jillsy,' he said sternly.

'Jillsy?' I said in astonishment. If only I had thought of that. . . .

'Of course you've met,' she said. 'That's how we met, isn't it, Paul?'

'You two engaged?' I asked.

'Mmm.' Potosky sucked her grasshopper through a straw. 'We're going down to Steubenville to meet Paul's folks this weekend. We were up in Westport last weekend to see my Mom and Dad.'

I looked Goldburg over. All I could see was a dumpy, resentful bureaucrat with sweat stains around his collar. What was his secret? Hopeless male chauvinist that I am, I flashed to a nude Goldburg uncoiling a phallus like a ship's rope while a nude Potosky watched in wonder.

'You know, I really have you to thank for all this,' she said.

'How so?' I asked, still trying to guess Goldburg's mysterious allure.

'Well, because of that dirty trick you played on me with Bill De Forrest.' She stroked Goldburg's pallid hand and looked adoringly at him. 'My God, I never would have met Paul if I hadn't started seeing Bill.'

'You were seeing him?' I asked. Potosky had turned into a Coast Guard groupie. There must be something about a uniform, I thought.

'Bill and I dated for a while,' she said. (Even her language was appropriate. Old Protean Potosky. I wondered how she'd end up after having sampled and absorbed every variety of male behaviour.) 'One night we doubled with Paul, and. . . .'

Goldburg belched in embarrassment. I grabbed his free hand and shook it until his Good Conduct Medal rattled. 'Well, it all worked out for the best, didn't it,' I said. 'If I may, I'd like to offer you both a drink.'

'Not for me, thanks, I'm OD tomorrow,' Goldburg said.

'Overdose?' I asked.

'Officer of the Day,' Potosky said with a tolerant smile.

'Where's the head?' Goldburg asked the bartender.

'Listen, are you really going to marry that young salt?' I asked when he had gone.

'Yes, absolutely.'

'Go to a split-level in Steubenville, cake sales, and ladies' auxiliary, officers' club? . . .'

'I'm going to wash a man's socks, cook his dinner, all the things you talked about that night. I've finally found someone I want to do that for.'

'You're into normalcy now – is that it?' I asked. 'You know, that's the biggest trap of all. It leads to children. . . .'

'I hope so,' she said. 'Paul wants four.'

'. . . Recipes, boredom, and don't forget infidelity.' I leaned in as Goldburg approached, listing a bit to starboard. 'You think after a few months you'll be ready for a little fling?'

'If I am, I'll have it with the chaplain,' she said. 'That is standard operating procedure for military wives. . . .'

'C'mon,' I whispered, 'tell me, what's he got? C'mon. . . .'

Potosky gave me a smug, soap-opera smile and turned to her respectably tipsy fiancé, who was holding her coat for her. 'Thank you, dear. Night, Josh.'

Goldburg gave me his hand. 'No hard feelings, buddy. G'night.'

And out they went. Of course, he was the height of exotic for her. She probably came every time he called her Jillsy. Or Jujiepoops or whatever other little nicknames they had conceived. She'd end up putting on his uniform and whipping him with his swagger stick. They'd get embroiled in a mate-swapping ring in Greenland, and I'd cover the story.

'I want to buy those people a round,' I told the bartender.

'They just left,' he said.

'What's that got to do with it?'

He put a beer and a grasshopper in front of me and stood there with his arms folded. I threw the grasshopper down and chased it with the beer.

'That your ex-old lady?' he asked.

'Yup, and she's marrying my best pal,' I said.

'Well, you deserve one with me for that. . . .'

'No.' I held up a martyr's palm. 'I've had enough.'

I would not get drunk. There were no grounds here for a bender. Besides, I had to be at Brooklyn police headquarters in a few hours, and I still knew where my car was.